# BLACKQUEST 40

### JEFF BOND

Thanks, Dr. Forth!

MB

11-26-19

# PART ONE_

# CHAPTER ONE_

I AM IN THE MIDDLE OF SOLVING HOMELESSNESS WHEN MY boss raps his knuckles on my cubicle border. I know it's Paul—my eyes stay on the computer monitor, what with an intractable social ill hanging in the balance—by the timid *tap...tap-tap* pattern. Also the smell. Paul eats McDonald's every morning for breakfast. He's a Sausage McGriddle man.

"Deb, we're heading up to the meeting—"

"Busy." I squint around the San Francisco street map on-screen, mousing over a blinking dot labeled *Wanda*. She isn't moving. None of them are moving.

Paul sighs. "We're all busy. But it's a Company-All, so if you—"

"Is it a Susan meeting?"

"No. It's the kickoff for Blackquest 40."

"Means nothing to me." I click Wanda. *Why aren't they moving? Database problem?*

Paul says the meeting invite should have explained everything. Blackquest 40 is a training exercise, mandatory for every employee in the company.

I look up and see that, indeed, he has the whole team in tow.

3

Jared in his *My Code Can't Fix Your Stupid* trucker hat. Minosh fingering his spiral-bound notebook, peeking at a clock. They are watching me—all 5'2" if you count the platinum spikes, and a decade younger than them—like zoo visitors wondering if the glass is thick enough around this freak-colored poison frog.

"Susan hired me," I say, invoking our rockstar CEO again. "Susan said I don't have to participate in anything I don't believe in."

"Look, this project—"

"Is corporate training. High on my list of things to not believe in."

With that, I pop over to the log file, which confirms my worst fear: the Carebnb database isn't refreshing. The last GPS coordinates are from eight minutes ago, meaning Wanda and every other unhoused person on that map is misplaced.

Ugh.

The timing is brutal. Today is my launch, the day I am supposed to start demonstrating to all the venture capitalists not funding my side project that a little technology plus basic human decency can equal disruptive positive change.

Across the city, 137 unhoused San Franciscans are wearing 137 smart wristbands, produced at great expense by a local micro-manufacture co-op, in the hopes of connecting with a beta host. I signed up 344 hosts, but that number is dicey because many I bullied into joining. Some will have uninstalled the Carebnb app, not anticipating that I'll soon be combing my list for chicken-outs and visiting their apartments to measure, then post on social media, just how many square feet of covered living space they waste nightly.

My brain races for solutions, but Paul's voice and *eau de McGriddle* distract me. He's explaining that Susan is out of pocket tying up loose ends in Davos, that Carter Kotanchek has the ball until—

"Okay Paul, honestly?" I click over to the T server, the probable source of my issue. "There is no combination of words or faux-words you can say that will get me off this workstation."

"You're the principal software architect, Deb," he says. "We need you. I'm still in the dark myself, but I'm hearing Blackquest 40 is enormous."

My mouth twists. "Getting colder."

Paul hates managing me. I'm sure he goes home every night to Li Wei, his former-secretary-now-wife, and curses Susan for poaching me away from Google.

Now, as his eyes roam my workspace—hemp satchel, bin of droid Hot Wheels, Polarity of the Universe toggle currently set to *Amoral*, my toes in their sandals (he has a pervy thing for my feet)—his face drops another shade closer to dough.

He looks at my screen. "How much time are you spending on Carebnb?"

"Twenty-five percent, just like my contract says." I manage to keep a straight face.

"It's a *required* Company-All. You don't badge in, you lose network privileges. It would set you back."

"You can void that."

"I can." Paul taps his ample jowls, thoughtfully paternal. "But I won't."

I've been working throughout our exchange, deciphering error messages, rebooting, tweaking this and that...nothing is helping.

I grit my teeth. Resetting my network privileges would be a big, sticky wad of red tape.

"Fine," I say, "I'll do the meeting. But I am still not participating in this Blockquest deal."

"Blackquest."

"Whatever." I can bring my laptop and troubleshoot from

the conference room. "Our queue is about ten miles long—whose bright idea was some lame time-suck training?"

Paul grimaces. "Carter is driving it."

Carter Kotanchek, our chief financial officer, is warring with Paul about the makeup of the Codewise Solutions workforce. Paul favors programmers in keeping with our reputation as the leading machine-learning and optimization company on the planet.

Carter wants more salespeople and has a knack for finding third-party vendors who sport the same Gatsby slickback he does. Inexplicably, Carter is winning.

The engineers behind Paul knock in place like pens in a mug, waiting.

I flop my wrist toward the elevators. "Go, go—I'll catch up. Two minutes."

They go. Paul lowers his gaze in a final *I know you will choose wisely* appeal.

I focus on my screen with a wonderfully McGriddle-free breath, then try refreshing the database.

DENIED: CONNECTIVITY ERROR 612.

I rejigger a script and try again.

DENIED: CONNECTIVITY ERROR 612.

Same error every time.

This is infuriating. Have I been found out? I never officially informed Paul about routing Carebnb's unhoused-person GPS data through T, Codewise's least busy server. Did he shut me down without telling me? Coincidentally on my most important day of the year?

No way. Paul would write a huffy email or file a ticket. He

won't refill our departmental stash of teabags without paperwork.

My calendar bleeps. *YOU HAVE NOT BADGED INTO BLACKQUEST 40 KICKOFF (ORGANIZER: CARTER K.); NETWORK PRIVILEGES WILL RESET IN 4 MINUTES.*

I stand and grab my laptop, then remember it doesn't have the software to access the T server. I won't be able to troubleshoot during the meeting after all. I'll be forced to sit there and eat an hour's worth of corporate mumbo-jumbo.

"Raven!" I call over my shoulder.

My trusty solar-powered quadcopter perks up. She hums around to my sightline, her underside dome blipping green to indicate her attention.

"Attend meeting in conference room 6-A. Badge in. Watch, back row. Record."

Raven processes each command using natural language algorithms I wrote in grad school, then lowers her claw—repurposed off a junked arcade game—to accept my keycard.

As the drone whispers up the hall, I feel a twinge of unease. She's attended meetings in my stead before but never on a different floor. She will need to push a button, read a floor indicator, possibly accommodate human riders...logic I have given her but not thoroughly stress-tested. It's asking a lot.

I work another five minutes without success.

Air blasts through my nostrils.

I need eyes on a live wristband.

I grab the phone and dial Cecil, my go-to trial user. Cecil has known me since I was a baby, when Mom would push me around in her cart, snuggled in among dumpster scraps and Styrofoam peanuts. Cecil walked me through the roughest part of the city every day of second grade, and taught me the nutcracker choke after a kid pushed a shiv through my septum in fifth.

"Lil Deb, yo," he answers in a deep baritone.

"Cec! Hey Cec, I'm seeing weirdness on my end and I need to know if you—"

"How's your mom?"

"Oh, she's cool, I talked to the orderlies and—"

"They're keeping her meds straight?"

"No no, yeah, it's all good," I say—Cecil is so unfailingly polite you have to move him along sometimes—"listen, what are you seeing with Carebnb? Is your wristband working?"

"Think so."

"Green light?"

"Yep."

"Map of available host beds showing up?"

"Yep."

"How many hosts in range? My database wonked and I gotta know if the problem is local or if peer-to-peer transfers are broken too."

A guttural breath over the line. "English, Deb. Regular English please."

I grip the keyboard tray, slow myself down. I don't expect non-techies to understand every word I say, all the nitty-gritty. They just need the gist.

I lost the gist there. "Could we possibly meet? I think I have to see the wristband myself to diagnose this. Sorry, I hate to inconvenience you."

"I'm homeless. Where else I gotta go."

"Right. How about our usual spot, say twenty minutes?"

Before he can respond, the call drops. *Bzzzzzzzzzz.*

I clench my jaw and redial.

NO SERVICE.

I stand and waggle my phone outside my cube, I walk to

the window, I glare at the Verizon logo and telepathically threaten to hack their transceivers to mush if they don't find me a signal.

Nada.

I plunk back down. I'm contemplating flipping my Polarity of the Universe toggle to *Evil* when a tinny sound announces the presence of a new window on my monitor: Raven's livestream.

She made it up to the Blackquest kickoff meeting. *Atta girl.* I resize the window to span my entire screen and watch as the big conference room comes into focus.

The Company-All is underway. Carter Kotanchek stands at the podium in a dapper summer-weight suit. Raven's camera won't win any TechCrunch awards, but Carter's teeth still gleam from the middle of a plastic grin.

"Like y't'meet Jim Dawson," he says, introducing a stone-faced man in chunky glasses. "Jim here runs Elite Development, the company that will be facilitating Blackquest 40. Guys are doing phenomenal stuff in a new space called Extreme Readiness. Helping organizations build capability to complete projects of extreme complexity, requiring extreme teamwork, on extreme deadlines. So far they've been working with high-leverage government agencies, paramilitary, et cetera. We, ladies and gents, are fortunate enough to be corporate client number one."

Dawson, in a bland accent—Ohio? Indiana?—thanks Carter and says he's pleased to be here today. *Excited for our shared journey.*

Gag. So not participating.

As my focus returns to Carebnb, I groan at the ceiling. I need to test a wristband, but if I can't meet Cecil...hmm. I have a few spares lying around, but none are initialized.

I'm figuring how long initialization would take—and how

true a read I'd get from a wristband not in the field—when I hear something that stops me cold.

"...campus quarantine and data blockade will remain in place for the duration of Blackquest 40. If you absolutely require outside contact, in case of emergency or vital family obligation, a protocol exists..."

Wait, *data blockade*? I rewind Raven's feed and replay the last fifteen seconds. Elite Development, in the name of "improved focus and personal efficiency," is collecting every cellphone in the building and blocking all inbound-outbound internet traffic.

I feel slight queasiness at the authoritarianism of the whole setup, but mostly relief. Because now I get it. These jerks shut down T. They killed my call. Probably they're using some military-grade antenna to zap cellular signals, and a simple software block on the servers.

And that won't stop me.

CHAPTER TWO_

THERE ARE A FEW DIFFERENT POINTS WHERE JERKS COULD stick a software block. All are accessible from the server room on the second floor.

I head for the elevator bank, fists balled.

My floor is a ghost town: everybody is upstairs at the Company-All. Here is Jared's La-Z-Boy swiveled from his keyboard, with its broad butt imprint. Minosh's sit-stand workstation looking like some giant mechanized praying mantis that ran out of juice mid-attack.

My coworkers aren't awful. Yeah, they resent my age and salary—which got reported around when Susan did her press circuit heralding "the Codewise commitment to acquiring bleeding-edge talent." Yeah, they're homogeneous as Safeway milk. Neither is their fault.

Susan wants me to be a "disrupter" here, to "jog the culture." This sounded cool at the time, as she was recruiting me over pastries at du Soleil—resembling Reese Witherspoon, fresh off a CNBC roundtable—but progress has been slow. I have discovered that the word *diversity*, uttered in a 90 percent male office, produces mostly dyspeptic winces and hands stuffed in pockets.

Off the elevator at Two, I stalk up the east hall and round a corner, then freeze.

Standing at entrance to the server room is a man. He wears the same polo shirt as Jim Dawson, yellow with a blue "Elite" logo, the E's top horizontal curving into a skyward arrow. (This denotes excellence, skyrocketing valuations, and generalized corporate Goodness.) His wrists are crossed over a belt buckle.

I flash back to Carter's introduction. That term, *para-military*.

The server room has a second door that spills out nearer the elevators—too bad IT keeps it locked from inside or else I'd slip in that way.

I angle for the door. The man doesn't make way.

"Need to get in there," I say.

"All employees should be at the meeting." He has Dawson's bland accent, like some appliance instruction manual if they could speak.

"Right, but I'm not, and I have important stuff to do inside, so..." I twirl my thumb ring in a hurry-this-along gesture.

"Access to the server room is restricted."

"Restricted?" I recoil. "Well, although I look like a bike messenger, I'm actually the principal software architect here. All good."

He plants one foot against the door. It's not a plain shoe poking out from underneath his slacks, more of a boot. High-lacing. Black.

"I cannot allow access."

I feel my pulse accelerating in my wrists. "You're corporate trainers, yes? Your company? Meaning you work for us. Meaning *you* don't grant *us* access to squat. Other way around."

The man's boot does not move.

I whip out my phone.

He says, "Calls are not allowed."

"What? Oh shut up, I'm calling my boss. Or Susan. This is over."

"They will not answer," he says. "Employee cellphones are being collected. Upstairs at the kick-off meeting, there is a box."

A box. What the hell.

I dial Paul, forgetting the cellular block.

More *bzzzzzzzzzz*.

"This is moronic," I say, head ticking back and forth. I consider puffing up, asking for his name and explaining what trouble I could make. But I can see it wouldn't work, and anyhow it's not his fault. He isn't the one who dreamed up this bozo training.

I head for the elevators, pissed. I slept badly and skipped breakfast and my boobs are sweating a little. It's after ten o'clock in the morning, and all my beta users have stale information about available hosts.

When I took over planning duties from Mom after her schizophrenia hit, age ten or eleven, I tried to have our nighttime arrangements made by noon. That way I had a rough idea how we needed to move throughout the day. Some shelters have check-in times. Greenspaces fill up.

If I don't fix the database soon, day one of Carebnb will be a disaster.

I turn back.

Discreetly, I retrace my steps to the server hallway and peer around the corner. The guard is still there. I summon Raven with a tap-swipe of my phone. She exits the big conference room by bumping the handicap-access door button, then purrs away. I watch this on her livestream, back flush to the wall. The feed fizzles once she boards an elevator.

I wait. Just before I start to worry—Elite can't be blocking

Wi-Fi inside the building, can they?—my ear detects the slightest thrum.

Moments later, my girl appears.

*"Nice work,"* I whisper.

Raven descends eighteen inches, responding to my reduced volume. I put her into remote control mode and, dragging slowly along my phone's touchscreen, send her into view of the guard. Then spin her slowly until he becomes visible on the livestream.

Raven is extraordinarily quiet. I gave each of her four propellers its own motor, which allows the RPMs to vary and effectively makes them noise-cancel each other. NASA calls this "frequency-spectrum spreading" and thinks they're the only ones doing it.

The guard does not notice until she is on top of him. His face, pixelated on my phone's rendering, pops, but he composes himself quickly and eyes her down the hall.

Raven skids to a tilting UFO-esque stop, then turns her "face"—a line of cooling vents below the cyclops front camera— toward him. I move her coquettishly around the corner, out of sight.

I lean forward, exposing only my left eye, and check the guard. His head is turned in the direction Raven disappeared, but he doesn't leave his post.

Really? A solar-powered quadcopter traipses by and you're unmoved?

My coworkers are used to Raven by now, but the first time she met Jared, he dove behind a printer. This guy barely flinched. Possible he was prepped, or somehow knew about her in advance?

I send Raven up the hall, panning around her livestream for something useful. There isn't much. This floor used to be half-Engineering, half-Backroom Ops, but after the last downsizing Engineering fits wholly on the third floor.

What can I work with? Bathroom. Locked conference room. Dozen empty cubicles. Water cooler.

Water cooler.

I focus Raven's camera. The cooler is of the upside-down-jug variety. *I wonder...*

Usually these coolers are very heavy, and of course Raven being avian in nature is very light. But the jug is only a quarter full.

Worth a shot.

I back Raven up, elevate until her carbon-fiber propellers skim the ceiling. My tongue traveling high up my cheek, I give the *MAX_ACCELERATE* command. She zooms for the jug using gravity and every last kWh she's harvested from this cloudy San Francisco morning.

The water cooler grows quickly in the livestream, then disappears.

*THOINK.*

Then a loud crash, then strangled gurgling. I am blind for a moment, Raven presumably filming carpet from her derriere, until she restarts her propellers and gets aloft.

It worked! The cooler is toppled, water spurting from the jug's narrow neck.

I peek again around the corner. The guard is moving toward the noise, his back to me.

I sprint for the server room, arms pumping, sandals slamming. I don't know how long he will take investigating, but I seriously doubt he'll go hunting for paper towels.

I need to hustle. I reach the server room door. I push with my palm but it isn't propped. I yank the handle so hard I feel it in my chest, can't open it.

The keycard reader shows red. Of course—the server room requires badge-in!

I slap both hands simultaneously about my waist, searching,

clutching, sliding my fingertips down my badge's lanyard...and find it bare.

## CHAPTER THREE_

My badge is on Five at the Company-All. Raven either left it on her chair or dropped it after badging in.

I glance up the hall. I don't see the guard, but creaks in the floor tell me something is happening around the corner. He'll be here soon.

I have to move—either beat my retreat or power ahead into the server room. I grope around the keycard reader. Backing out these tiny Phillips-head screws will take forever...blunt force, a kick or some elbow-smash, would have zero effect on a magnetic lock...

Panic and despair stretch my face. I need to fix this dataflow *now*. If Blackquest 40 proceeds as described, Carebnb will stay dark for two nights. Launch fail. My credibility shot—with venture capitalists, sure, but more importantly with Cecil and Wanda and my 135 other unhoused volunteers.

My gaze falls serendipitously to a wall outlet. I think, *electricity*.

No electricity, no magnetism.

The first tool that leaps into my head is a fork, but I don't generally keep utensils on my person. I begin a frenzied inventory from the sandals up—buckles, toe ring, keys, phone.

Wait, backup.

Keys.

I whip out my house key, which I carry around on a carabiner clip. The clip doesn't have tines like a fork, but maybe if I open its gate and align its angular teeth-grabs just so...

I grab the carabiner with the tail of my shirt, doubling- and tripling-up the fabric, before realizing I have no clue how far this circuit extends. Will I zap these hall lights? The servers themselves? The whole floor?

The risk is significant. Job-jeopardizingly so. Working at Codewise Technology is not my life's ambition, but that biweekly paycheck is nice and meaty: meatiness I need to pay for mom's care—assisted living is outrageous in San Francisco—and keep Carebnb afloat.

I drop to one knee and regrip the carabiner. Metal glints between my quivering knuckles.

I inhale hard. For resolve, I imagine the parallel outlet openings are the jolly faces of Carter Kotanchek and that Elite stooge Jim Dawson.

I ram the carabiner forward. Through my shirt fabric, I feel the bite. An angry, concentrated tickle. A toast smell worries the air.

I check the keycard reader. Its indicator is dark. The server room door hangs slack between its jambs. The nearest hall light has blown too, but I can't fret over that. I scramble inside.

To make the door appear closed, I drag over a rolling cart and lock its wheels. This may take a few minutes, and I need the guard to stay incurious.

I head for T. The servers are all blipping and whirring in their racks—they have emergency failover power. The lights are off and the aisles are narrow and I wish I'd brought my hoodie because my arms are *freezing*. Paul Gribbe believes a server room must be kept at arctic temperatures despite modern thinking to the contrary.

I am scampering half-blind toward the last row of machines when a giant tower, jutting into the aisle, trips me. I crash to the concrete.

Cursing, raising up onto my throbbing shoulder, I squint at the tower, which bears the Elite "E"—blue, topped with the skyward arrow.

It's one impressive machine. I can hear the disk platters spinning, cranking—they could be compressing coal into diamonds inside.

What does Elite need with their own server?

Just transporting this beast up from the garage would've been a chore. Why? *What are these guys about?*

No time to ponder; I gotta move. I shrug off my aches and locate the T server, whip out a USB cable, and stretch on tiptoes, plugging one end into the back and the other to my phone, which will have to serve as my input device.

Raven's livestream still plays on my cell. Before swiping it away, I note that her hallway looks empty. The guard must have returned to his post.

I am just praying he won't notice the blown keycard reader when a series of progressively louder thuds begin behind me, followed by a crash that can only be one thing.

A toppled rolling cart.

The server racks are eight feet tall, leaving a short gap below the ceiling. I climb the boxes two at a time, sandal treads digging off their chassis edges, which groan but don't break under my hundred-odd pounds.

Bless Paul for his priggish insistence on titanium.

I heave myself over the top. *Ow!* My shins and groin bang into the top server, whose surface burns my exposed wrists. I flatten out until my elbows and ankles find the cool edges of the rack, then lie in this excruciating position—spread like a squirrel pelt—to listen.

The guard's footsteps boom around like rifle-shot. He walks down one row, up the next. Ambient computer noise worms around my brain. He pauses several times—inspecting? receiving a message on his phone?—and I hold my breath. I hear him flip the light switch. The room stays dark. The guard says nothing.

When he nears my rack, I shrink back from the aisle with small, crab-like movements. My USB cord remains plugged in but is hardly visible, just a sagged section between racks.

"Ehhhn."

I can't tell if this exhalation is pensive, or bored, or what.

I keep perfectly still. My thigh muscles, flexed to keep me off the surface of this top burning-hot server, scream with exertion.

Finally the guard moves off. In another minute, he's left the room.

I half-climb, half-vault to the floor. There's no time to regroup. He might be reporting these irregularities, the blown reader and barricaded door, to his superiors. Tapping my cell keyboard, I access T and navigate to the Carebnb database.

Within seconds I see the problem. As suspected, Elite is blocking network ports. I try all the biggies, including 3306 which Carebnb uses, but can't get data in or out. I kick off a nifty scanning script I wrote at Google that quickly checks each port. I squint down the results, spilling out ten rows per second.

The text is all green except for a single red entry: 9009.

Interesting. Elite has kept a single port open, way up in the high range. Probably for their own email and cell traffic. It's clever, hiding their little data-tunnel in this spot nobody would ever look.

Again, I wonder about this outfit. The technical sophistication of corporate trainers generally tops out at PowerPoint.

Again, though, I have no time to puzzle. It takes me nine minutes to reroute Carebnb's GPS traffic through 9009. This requires a tweak to the data format, which makes me cringe. My wristbands in the field *should* handle it, but without testing, you never know.

I punch up the master map of San Francisco. The dots are moving. Wanda is all the way into Haight-Ashbury now.

Quickly I cover my tracks, logout, take my cord. I tiptoe past the giant Elite tower that tripped me. Assuming the guard has returned to his post, I leave by the secondary door near the elevators.

Feeling returns to my shivering arms in the hall. I check the time. Ten past. The Company-All should be over, everyone returning to their desks. It's great the Carebnb data is fixed, but I still need to confirm my wristbands are understanding the tweaked format. I need Cecil.

Walking faster, I issue a command for Raven to meet up at my cubicle. I reach the elevators. I jab the button and peer at my notifications bar, hoping for some Verizon love. Whatever Elite is doing to block mobile, it must be wireless—meaning there could be random holes.

All four bars are faint, gray. Randomness is not favoring me today.

The elevator chimes. The door panels split and I stride forward, head down, slamming right into Jim Dawson.

## CHAPTER FOUR

Dawson gives not an inch. I could have run into a Market Street lamppost.

Elite's head honcho is brawnier in person than on Raven's livestream, his chest etching ridges in the yellow polo shirt. A scar pocks one temple. His eyes pulse from black, horn-rimmed glasses. He wears khakis and those same high-lacing boots, company-issue apparently, looming over my sandals like thugs cracking their knuckles.

We're a step outside the elevator. He holds out a box. "Your phone."

I say, "Don't bother, I'm not getting service."

Dawson explains he doesn't need to make a call. Cellphone use is prohibited during Blackquest 40.

"Oh, okay." I pat my jeans pocket. "I'll keep it in my pants then."

He smiles, but his left hand is clenching a foam stress ball. With his right, he raises the box. "Please, Miss Bollinger."

He knows my name. *Interesting.* "What's the fashion logic on those boots. You guys are, what, commandos? Business commandos?"

"Dress is one tool in the organizational quiver. Used properly, it binds employees together and promotes a culture of discipline."

I find myself straightening up—it's automatic in this guy's presence. "You recommend brownshirts or blackshirts?"

Missing the reference, or more frighteningly not missing it at all, he says attire is out of scope. The man speaks with this irksome schoolmarm composure—a librarian walking third graders through the Dewey Decimal system.

I've crossed paths with a few of these corporate training types, who act like their product-insight-worldview is unassailably obvious. Once you've shelled out tens of thousands of dollars to have them explain it.

"So," I say. "Forty straight hours. People are going to sleep here? At their cubicles?"

"We have cots."

"Food?"

He nods. "Meals will be catered, high caliber."

"I'm supposed to take my girlfriend to a doctor's appointment at four o'clock." In fact, I'm between relationships. "She's counting on me, I'm her ride."

"A protocol exists in cases of essential family duty. Which taxi service is not."

This guy. Unreal.

"She'll try texting," I say. "You're gonna have 200 people not answering text or email for almost *two days?*"

Dawson says auto-responses will be sent to all outside persons attempting contact, explaining the nature and duration of the exercise.

It's simply insane. "How is this legal, keeping people here against their will? If OSHA hears about this, I'm guessing the game is up."

"Each Codewise employee signed an addendum to his contract."

"I never signed anything."

"You did," Dawson says. "Electronically, ten weeks ago. The addendum acknowledges the unique challenges posed by today's software industry and the employee's assent to a broad range of company actions. We worked closely with your Human Resources department in crafting the language."

This does sound like an email I would scroll through and click away, just to get the ick off my screen.

But why did everybody else essentially sign away their rights? Ten weeks means the email went out in...early May.

*Ahhh.* Now I get it. The big layoff happened in April. Nobody would've been eager to rock the boat, to make a nuisance of themselves over some hypothetical rider on their employee contract.

Speaking of rocking boats, I'm started to feel nauseous. This Dawson guy and his rhetoric.

"Well, listen, I'm enjoying the heck out of this," I say, "but I have work."

I try stepping around to the elevator, but Dawson blocks me with his box. "Phone surrender is not optional."

The box physically brushes my shoulder. "Number one, you always have options. Number two, *this*"—I cock an eyebrow at where my shirt got touched—"is stopping immediately. Yesterday. Last week."

He keeps his box stiff. "Why are you on this floor, Miss Bollinger?"

I mumble indistinctly.

"The only room still being utilized on this floor is the server room."

I frown as though the term *server* isn't ringing a bell.

He says, "I expect you were maintaining Carebnb. Your launch is today, correct?"

My face takes on a sideways tilt, and I feel chills walking up my neck.

*Should I deny?*

That seems pointless. "What do you do, hack everybody's email before you start a gig?"

"A thorough understanding of personnel is vital." His gaze travels the length of my body. "We make a point of knowing each employee in his totality."

"For the record, I'm a 'her.' But I think you know that. You're looking hard enough."

Dawson chuckles. He does lower his box now.

"Deborah Maurine Bollinger, born 1990 to Celeste Bollinger at San Francisco General Hospital. Raised indigent. Subjected to frequent and scarring violence as a juvenile. Gained hardship admission to Massachusetts Institute of Technology at age sixteen. Double-majored in robotics and gender studies. Awarded PhD from Harvard in three years, computational science and engineering. Hired via on-campus interview by Google, where advanced self-driving technology several generations beyond competitors. Promoted to lead engineer for darkest of Google Labs projects. Details unknown, rumored to be company's top priority. Left eighteen months later to join Codewise Solutions."

I scratch behind my ear. "Who told you I was scarred?"

He ignores this. "In order to sufficiently stress an organization, to deliver the max-out training we promise, we must assess each client's team fully. This is why the Blackquest 40 requirements are the most demanding, the most grueling we have yet conceived. Because of you and what you're capable of."

Flattery in general works on me, but I'm just not feeling it now.

"That's going to be a problem," I say.

"Why?"

"Because I'm not participating."

"Your superiors assure me otherwise."

"You mean Carter Kotanchek? CK Slick? See, he looks like my superior on the org-chart, but—"

"You will participate, you *will* hand over your phone." Jim Dawson lifts the box. A tendon bulges in his elbow, and he's pulverizing that stress ball. I half expect his eyeballs to start filling red.

But I'm mad too.

"Get your sorry ass out of my way."

I slam through his box and the arm holding it. Phones tumble to the floor, clattering in heaps. Dawson squats over his high-lacing boots and begins deliberately refilling the box.

I don't help. I'm on the elevator.

"Be aware," he says before the doors can close, "that any device requesting data from the network will have its circuits fried. That's why I came down. To activate this countermeasure."

I scoff. "*Fried?* Nice use of layman's terms. How exactly does said frying occur?"

"A rootkit disables the chip failsafe. Simultaneously, a circular virus creates heat and voltage spikes that melt the motherboard."

I scoff again. More like a half-scoff. "A rootkit *and* a virus? Sure thing."

He continues collecting phones from the carpet.

I say, "I don't have time for web surfing anyhow, so I guess it won't matter. Phone's just going to be sitting on my desk."

"It will still fry. Even background processes—simple time of day updates—will trigger the malware."

I feel my forehead crinkle. Is he bluffing? *Could* a rootkit-virus combo fry my motherboard? It's impossible to know without testing.

My real question, though, is this: how is this character, this glorified motivational speaker, versed in rootkits?

I think about the big tower that tripped me in the server room.

With the corner of a fingernail, I poke the pinhole on the side of my phone. A tray pops out and off it I pry my SIM card—which has all the important stuff like passwords and Raven logic. I stash the SIM card in my pocket and chuck the phone at him.

"Choke on it."

Dawson catches the phone on its fourth skip. "Quite careless for a device you fought so hard to keep."

I shrug. "It's shatterproof. Specs don't say so but it is."

He smiles dubiously. "If the feature is not in the specifications, how would—"

"Because I built it, douchenozzle."

As I walk away, he turns the phone over and reads the logo.

G.

CHAPTER FIVE_

Upstairs in the Latrine, the largest conference room on Three, Paul Gribbe and team are digging into the Blackquest requirements. Elite has provided a spread including bagels with smoked salmon, pastries, and a tower of sculpted fruit. Yellow-shirted "coordinators" stalk about answering questions, gesturing at screens. A woman smiles and nods with Minosh. A man with windswept hair talks to Jared, whose lips purse in the toad-like expression he uses to feign deep thought.

After my nasty exchange with Dawson, I'm encouraged to see normal people on their team—people who aren't scowling or squeezing the foam guts out of a stress ball.

I linger at the door to the conference room, officially 3-C. The name "Latrine," as Paul explained during my first-day tour, traces back to an old project that involved rewriting copious amounts of CRUD (Create, Read, Update, Delete) logic, the type of tedious work you almost wish got farmed out to rent-a-coders. Someone said, "We're so deep in CRUD, we should call this place the Latrine." The name stuck. I said to Paul, "I bet it also makes you guys feel tough, right? A little?"

Now Paul stands at the projector, a bracing hand on his half-donut-bald head. Sprawled across the screen are 187 interfaces represented by plain black rectangles. He's begun grouping them with blob-shaped outlines: a loose green L across the middle is labeled *Jared injection piece*; most of the top is purple *Deb under the hood*; etc. His first try at assigning who will do what.

"Deb, good." Paul waves me in. "I need to get your take on these requirements. This thing is enormous."

"Oh, no—I was just rubbernecking," I say. "I'm not coming inside."

"No, you need to. Now."

I shake my head. "Pass."

He peeks back at the Elite coordinators, then approaches confidentially. "First checkpoint happens in two hours. We have to file our initial design."

He gestures to a timer mounted in the corner, ticking down from 01:43:52. I saw a few others on my way, these digital red readouts clearly meant to suggest Jack Bauer lurks somewhere, prepping hypodermic needles behind a two-way mirror.

"Or what?"

"We get docked. Apparently Elite has the authority to dock our Q4 stock options—they believe in incentivizing 'at the micro level.'"

"How does Elite have any authority whatsoever over our options?"

Paul shrugs. I think about that addendum Dawson mentioned. What other powers has Elite usurped? Can they boot our vehicles? Restrict bathroom access?

One of the coordinators, the woman, strides forward with hand extended. The polo shirt is slightly huggy on her and gives off a can-do, worker vibe.

"Katie Masterson, communications specialist." Her grip is firm. "Can I assist? Is there some confusion I can clear up?"

My sandals remain in the hall, such that our handshake occurs across the threshold. "No confusion. I'm just headed back to my cube."

"But you're an engineer, aren't you?"

I can't tell whether she is assuming based on appearance or has my bio memorized like Jim Dawson. "I have too many deliverables for corporate training. Sorry. Your scones look yummy."

Katie is preparing to respond, the corners of her grin rising dangerously, when Paul says, "I'm just bringing Deb up to speed. Thanks."

Once she's left, Paul faces me. His eyes drop for a sketchy peek at my feet.

"It'll be remarkable software," he says, "if we pull it off."

My attention drifts unwittingly to the projector screen. The interfaces paint a complex tapestry of function, littered with obtuse variables that defy the accepted industry standard of English-readable names. The gist, I perceive in a blink, is that the code needs to (a) inject itself into a foreign operating system, (b) perform some optimization, transforming a matrix of inputs into output, and (c) persist in the host with minimal footprint.

It's an odd mix of systems programming and heavy algorithm work, with a dash of old-fashioned hacking thrown in for good measure.

Paul notices my gaze. "Thought we might carve out the optimization piece."

"Can't be black-box," I say. "That middle piece—whatever it does—will need context."

He winces in grudging acknowledgment. "True."

"Do you know? What that middle piece does?"

"I asked that at the kickoff. Jim Dawson said it shouldn't

matter. 'Code to the requirements. Do not worry about use cases.'"

With uncharacteristic humor, Paul delivers the line in a decent imitation of Dawson.

Paul can be tolerable. I enjoy talking shop with him. The guy knows his stuff. People say he was an absolute code ninja during Codewise's startup days, when he, Susan, and Carter Kotanchek were fresh Carnegie Mellon PhDs, spinning off research started with their professor. While the other two moved into executive leadership, Paul stayed in the salt mines, architecting the groundbreaking optimizations that fueled the company's rise. In time he was convinced to take his current role as head of development—an office, a dozen direct reports.

I think he misses coding, though. I think a tiny part of him envies me, not having to sit through meetings and wrangle bureaucracy, wholly compensated to solve (real) problems. In a way, I'm the new him: Codewise's revenues last year missed analyst expectations, and Susan expects my arrival to ignite a resurgence.

Still, there's only so much sympathy I can muster for a man of Paul's net worth. When the founders finally did sell out to private equity three years back, the price tag was 1.8 billion dollars.

He says now, "One possibility is to go with small teams using parallel approaches."

"Like Boeing," I say.

"Exactly. Boeing was complex, too, lots of moving parts."

"Not 187-interfaces complex. And we delivered in two months, not two days."

"Right. Probably impossible."

He is baiting me of course, and I am halfway considering chomping when a plastic grocery bag drifts by in the window below. The dumpster at street level is a common foraging spot for the unhoused.

"Nope." I shut my eyes, grind both palms into my ears.

*Must focus.*

"Sorry Paul," I say. "I'm not getting sucked in. Not doing it."

CHAPTER SIX_

I RETURN TO MY WORKSTATION. AS I PLUNK DOWN IN MY chair, Raven greets me with a friendly blip-de-*bloop*.

"How goes your day, lady?"

She plays a high chirp, indicating her battery is fully charged.

The cube salves my mental health, which needs salving after the morning's drama. Here, surrounded by stuff I built with my own hands, I feel safe. I flip Polarity of the Universe from *Amoral* to *Evil*, easy call. I turn Raven this way and that, making sure her kamikaze run at the water cooler hasn't damaged any components. Her rotor blades are vermilion—the drone equivalent of painted nails—and one is scuffed, but all four level out perfectly.

Google gave me an office, and Susan wanted me to take one here too. I just couldn't—not when the eight engineers who report to me lack the Codewise HR cred to get one themselves. Would Raven and I enjoy our own window? Would it be nice to have the luxury of tweaking the spikes of my hair privately, without risk of colleagues discovering my secret vanity? Sure. A cubicle sure beats an alley, though.

Next on my list of comfort tasks: scanning the mechanical dragonflies' surveillance images. Primarily what I'm looking for is confirmation Jared hasn't been harassing Prisha, the Cal grad Susan and I just hired. It's an abuse of power on my part, I admit, but also necessary after The Incident three weeks ago.

I punch up the images. Let's see...*Jared surfing MMORPG forums...Jared squinting at the Blackquest meeting invite...*

He thinks the dragonflies' swerving forays around his area are debugging runs, a believable cover story given they really are lousy fliers. Their algorithm approximates a real aircraft's, calculating required lift based on a complex range of inputs, but the resultant flight paths are all over the place. I have a month to fix this or else Universal Studios' new *Bailey's Buzzy World* attraction is going to seriously disappoint.

*Jared scratching...Jared turning his trucker hat around, (off-camera) muttering "Git 'er done, kid"...*okay. More or less docile.

Restored, I get back to Carebnb. The logs show data still flowing in and out of the T server, which I like, but it's impossible to tell how my wristbands are doing.

Are they interpreting that tweaked data correctly, giving an accurate picture of available beds? Or are my unhoused beta users being sent toward nonsense coordinates halfway across the Pacific Ocean?

Again: I need Cecil.

During our call, he said he could meet. Sort of. If I show up at our usual spot outside the parking garage, will he be there? Did he hear me say "twenty minutes" before the network cut? Even if he did, will he have stuck around? We talked more than an hour ago.

I have to try.

I stand and go. Past the breakroom, the Latrine, the print station. Leaving the office always invigorates me, the promise of urban noise and non-climate-controlled air. Today the pull is even greater, this Blackquest 40 nonsense a pall over the building, looming, so male and steroid-reeking. I feel my knees dip and break into a jog.

I whoosh by Carter Kotanchek, white teeth and a cloud of aftershave.

"Deb!" He double-takes at my direction. "Was just coming to find Paul, check out the game plan. Assumed you'd be in the thick of things?"

"I'm stepping out for air," I say. "Maybe I'll catch you there in a few."

He frowns. "You know about the campus quarantine, right? Blackquest. Nobody in, nobody out."

"Yeah, I'm not participating."

"Sure y'are. All hands on deck, aye? Fourth quarter. Everything we got."

His hands form triumphant fists, then rub devilishly, then snap-point in unison. I feel oily just being this close. Happily I don't deal much with Carter, whose CFO duties keep him busy counting money and brown-nosing Wall Street.

"I told Paul, and that Elite guy, and now I'm telling you. I am not participating. Talk to Susan if you don't like it."

"I have. Susan's behind Blackquest all the way, thousand percent."

"That may be, but we have an agreement. The only person who gets to manage my queue," I say, lowering my eyes, "is me."

Carter fingers the lapel of his linen suit. "These guys built this whole shillelagh around you. Can't do it without you. Don't have the horses."

"Try hiring back those thirteen engineers. See if that helps."

"Deb, I know financials aren't in your wheelhouse, but we're swimming upstream. Used to be Codewise Solutions could charge whatever we wanted. Now? Got lower-cost competitors squeezing us."

I scratch my chin. "How does bloating our costs with some fat, elaborate corporate training help? Excuse my ignorance—it's so out of my wheelhouse."

"It's a differentiator. If we complete Blackquest 40 to spec, on deadline, Elite certifies us FPP-1. Flash Project Prepared Level One."

"Another acronym for the website."

"No, clients! This opens up a ton of new business. They're working their government ties to get these different cert-levels standardized. You make level one, you're looking at DOJ work. Cybersecurity. Cyber*warfare* for U.S. Cyber Command. That's just public sector. Once the private market catches up..."

Carter whistles, a lascivious noise that grates on me.

When his money-lust clears enough for him to notice I've turned my back and am walking away, he calls, "This is a big deal. No way we're making FPP-1 without our quarterback on the field."

I keep moving up the hall.

He says, "I know Susan brought you aboard with some...well, unique privileges." Fussing more with his lapel. "But we hired you to do a job. We hired you with an expecta—"

"*She* hired me. Susan. You weren't involved."

A sweat bead appears on Carter's forehead. Strange—I haven't seen him like this. He never shows nerves or admits a setback, full of that salesman's reflex for glossing over. But he's worried now.

I have to say, I'm enjoying it.

"Listen. Deb." His eyes harden. "If you aren't fulfilling the baseline needs of the company, we'll have no choice but to revisit the terms of your contract. Some of these more extracurricular pursuits"—he flails, lolls his tongue—"might be curtailed."

I am aware of eyebrows halfway up my forehead. "Was that

your hobo face? Just now, were you impersonating an unhoused person?"

"Honest to Christ, could we please—"

"A mentally-disabled hobo perhaps? That's a whole new level of insensitivity."

"I'm serious. This is not—" He looks over his shoulder, continues in a hiss, *"This is not a joke. There is a lot riding on this!"*

"On corporate training. There's a lot riding on this fake, busywork assignment."

Before he can bloviate further, I turn my back on him. I need that air.

## CHAPTER SEVEN_

B1 IS THE LOWER OF THE TWO PARKING GARAGES. I RIDE
the elevator to the bottom, disembark, and stride over sharp-
smelling concrete.

There are fewer than a dozen cars. The garages, the whole
building really, was built for a larger workforce. The latest
round of layoffs left some floors empty or nearly empty. Susan
assures me this is merely cyclical and our reputation remains
intact—"We're Rolls Royce, and people can't always afford Rolls
Royces."

Now I'm pulled along by cool outside air, tugged toward sky
and freedom and—I'm desperately hoping—Cecil.

My mouth still tastes sour from the Carter exchange. The
hobo face is one thing; latent bigotry emerging in a stressful
moment from people like him is no shocker.

The threat is another. *Curtailed*. Please. When Susan gets
back from Davos this afternoon or evening, she'll shut this
down. She'll blow into the lobby and immediately feel the BS,
the testosterone-film on her skin.

I wonder what Carter told her about Blackquest 40 to get
that "thousand percent" support. Not the truth. He certainly

would have needed her sign-off on that stealth HR addendum authorizing all this. Maybe he got an admin to stamp it when she was off jet-setting?

My steps slow at the sight of an unfamiliar vehicle parked near the fire extinguishers. A hulked-up commercial van. Fifteen-passenger. Windowless black sides. I hear a soft chugging coming not from the engine, but closer to the rear wheelwell.

The sliding door reads *ELITE DEVELOPMENT*.

I take only a moment wondering what lives here—this van perfectly complements their big honking server—before rushing on. I see light from the street and am already formulating my first Cecil question.

"*No!*"

A tall, angular man bursts off a stool. He wears the yellow polo shirt.

The command startles me. I knew about Elite's "campus quarantine" but didn't figure they would post actual guards for a training exercise. It's like igniting staircases for a fire drill.

I keep walking, saluting two fingers off the top of my head.

He repeats, "No!" and shakes his head vigorously.

I pass him, onto the ramp now, hearing the thrum of traffic. I lean out over my thighs, hiking the grade. Usually Cecil waits for me here at the halfway point.

I don't see him. *Why aren't I seeing him?*

"No! No, no, no. *No!*"

The Elite guy, still. I peek back. His face is contorted—he's trying to amplify his warning with his expression—and his limbs seem too long, as if they have extra joints. That his vocabulary is capped at one word—*No!*—says something about his likely job qualifications.

I feel bad for him. Occupying the bottom rung at some corporate training firm is nobody's idea of a sweet gig. I bet he's working on his night-school MBA and thought this would look good on a resume. *"Elite Development."* Bay Area address, nice generic name. Twenty bucks an hour. Figured he'd be collating reports or conducting employee interviews. Now they have him playing rent-a-cop.

I turn back to the alley. Scan left, scan right. Still not seeing Cecil.

Could he be at the dumpster? Getting in a quick forage? The other day he bumped into Jared by accident, and my wannabe-hipster coworker chatted him up about favorite Coltrane albums. Maybe he's hanging back to be sure it's me.

I start for the dumpster. A hand seizes my arm.

"Hey," I say. "That's not cool."

The Elite guard furrows his brow and keeps saying, "No," only I'm not even sure it's "no" anymore. It's changed into something guttural, animal.

"I'm serious. Let go."

I whip my arm but can't get free. He tightens his grip—pinching bone in my upper arm—and forces me back into the garage. The move is quick and cruel: he jerks my shoulder without regard for the rest of my body.

"Are you *insane?*" I choke. *"What're you doing?"*

He doesn't care, or understand—it is impossible to know. As he keeps dragging me, and I keep chopping my steps to get away, all is scrambled in my brain.

*This is an office building.* People do not touch each other. People do not grab, or gouge, or use shivs—that's been my reality since I headed off to MIT.

I look at my attacker. His eyes are cold, oaken. I don't feel bad for him now. What I feel is diminished. The way I used to feel as a child with Mom whenever a man, or men, approached our rat-gnawed bedroll in Golden Gate Park. It never matter what I screamed—that *I knew where they slept!, I could ID them!, they were going to be held accountable!* They would take what they wanted. I was weak. I made no difference.

"Okay, fine." I huff heavily and stop struggling. "I give up."

He makes no move to relent, his thumb stiff in my armpit. I raise my hands, palms out, and smile. Both are extremely difficult to muster. Finally his teeth unclench and he lets go.

We both exhale. A purple-red welt has formed on my arm.

"Thanks. You guys aren't messing around with this quarantine, huh?" I force a light tone.

Though he doesn't answer, I can see his relief. He fixes the tuck of his polo shirt. The sleeves make his long arms look like noodles.

My heart hammers in my chest.

"So I'll head back up," I say. "Is the stairwell open, did you notice?"

He stares back quizzically. I gesture around a concrete pillar, inviting him to check.

He takes one step to see past the pillar. It's all I need.

## CHAPTER EIGHT_

I sprint for the alley. Sandals pounding, lungs searing. My arm feels like a wasp got trapped inside my shirt and is savoring an extended sting. I reach the ramp in five strides. I stumble at that first short step, knee banging chin, but keep moving.

"Help!" I yell the instant I'm to the alley. "Somebody *help*, call the cops!"

I glance around feverishly. Nobody is here. Not cops or Cecil, not anybody. My fingers open and close and saliva floods my mouth.

The Elite guy catches me by the ankle. I stomp him off with fury I haven't known in a decade and run toward Second Avenue.

"I'm being attacked!"

I spot a group of office workers crossing Howard, thumbing their phones.

"I'm *being attacked!* Call the cops, quit outta your profile and *help!*"

Before I can tell whether they've heard, an arm closes around my waist. I buck forward another step or two, breaking the hold, but the thug hangs onto my sandal. My one leg flies out from underneath, flattening me to the street.

"*Stop* him!" I try. "*Somebody help, dial 911, get this guy off me...*"

But I am being dragged through the alley, and soon we're back underground. The thug yanks the metal grate down over the exit. It locks with a *clang*.

My cheeks are scraped raw from the asphalt—I can smell blood—and tears are streaming from my eyes. I swing my elbow blindly backward.

"I need doctors!" I say. "You assaulted me, I need a hospital doctor *now...*"

The man throws me over his shoulder in a fireman's carry. As we enter the stairwell, I scream and pound my fists into his back. His grip shifts across my arm, over the spot where he was squeezing before. The pain is bright-hot.

I howl into his yellow polo shirt, then once my breath returns, bite through the fabric.

He totes me up what feels like a dozen flights, but must not be, because we exit the stairwell at Three.

Carter Kotanchek and Jim Dawson are standing together, delivering some joint address. Elite has set up a command station, an open area between cube farms with phones, computers, and a doomsday countdown timer.

The guard dumps me into this area like I'm feral, peeling my nails off him, leaving me in a heap and then hurriedly backpedaling.

"Police, *now!*" I scramble to my feet. "This maniac needs to be in handcuffs!"

Behind the two principals, people drift over to watch. Minosh's eyes are saucers. Prisha grips a notebook over the bottom of her face. I heard a few grumbles this morning over Elite's unorthodox methods, but now people are full-on freaked:

their coworker is screaming about police and looks like she just crashed her dirt bike going a hundred miles an hour.

On the other hand—I can read the doubt in their stances—that coworker is me. Who knows what I might've done to provoke this?

Carter makes a flattening gesture for calm, then faces me. "We'll get you care, Deb. Blackquest contains a protocol for on-site medical. This is a terrible misunderstanding and I feel awfu—"

"*Misunderstanding?* No, it's not a misunderstanding, it's assault—and this dude here is going to jail. And *you*"—I whirl about finding Jim Dawson—"*you*, you neo-Nazi, you get to be his cellmate."

Dawson steeples his fingers, considering me. "You were informed that campus was closed. You willfully violated the rules."

"I tried to exit a building and *walk up an alley*. Like a regular, non-incarcerated citizen of the United States."

"You were warned. The consequences—"

"I was not warned!" I stab my finger at the guard. "He kept growling, '*Nn, nn, nn,*' like some dumb frickin' beast in the woods. He never told me he was going to physically lay hands on me."

Dawson lets my vigor dissipate. "Matthew cannot speak. He is mute."

I rear back like this is ludicrous, then consider the man in front of me. He crosses his arms.

"Well, now I feel like the Insensitive Clod of the Century, but that doesn't change what happened. He assaulted me. I'll let the cops sort out who said what."

"Your wounds are superficial," Dawson says. "Far short of the standard for terminating participation. Our medic will have no problems."

The arrogance in this statement is staggering. "I wasn't going to participate in this lame training *before*—but now, after your guy essentially mauls me, you think I'm good to go?"

He clenches his stress ball. His brow knits, making the scar at his temple twitch.

"I'm gone," I say. "I'm marching right out of here to a police station."

"Campus is sealed."

"I'll find an emergency exit. Apologies in advance for the ear-splitting siren."

"These exits are also sealed."

"*What?*" I scan around for Carter. "Have we talked to the fire marshal about this?"

Dawson says they did. A temporary exemption was granted.

I splutter, struck dumb for a moment. "I don't know what's going on here, but I'm leaving. You wanna make it two assaults? Go for it. Hope you've got good lawyers."

I start for the stairs. My legs are quivering and I'm seeing double. The guard looks questioningly at Jim Dawson. *Want me to stop her?*

Dawson says, "Blackquest 40 has a separate protocol for insubordination. The kitchen of this floor can be retrofitted as a detention center."

"Ooh, your own personal Guantanamo Bay. I suppose you have some attachment that turns the Keurig into a water-boarding machine?"

Now Carter rejoins the conversation. "I am sorry for all'a this, Deb. But the campus closure was made crystal clear. You heard, you were at the kickoff."

"Yeah," I say even though I wasn't, "but why would anybody expect that to be an actual thing—a thing enforced with violence? This is Corporate America. None of this macho talk is real."

"Blackquest 40 is different. As I explained, these guys approach stuff from a more serious place. *Paramilitary*." His cool-blue eyes gleam.

"You can't just sent around an email, people click, *I agree* and suddenly the place changes from an office into an internment camp."

As Carter counters with his FPP-1 spiel, Blackquest 40 being vital to the continued health of Codewise Solutions as a market leader blah de blah blah, I start feeling sloshy. It's a thing that happens to me—I don't know if it's a precursor to Mom's schizophrenia or what. One ear seems to accelerate to the floor while the other flies off my head, then they flip, then flop, then flip again—like some sadistic kid is yanking kite strings. I don't breathe well. Arteries pulse in my brain.

These shiny lips. Slithering, emitting noise. I need to stop the noise.

I walk close to Carter Kotanchek. Very close. His teeth are less white at this range, yellow-flecked near the gums.

My own molars lock and I suck from the base of my tongue. When it feels like enough, I squeeze off a ferocious grin and hock in his face.

Now an arm is around my waist. Paul Gribbe's.

"Let's go." He gestures to a conference room. "Let's go talk."

Half delirious, I allow him to lead me. Carter Kotanchek wipes his chin, then looks for someplace to wipe his hand—it's quite the gob I expelled. After settling for a wall, he takes a step to follow.

"Alone!" Paul says, waving Carter off. "You stay here. You talk to these animals. My team is *not* working under these conditions."

## CHAPTER NINE_

BY THE TIME WE MAKE THE CONFERENCE ROOM, PAUL guiding my woozy steps, I'm better. My eyes have cleared. The slosh has morphed into manageable disorientation. I sit beside Paul at one end of a table and am able to touch the chair arm, to process its sponginess with my finger. I can even smell.

McGriddle.

Paul hunches over our knees. "That's quite a bruise. Does it hurt?"

I shrug. "Not half as bad as Carter and that wannabe drill sergeant after I finish with them."

"That's the wrong approach," my supervisor says. "Don't let anger be your driver."

But I'm not really going to fight them. Not like that.

I scan the conference room, considering possibilities. The computer here will be blocked from the outside world...the phone is not going to reach 911...the window has potential—maybe I could sprawl, "SEND HELP NOW, FASCIST CORPORATE TRAINERS ARE HOLDING US HOSTAGE!" across several sheets of copy paper—except we're on the third floor and the adjacent building is windowless.

Through the door, Carter watches us. Jim Dawson is frowning at his doomsday countdown timer and hassling people back to work.

Paul asks what happened in the garage. I tell him.

"It was savage," I say.

"But you did try to leave?"

"Yeah, I tried to leave. So? You're taking their side?"

He kneads the bridge of his nose. "I know it feels good to follow our impulses. But as adults, sometimes—"

"Think they blocked Bluetooth? If not we might get an SOS through that way."

"You're not listening, Deb. You're not being rational."

"Oh, I think I'm being extraordinarily rational."

"No. You aren't. Look, I realize you disdain protocol—you've succeeded largely in spite of it. You have the kind of talent people accommodate. But there is a limit. There are times when compliance is required."

"Says you."

"Yes, says me!" His eyes bulge like Mr. Magoo if he ever stopped squinting. "Carter and Susan want Blackquest 40 to happen. They wouldn't have brought these guys in if they didn't see a concrete financial benefit."

"What, this FPP-1 junk?"

Paul wheezes. "I suppose. These executives...the logic can be circuitous, I admit. They have a plan. We need more revenue, and they have a plan to achieve that."

"Are you sure they have a plan? Because I'm not."

"I've worked sixteen years in this industry; I know how these business types operate." He fixes me with his thickest gaze. "You don't."

"Wait, you *are* these business types. You co-founded Codewise with Susan and Carter—you're rich and white, and you married your secretary."

Paul falls silent, taking sudden interest in the table's woodgrain.

As soon as the words are out, I feel terrible. What do I know about him and Li Wei? Paul doesn't throw my personal life back in my face. In fact, he once called out the whole team after a racy ad featuring lesbians entangled with Armani ties found its way to the kitchen corkboard. It didn't bother me a bit, but his concern was sweet.

"I am white. I did marry my secretary," he tells the table. "But the rich part..."

"Huh?"

"I have three kids, and Sunnyvale's expensive. Not much is left after the mortgage payment."

"How do you even have a mortgage?" The founders got 1.8 billion dollars—even split three ways, that should've been enough to support a family of three *hundred*. Does Paul have the mother of all gambling problems? Did he sink his windfall into Vonage shares?

He seems to read my thoughts. "I cashed out early, two years before the buyout."

"Seriously? Why?"

"I thought..." He pinches his forehead, then sighs. "Well, 900 K was 900 K. When Carter walked into my office and made the offer, I was shocked. My parents taught elementary-school math. I was driving the same Jetta I had at Carnegie Mellon. It felt like a no-brainer."

"But didn't—I mean, did Carter suggest maybe keeping a *little* skin in the game?"

Paul shakes his head.

"What a bastard," I say.

"I was a grown man, I took the deal."

"Did Susan object?"

"Oh, Susan was part of the deal—the offer was on both their behalves. They split my shares fifty-fifty."

I open my mouth to speak, but cotton balls are clogging the base of my throat.

I can't imagine Susan screwing him over. Maybe it was Carter's idea and she just went along, too busy to get involved at a detailed level. Maybe she thought Paul was being shrewd—playing safe, the only one of the three with a family.

Paul continues, "To their credit, they believed the growth would continue. They had faith. I didn't. Carter had just bought the Cray"—the Cray XK7 supercomputer currently mothballed in a broom closet—"and I thought his ambition would bankrupt us."

"But you're the one who built all those whizbang systems that put Codewise on the map! They became managers and you kept coding. Like those genome algorithms—that was all you, right?"

His mouth quirks at the memory. "It was."

"You were just hired help by then," I say. "Like the rest of us."

So much makes sense now. Paul and Carter always bicker—in meetings, over the dev queue. I've seen them fight over which grayscale is most appropriate for presentation drop-shadows.

*Of course.* I'm surprised Paul can stomach working in the same building.

Paul says, "Can you believe that stunt he pulled at kickoff, what they've got biz side doing?"

He has no clue about my server-room adventure. "Uh, I..."

"Did you even go?"

In this moment, I'm finding it hard to lie to his face. "Raven badged in for me."

He raises a shoulder, unsurprised. "Well, you missed a doozy. Somebody asked what the rest of the company's supposed to be doing while we engineers slave away on those 187 interfaces. Carter says, 'Crafting a business plan.'" Paul gussies up his own doughy features in an imitation of his old grad-school classmate—what a hidden talent, these impressions. "Guy asks, *What business?* Carter says it doesn't matter. They should be capable of analyzing any industry.

"Then, get this, he picks a newspaper off the podium, reads the first headline he sees—*Bay Area Firm Bets Big on Space Tourism*, about that launch Thursday—and says, there. There's our business: private spaceflight. They're going to mock up marketing materials, budgets, a ten-year plan. I swear he's rubbing our face in it, the arbitrariness. How divorced from the actual work-product these businesspeople are."

"They're just dreaming up a random business plan?" I say.

"Right."

"Do the same rules apply for them? No phones, nobody in or out?"

"Yep. Carter wants, 'that same time-crunch capability, instilled throughout the organization.'"

Paul's jowls are quaking. His eyes do dart to my toes below, so I know it's the same old him in spite of our new intimacy.

"Screw 'em," I say. "Without us they can't build their big Lego phallus. So we bail. They already assaulted me—what more can they realistically do?"

"Fire us. I did mention my three children, right? And I know those Carebnb wristbands don't come cheap."

"Anything that goes down, Susan can undo." I walk to the window, edging my nail into caulk. "I'm getting out."

"How? You heard what Jim Dawson said. You'll end up locked in the kitchen, guarded. Then what chance will you have to keep tabs on the launch?"

I feel my tongue traveling up my face, pushing out the cheek. Through the door glass, Dawson is approaching. Gripping his stress ball, pounding those commando boots over office carpet.

"Play it cool," Paul urges. "Keep your head down, do your work."

I watch Dawson. And he is watching me, with a glare so penetrating—so possessing—that I instinctively hug both elbows across my chest.

## CHAPTER TEN_

HELL. PAUL'S BORING AND REPRESSED AND STICKLERISH, and maybe McGriddles are slowly pickling his brain, but he gets this much right: I need to cool it. I can't manage Carebnb under house arrest. The stupidity of doing the entire project solo—without a single partner to backfill in case of emergency—is glaring. There's nothing for it now.

I blow past Jim Dawson to the Latrine and tell the room at large, "Come on, let's do what needs doing to get everybody off my jock."

The conference table is littered with notecards, coffee, highlighters. I take the middle seat and, using the knob of my wrist, clear a swath. The room feels jittery. The engineers might be working again, but none have forgotten my confrontation with the guard and subsequent screaming match—my bloody face and flayed upper lip are vivid reminders.

The digital timer reads 00:38:49.

Standing at the whiteboard are Jared, frowning with a dry-erase marker in his armpit, and that Elite guy with windswept hair.

"Graham," he says, introducing himself as Elite's technical liaison. "In your absence, I worked with Paul and Jared here on the broad strokes of an architecture. We'd love your input."

My eyes narrow. Graham wears the yellow polo shirt but with the collar turned up—ironically? accidentally?—and over thermal sleeves. Trim black jeans. That buoyant, dishwater-blond hair.

I am a firm believer in establishing ground rules. "I'm gay."

"Lovely. I'm Sagittarius," he says, dimples winking. "What do you think? We've encapsulated where possible but tried to keep our layers thin."

Warily, I turn to the whiteboard and consider their design. One group of programmers is to craft the module responsible for penetrating the host system while a second takes the optimization-algorithmic piece, the two groups collaborating over the initial link but mostly working separately.

"Conventional," I say. "If you freeze that junction early"—the junction being the link—"you predetermine the approach. You sacrifice creativity."

Jared snorts. "Have to. Otherwise everybody's coding against a moving target."

I should let this go. What do I care if the project fails? But that snort.

"The target is always moving if you're any good," I say. "Writing 187 interfaces in forty hours can't happen if you think like a lemming."

Graham watches with a bemused expression. I don't get how he fits with Elite. You have Commando Bureaucrat Jim Dawson. You have the mute thug. You have Katie Masterson with her thousand-watt smile. It's a motley crew, but each has some defect or slight weirdness to explain why they took a job with this bizarre outfit.

Graham, though, has hair like Matthew McConaughey. He

looks me in the eye while speaking, a rarity in the tech world, and his easy posture displays none of the others' overcaffeinated aggression.

After the three of us arrive at a compromise on architecture —i.e. fix Jared's mistakes, I face Graham with a squint.

"What exactly is being simulated here? You guys did a phenomenal job making the whole thing totally incoherent. What's the use case?"

"None. This is merely an exercise to improve teamwork and recreate a high levera—"

"Save it, I heard the spiel. But *this*"—I thump the white-board with its sprawling diagram of interfaces—"did not arise from thin air. It *does something*. It wriggles in, then blasts a bunch of complicated calcs, then hangs out. Why? What for?"

Graham laces his fingers behind his head and says sure, he'll provide more color. The software must inject itself into a foreign system, slipping past sophisticated, algorithmically-randomized security. Once established, it needs to monitor system output and swap in alternative values in perpetuity, passing any data-quality checks encountered along the way.

It's a mouthful.

I say, "Testing environment?"

"We have a server on-site," he says. "For FPP-1 certification, the final Blackquest 40 code must grade out perfect."

"Yeah yeah, I think I saw it." It occurs that I shouldn't divulge this, but Graham's hazel eyes are drawing me out. "Server room, big yuge box? At first I thought it was a bomb."

The eyes flicker. "Oh, that? Yes, that is a bomb—the faint green glow comes from plutonium. But we also brought a test server."

My stomach bottoms out for one beat, two beats...before I get it. "Jesus." I pat my chest. "Don't do that."

Graham smiles rakishly, crossing one black-jean leg over the other.

I remind him, "I'm gay."

"And I detest water chestnuts," he says. "Always have. Ready to write some code?"

CHAPTER ELEVEN_

WE CREATE A NEW REPOSITORY DIRECTORY FOR THE
Blackquest 40 code and divvy up engineers. The haggling over
assignments takes ten minutes. Jared wants Prisha on his
module because "she knows regex, and mine needs regex." I say,
"We all know regex. First day, CompSci 101." Jared claims his
is rusty. I say, "Can't you watch porn at lunch and leave The
Female alone during work hours?"

Graham is chuckling when a voice behind us calls, "What
seems to be the problem?"

Something like conspiracy flashes in his face before he
pivots to face Jim Dawson. "Miss Bollinger was just providing
invaluable cross-peer feedback."

Dawson ignores this attempt at levity. "A full workplan
must be filed by the first checkpoint, which arrives at the top of
the hour. Where do we stand?"

Everybody looks to me. "I was proactively heading off a
harassment situation."

Jared slams his trucker hat to the ground. "You can't say this
stuff!"

I inch my feet away from the hat, which brushed my

sandals. *Ew.* I may need Raven to do a lavender-rain sanitizer run.

I tell Dawson, "You've demonstrated access to our personnel files—check it out. I guarantee HR has formal documentation of the history."

"Bogus," Jared counters. "You cooked up that complaint at that diversity meeting of yours. Prisha would've never filed it on her own."

He is referencing the monthly gathering I host in the big conference room on Six. The room is obscenely oversized for us —the only regular attendees being myself, Prisha, Susan, and a militant ferrets-rights activist from Accounts Payable—but that's sort of my point: to highlight how badly not diverse we are. I think of it as half-meeting, half-political performance art.

"Maybe not," I say. "Sadly for you, institutionalized female acquiescence is on the run."

Jim Dawson's eyes pulse between us. "This is precisely the waste I spoke about in the kickoff. The *muda*. It paralyzes an organization."

"*Muda?*" I repeat.

Jared says, "She has no clue—she didn't go. Sent her drone instead."

I scoff at his juvenile tattle. But Jim Dawson is not laughing.

His eyes and mouth shut in unison while his stress ball grip tightens. Controlled breaths swell his chest. I feel like he could strike us, or tear the projector screen down with his teeth.

Paul Gribbe moves into the room with a ready look on his face. Engineers huddle at the door.

Dawson asks, "Is this true?"

I shrug. He knows the answer—he saw me right after outside the server room.

Is this for show? Menace for the sake of menace?

His lips are a bowstring of purple. The Elite gang too seems to fear a meltdown; Katie Masterson strides toward us with arched eyebrows. As she comes nearer, I notice they have the same chin and beaked nose—she and Dawson.

Siblings.

In an instinctive flash, I'm certain of it. This is not good. Family businesses are insular, warped—there are no checks, no empowered outsiders to sound the alarm when Brother Jim starts basing hiring decisions on whose moon sign happens to be in phase.

This guy Dawson could be anything. Polygamist, meth head.

He continues, "*Muda* is the Japanese term for waste. Toyota has made a mission of identifying, and systematically eliminating, its *muda*." With deliberate fury, he shifts to Jared. "Indeed I have reviewed your file, Mr. Ackerman. The phrase 'lack of personal responsibility' figures prominently. Your last review concluded that 'an obsession with process' hampered the speed of your deliverables."

"*What?*" Jared tugs his hat back on. "Who said that?"

"You spent a week perfecting the color scheme of your bug-ticketing profile."

"I was getting fifty emails an hour! If every single one's red, how am I supposed—"

"Enough," Jim Dawson interrupts. "Perhaps you've learned that instigating petty squabbles can advantage you. I assure you, during Blackquest 40, it will not. Do what Miss Bollinger says. To the letter. Make *muda* of yourself, and we will treat you like *muda*."

He enunciates the term with gusto, almost turning "-da" into "-die", then leaves.

The pressure in the room eases. My fist, tight around a pen, relaxes. *Did he really just smackdown my arch enemy?* I figured Jared's brand of bureaucratic glug would play well with these guys, but maybe I have underestimated them. Or overestimated him.

We finish the workplan inside ten minutes, Graham and I defining the stepwise deliverables with Jared's mumbled assent. The moment our document hits the repository, a jarring *pling* booms over the office-wide public address system.

I whirl to find the timer reset, ticking down from 1:29:58, its digits changed from red to green.

"Okay then." I stand and shake out my hands. "Now that we've staved off the beheading, I'll get cracking on my piece."

I round up my module-mates and give a brief peptalk. I tell them Blackquest 40 is a high priority for "the bosses"—a blanket term that excludes me even though I'm theirs—and that I intend for us to seriously kick its butt. In general, I try to shield the people I manage from my own snark. If they want to become jaded, that's fine, but I won't be that loser making others into malcontents for personal affirmation.

After splitting up the work, I head back to my cube and dive in, thinking to gain some breathing room, then pivot to Carebnb. I took the hardest interfaces myself, and now review the gnarliest of the gnarly on my laptop. (Elite has forbidden print-outs in the name of sustainability.)

At the module's core is a seven-variable matrix, which gets passed around and calculated upon. I squint and splay my hands and meld my soul with the problem—the only way I know, the method that got me through Lowell High and MIT and Harvard.

I slip into functions and carousel through FOR-NEXT loops, am divided by, and taken the cube-root of, and all this I *feel*. I have to or else it doesn't work. Without living in the algorithm, coursing through its guts, drowning in its veins, I can't express it in code.

My fingers find keys. I am vaguely aware of tapping, quaternions and helper classes and inner functions materializing on-screen, flowing from my brain like juice through jumper cables. I know narrow things—my left sandal is mis-Velcroed. I hear chatter from adjacent cubicles interspersed with recent memories, Graham dodging my question about use cases, Carter Kotanchek's plea to participate. My arm hurts. I smell blood again. I see cots and guards and disappearing stock options, and my overpowering sense is...specificity.

Purpose.

This algorithm has a mission. Psychically, I enter a different place. I jackknife into Jim Dawson's skull and that giant server, then lower to B1, to the hulked-up commercial van.

I hear that soft chugging.

CHAPTER TWELVE_

Minutes later—three, or thirty, or eighty—I come up with a shiver. My screen is awash in commands and variable names. Random comments I have no recollection of writing pepper the code. The interface is maybe four-fifths complete. A single conviction anchors my thoughts: I need eyes inside their van.

A secondary thought, tactical: Hedgehog Eleanor Roosevelt is coming with.

All my little pals are meaningful to me—the droid-Hot Wheels, the buggy dragonflies, Raven of course—but Hedgehog Eleanor Roosevelt claims a special place in my heart. She was my first, built back at MIT for a battle bot tourney. A protest entry, she had only soft spikes from a whimsical bike helmet—her "quills"—for weaponry. The chassis is an old toy tank whose plastic treads limit her to sub-snail pace. She makes flatulent noises whenever her fan spins, and she has zero long-term memory. Literally zero: her hard disk cracked during a prank at Google and I never bothered replacing it.

What the old girl does have, though, is input/output.

Keyboard and screen. Tiny ancient ones that flex across her back—awful to type and read on, but without my phone, she's all I have.

I find her in the bottom of my hemp satchel. Pulling on my hoodie, I carry her overhand to the elevators, quills between my knuckles.

Elite tech-hunk Graham is consulting with Jared and team. He crimps his brow in my direction.

"Hedgehog Eleanor Roosevelt!" I call over.

Graham strokes his stubble, and I see the word *naturally* in the top half of his face.

I keep walking. Back onto the elevator, down again to B1. I creep through the garage, hugging the east concrete wall toward Elite's van. An asphalt smell haunts my nose, possibly sense-memory from being dragged over it. Street noise sounds distant, like voices from the bottom of a swimming pool.

I move through dark, vacant spaces. The cage LEDs don't reach here, recessed as they are beyond the pillars. I pick my steps carefully, wincing each time my sandal contacts the ground.

I reach the fire extinguishers. I peer around one of the red canisters, past the van's tailgate, and see Matthew—mute Matthew—at his post.

He's twenty feet away. If I keep to this side of the van, he won't be able to see me. But will he hear, if I need to smash a window or destroy a door handle? There is still that chugging, which this near the wheel well has a high, rhythmic quality—a spinning belt?—that might camouflage a minor ruckus.

I approach the van with squatting steps. Through the driver's window, I see keys in the ignition. Whatever is chugging must need the current.

The other windows are nearly opaque, but I do make out

pillbox-shaped devices attached to the inner glass. Each is located near a door frame and pulses red.

Meaning *ARMED*.

No surprise there—Elite's security is bound to be state of the art. That isn't necessarily a bad thing.

Sitting cross-legged on the chilly floor, I prop Hedgehog Eleanor Roosevelt in my lap and scan Bluetooth. I then have to spin her around to check the two-by-three-inch display. (A rectangular cutout in her left quills houses the keyboard; a similar cutout in the right, the screen.)

The scan runs...runs...runs some more...Hedgehog Eleanor Roosevelt sports a chip roughly eight generations obsolete...and finally reports one secured and five unsecured networks.

One of the unsecured is *ELITE_AUTO728*.

Gotcha.

I select it with an eager tap and transmit several stray messages, generic unlock codes like 001, 999, 109. One causes the closest pillbox to blink faster, and I have a premonition of alarms blowing out my eardrums. Hurriedly I repeat the code.

The pulse-beat returns to normal.

I exhale. My palms press Hedgehog Eleanor Roosevelt's nubby rubber quills for calm. *No worries. Nicked the alarm code, that's all.*

Since 109 was significant, I try varying the first digit, shifting by one, transposing back-to-front. Hedgehog Eleanor Roosevelt doesn't benefit from regular compressed-air cleanings, and her keys stick—I have to retype often.

Transposing does the trick. I enter 901 and the pillbox shines green.

*DISARMED.*

I grip the van's handle, gulping. This will be my first break-in in maybe a decade. My thumb quivers against the sliding door as my forefinger tugs ever so gently. No alarm sounds.

I support the door's weight with both hands, keeping it quiet in its track. The door slides open. The first thing I register is smell, and it's terrific.

Steel, gas, Kevlar.

## CHAPTER THIRTEEN

THE CHUGGING IS COMING FROM A GENERATOR IN BACK, which powers a ceiling-mounted block of pure silicon might. *Where did they even find a chassis this big?* It spans the entire canopy of a fifteen-passenger commercial van. That box I tripped over in the server room was nothing. A faucet tap. This here? This is the cyclone.

I am walking forward slackjawed, staring up, and so miss the crate of guns.

"Oww!" I clutch my shin and look down, and all breath is sucked from my chest.

It's a minor arsenal. Short guns, long guns, fat guns.

There is more. My thoughts are wild tumbling starbursts, but in adjacent crates I dimly perceive vials and ammunition and coiled wire and hypodermic needles in shrinkwrap, and I just...struggle...am really struggling...to stay in the moment.

That sadistic kid is jerking my ears again, wrecking my equilibrium. The air is close and mineral, and it feels like metal filings are cropping up in between my wrist hairs.

I flinch away from the weapons. I have to—the aversion is

sudden, physical. I stagger sideways and brace myself by a file cabinet.

A file cabinet. Documents. Information on paper.

Yes.

Yes, please: paper I can deal with.

I pull the top drawer handle. Locked. My senses gradually returning, I see that it is a simple mechanism, no different from what Mom and I used to pick sneaking into abandoned buildings on rainy nights.

Several of Hedgehog Eleanor Roosevelt's treads are loose and ready to slough off. I pry one free and fit its thin body into the keyhole. I twist clockwise while jiggling up and down, which should work.

Only it doesn't.

I ram the hard-plastic piece deeper. *Screaaack.* I cringe at the noise. I twist again, jiggle. No luck. I'm out of practice. I ram harder, tearing my thumb on the piece's back corner. Blood drips onto the lower drawers.

*Perfect. Here, have my DNA.*

On my fifth try I keep enough tension in the plastic to unlock the drawer. Inside are manila folders. I begin rifling through. Sample workplans, promotional materials, printouts about motivational techniques. A file labeled *Containment* full of stapled briefs on cellular signal blocking.

Here, in a folder with a red tab, are the Blackquest 40 interfaces. They aren't labeled as such but I recognize them, that seven-variable matrix. I lift pages out, smearing blood in the margins.

Wait.

These aren't empty interfaces. They have code: implementations for all the interfaces, not just my algorithm piece but Jared's infiltration too. Have I just discovered the answer key?

I consider stuffing the pages into my hoodie or snapping a

photo. Except Hedgehog Eleanor has no camera. Then I notice a note scribbled at the bottom of one. *Too slow, host disallows.*

Now I look more closely. Several interfaces have comments like this, or incomplete code—a FOR/WHILE loop with no WHILE—or just preliminary declarations. As if somebody began the project, then gave up.

Is this some other company's attempt? Wasn't Blackquest 40 supposed to be tailored specifically to Codewise? "The most demanding, the most grueling we have yet conceived," Jim Dawson told me.

The lying sack of pus. It's all recycled from another training.

I try the middle drawer of the file cabinet, then the bottom—destroying two more of Hedgehog Eleanor Roosevelt's treads in the process. I make more noise and leave more blood, and I don't care.

I am flipping, scanning, comparing. Paper edges keep scraping my cut and making me angrier.

Finally, in back of the lowest drawer, I find what I'm looking for: personnel records. Time to pull back the curtain on these scammers.

The first stack of paper-clipped documents pertains to Graham Davidson. A United States passport featuring a younger photo—carefree eyes, crooked smile—and a single visa stamp. Portugal. A personality assessment tersely praising the employee's "pliability" and "ingenuity" while noting "a frequent disregard for authority."

*I knew there was a reason I half-liked that guy.*

Here is his credit report. A San Francisco driver's license. An index-sized scrap headed VERBAL with a check-mark indicating PERFECT, UNACCENTED.

The label on the next stack means nothing to me. Mikhail Stepanoff. When I flop open the passport, though, I freeze.

The guard, Michael! His overexposed photo is ghoulish, like

some electrocution snuff shot, bright-white skin screaming through the laminate.

Something else is off, too. The passport itself. Ns and Ps all backward, magenta instead of blue like Graham's.

I flop back to the cover.

## REPUBLIC OF BULGARIA.

I lose track of my hands. The stack of documents scatters to the van floor. *A former Soviet satellite.* I'm thinking oligarchs and daggers and secret police.

I bend to gather the mess, dizzy, unsure whether I'm covering my tracks or collecting evidence or what. The top item is another index-sized scrap, VERBAL, checked RUSSIAN ONLY with a handwritten note, "No time for retraining/accent mitigation. Recommend alternate cover."

Alternative cover. Like pretending you're mute.

I am just returning to the files—imagining what house of horrors lurks behind the automaton calling itself Jim Dawson—when the rear doors burst open.

## CHAPTER FOURTEEN_

Matthew—Mikhail, apparently—barrels inside, powering over the bumper, dominating my field of vision, as though the passport photo conjured him through some Eastern Bloc sorcery. The van interior illuminates but his face is so high, up near the generator, that I feel him as nothing but a swarm of knees, thumbs, elbows.

A pair of walkie-talkies sits on a shelf. I throw one. The other falls and I kick it. Both glance off him.

He keeps coming.

*The file cabinet.* I bend and, hooking my fingers underneath, heave. The cabinet topples to an inverted V-shape. Together with its spilled contents and metal rails, it partitions the cabin.

"I know—I know what you are!" I backpedal, thinking. "You're some kind of Russian muscle."

As Mikhail clears a path toward me, I keep shouting, hoping to distract him or possibly be heard from the alley. The words aren't registering—his gaze remains thick—but my physical volatility seems to give him pause. He strides delicately over the file cabinet, his stance broad and balanced. *Are there explosives in here? Is he worried I'll set something off?*

I am retreating, crab-walking in reverse, when my palm knocks something solid.

The crate.

With exploding hope, I snake my arm over its edge and feel around. My fingertips roam over cold steel, across dimpled surfaces. I grab the first thing that feels like a barrel.

Mikhail clears the file cabinet. I thrust forward the thing in my hand.

It's a crowbar. I am staring at him through its pointy claw.

He smirks and keeps advancing. In one spastic motion, I hurl the crowbar at his face and myself at his midsection. The crown of my head strikes his pelvic bone—hard, I feel the *crack* in my molars. He crumples to one knee as the crowbar rattles away.

Momentarily we both reel. I recover first and, scrambling away, use my left foot to sweep Hedgehog Eleanor Roosevelt into his path.

Mikhail rises. Reacquiring his target like a bear roused from hibernation, he rushes me. His second step catches Hedgehog Eleanor Roosevelt's quills. The stumble is just enough; I reach into the weapons crate and come up cash this time.

A gun: black, trigger, hole in front for bullets to exit and kill stuff.

"Dude, *freeze!*" Is it loaded? I have no idea. "Stay where you are—*right where you are*—and maybe I won't blast you to the East Bay."

He is looking at the weapon with an expression either solemn or dubious, I can't tell.

I press, "*What're you guys here for?* I just found the files and all those weapons—this ain't corporate training. No way."

He points to his mouth lamely.

"Cut the crap—you can talk. WHAT ARE YOU DOING HERE? TELL ME!"

Again with the mouth-pointing. He gestures for me to lower the gun.

"Not a chance." I thrust it forward, shuffling in place. "Talk now or I put you down."

Again my words don't seem to register, but the barrel in his face is clear enough. He tries, *do no English,* in a pea-soup accent.

I gesticulate at the ceiling-mounted hardware. "This monster server!" I turn my free palm up. "What purpose? *Que propósito?*"

Why Spanish? Why not? Mikhail continues to feign ignorance.

I am getting very irritated—holding a firearm must stimulate some anger-center of the brain. *Russians.* I cannot believe it. They couldn't stop at delaying the election of our first female president. Had to come to San Francisco and screw with my day. I liked the ones I worked with at Google, but I'm not getting that same brusque, brilliant, only-10-percent-crazy vibe the Google Russians gave off.

Maybe it's only Mikhail. Graham was American. Maybe Jim Dawson is too—maybe he needed a goon and this Cold War scratch 'n' dent was the cheapest available.

While I puzzle over all this, I sense Mikhail's angular face growing in size. I look down. His feet are inching forward.

"Nope. Cut it out *now,* or I blast you!"

His feet keep encroaching, sneaky little nudges. With every millimeter, he is growing more confident I won't fire. I can see it, those noodle arms growing freer, his gaze darker.

The pressure puts me back on the streets with Mom and Cecil. My knees pinch together, and a core of rage builds—hot, barbed.

I pull the trigger.

Nothing happens.

For a moment I think I'll be able play it off, poise my finger again and pretend that harmless click came from the generator.

But Mikhail is smiling. "Bullets no."

"You're a big talker now, huh?"

I brace myself to fight, gripping the gun like makeshift brass knuckles. If I can buy five seconds, maybe I can scale the side of the van and reach the ceiling spring-gate, then drop that server onto him like the anvil flattening Wile E. Coyote.

The percentages are not good, but it's what I have to give. And I'll give it to him like cancer.

His hand starts forward. I swing my gun-fist and scream through bared teeth, and connect, and now my throat is closing —being closed, by force of human fingers—but still I feel great.

I'm rearing back for another punch when the van's engine roars alive.

## CHAPTER FIFTEEN_

WE JOLT BACKWARD. TIRES SQUEAL. I'M HURLED AGAINST the wheel-well and Mikhail flies into the file cabinet, and now we're fishtailing, the skidding van tossing us opposite, my arm smeared into my cheek. I don't know left from right or up from down. Glass shatters outside, but not our windows—is this thing bulletproof?

A keening alarm.

Sour smoke in my nose.

*Who's driving?* I crawl forward to see. Mikhail grabs my hoodie.

His grip is fierce but I work myself free, kneeing him in the nose, then barrel-roll to the far side of the cabin and struggle up.

He stands too. Bleeding, haggard, his face lumpy from the abuse I've doled out. Next to the crate now, he finds his own weapon.

"So?" I say, woozy, my field of vision rolling left. "Not like it's loaded."

He lifts a ridged object, roughly the size of a crayon box, and slams it into the gun.

Before either of us can say another word, the van screeches

forward. I lose my stomach as my feet fly out from underneath. My head slams the floor. I crumple to a fetal position.

We accelerate sharply, then seem to brake, then whip around a hundred-eighty degrees. Then, with a concussive roar, we stop. I take a gauzy look around.

The rear doors are shredded, a steaming tangle of vinyl and metal. I am curled atop Mikhail's high-lacing boots. He didn't fall.

*Why didn't he fall?*

I peer up. His chin is slumped to his chest. Underneath it, the triangular tip of a metal slide. Four inches of it—glistening red, protruding from his yellow polo shirt. He's dripping. On me.

I squirm away and tug at the red on my hoodie, desperate, grossed out.

*He's dead, oh man the guy is dead!*

I look into the slack face, panicked. I've seen dead bodies before but never ones I made dead—or was present for the death of, or whatever's happened here.

What *did* happen? I pant for a solid minute.

Bulgaria or no, this guy has a family. A mother and father. A person he kissed first.

My body throbs. My lungs take air in giant, quivering pulls. I hear a slow wheeze somewhere, below the chugging generator —which endured the crash. I can't pinpoint the source. Radiator? Gas leak?

I raise myself to an elbow. Questions swirl through my mind, vague notions of jail and courtrooms and orderlies packing up Mom's things, but one rings clear: *who is behind the wheel?*

A steel door partitions the driver and passenger seats from the mangled cabin. I peer through its small, latticed window but can't make out a thing.

I am afraid...but my fear is maxing out, changing into a different thing. It's becoming permanent, a living part of me the way it used to be around gangs or when hard drugs were being exchanged.

My fingers roam for that gun of Mikhail's.

If Jim Dawson bursts through the door—if anybody in a yellow polo shirt does—I will shoot. I won't have a choice. Whatever this gig is, I know too much about it. Too much to be left alive. I wonder if the van's mad-pinball flight was an attempt to take me off-site, someplace where I could be disposed of. Maybe they finally decided I couldn't be bent to their will and would only ever be a hindrance to Blackquest 40.

"Yo."

Even through steel, even in a single syllable, I know that baritone. Like clean water rinsing my wounds.

"Cecil!" I rush forward leaving the gun. "It's you—yeah baby, it's *you*! How are you here?"

He passes through the steel door and we hug. His belly is a pillow between us. I grip his surplus jacket tight, getting blood all over. A chuckle passes from his chest to my ear.

"You said to meet, I was waiting behind the dumpster. Came when I heard fighting. Figured if there was trouble, you were probably involved."

"I am so glad it's you, Cec," I say. "So glad."

We hold each other. The only longer embrace I can recall is the day we checked Mom into Crestwood Psychiatric.

He nods at Mikhail's body. "Who's this? Don't look like a programmer."

This brings me crashing back to reality. To the horror of this new life, in which a man died while I was committing a felony—breaking and entering. Which means murder.

Which means the next time I see Mom, if there is a next time, will be through Plexiglas.

It's weird and dazzlingly unfair that my life has arrived here. For years I have worried I was wasting myself in an office. Sure I volunteer weekends, sure I started Carebnb, but my actual jobs —at Google, now at Codewise—have never lined up with my passions. They followed naturally from my field of study, and I enjoyed the challenges and (if I'm being honest) praise that was lavished upon me. But I never cared. I took the conventional route. The safe route, you would think, compared with a thousand others I might've traveled from childhood indigence.

"Not a programmer," I agree.

I explain Blackquest 40 to Cecil, tell him about the Bulgarian passport, nod around at the weaponry surrounding us. Cecil listens with the imperturbable air of a person who knows violence.

"Could be everything takes care of itself," he says.

"What do you mean?"

"They aren't calling the police, how you describe it. They want quiet."

I work my tongue around my cheek. "That might be true."

We stand silent in the wreckage—in noxious, thick-hot smoke. I don't understand how or why, but I know in my bones what this is about: money. The rending of the material world in pursuit of money.

"Listen, Deb," Cecil says. "I can't exactly hang out. Cops come around, find all this? Homeless man in the middle. Black homeless man."

"Right."

"I'll help with the body."

"The what?"

"The body. This man is six-foot-four, at least. That's a job."

It takes another exchange or two before I understand Cecil means to help me move the body. More specifically, hide the body.

"But...should we?"

"You have a better idea, I'm listening."

I consider suggesting we take our chances going straight to the cops, but on reflection, those chances seem poor. By the time anyone hears us out and is convinced to come to the scene, Elite will have cleaned up. Guns, passports—anything incriminating will be gone.

The forensic story will be me, breaking into a van and killing their guy.

The investigation could even wind back to Cecil. Which I can't have. Cecil never gave me and Mom his backstory, and we never asked. I have no idea of his legal jeopardy. I only know he came to help me today, and is now offering to hide a body without batting an eye.

No. I won't drag him into this.

Half-dazed by the surreality of what we're doing, I help lug Mikhail's body to the dumpster, fortunately right across from the garage exit. Cecil props his cart to hide us from Second Avenue. He takes all the weight—I basically get the shins down—and backpedals to the green receptacle, lips tight with effort.

I circle ahead to prop the grooved lid. On the count of three, we heave the body onto a bed of bulging trash bags.

Cecil drags a few over to obscure Mikhail. Then for show—in case anybody is watching, I guess—he jiggles free a splintered office chair and props it among his stuff. Sneers skeptically, then hoists it back into the dumpster.

He gestures to my hoodie, which is caked with blood. I peel it off and toss it inside too. My arms feel ten pounds lighter. I catch a glimpse of my hair reflected in a window, all smooshed. Instinctively I spike it back up between my fingers.

Cecil disengages his cart's wheel-lock. "Want to come, get away from these fools?"

I look beyond him to the open sky. I am thinking clearer now, with physical exertion and the passage of time.

"I do," I say. "Absolutely. But I can't."

In the heat of the moment, I thought it was kill or be killed with Elite. Now I'm realizing it's more complicated. Bailing presents the same problem as going to the cops: Elite gets to frame the narrative. They can finish out Blackquest and sanitize the parking garage, then show SFPD to the dumpster with a pat story. I can shout from the top of the Transamerica Building about Blackquest 40 being a ruse, but the police aren't going to adjudicate that. They don't have the tech chops to get to the bottom of this.

They'll see a body, and a suspect who ran.

*I* need to get to the bottom of this. I need facts—or else these last ten minutes will hang like irons off the rest of my life.

Cecil opens his shoulder to Second Avenue. "Sure? There's daylight, right up there."

"Nah, I'm burnt if I take off." *You might be too*, I think but don't say. "I need to figure out what their game is."

"Want me to call the cops?"

"Not yet. I need time."

He nods, opening one massive arm for a hug. "What are you gonna say about the van?"

I collapse into his belly. "Nothing." I wrap what my arms can manage of his back. "I'll just keep my mouth shut."

"That's not your strength."

In spite of everything, I smile. "Be safe."

"And kind."

"And kind."

As Cecil disappears up the street, the warmth I feel from our ritual parting words fades. In its place comes dread. A cold knowledge that my range of outcomes has just shrunk tragically.

The best I can be today is a killer. The worst? I don't want to imagine. Since the advent of personal computing, the blessing of technology has been scale. The ability to spread code instantly at zero cost, multiplying the impact of a lone creator, leapfrogging brick-and-mortar stores, shattering barriers that have protected industries—and people—for centuries.

Whoever conceived Blackquest 40 understands this. Is counting on it. This software they're asking us to build, forcing us to build, has aspirations far beyond Codewise Industries.

It's not until I reach the elevator bank that I realize I never asked Cecil about Carebnb.

PART TWO_

## CHAPTER SIXTEEN_

THERE IS AN OUT-OF-THE-WAY BATHROOM ON THE SECOND floor, near where the laid-off engineers sat. I head there. Lugging my bones up from the parking garage, both arms pulling the handrail. Off the stairs, I ease open the door and pad softly so as not to draw notice from whoever Elite has guarding the server room. I reach the bathroom—single toilet, unisex— and slip inside.

Lock the door.

Dare a look in the mirror.

It's grim, but it could have been worse. A red disk circles my neck where Mikhail choked me. Blood spray dapples my fore- head. It scrubs off with water and gritty pink soap, but this welt under my temple—maybe from the wheel-well?—looks like a weirdly placed second chin.

What's my cover story? I could say I tripped over coaxial cable, or ran into one of the lobby's posh geometrical statues. That would have to be one heck of a trip or collision. And why was I even in the lobby?

I'll just have to play it off and hope the general bizarreness of today provides some small measure of camouflage.

I clean up the last flecks of blood and re-spike my hair, taking clumps between my fingers and thrusting up at angles. I tease my collar forward to hide the choke marks. Hedgehog Eleanor Roosevelt—who lost her personal skirmish with Mikhail's boot—looks sad, her left quills caved in, but remains operational.

I say to my reflection, "Mouth shut, got it? Just like you told Cecil."

The eyes staring back show a pique I don't quite trust, but I refuse to argue. Mom used to argue with her reflection. Muttering at the back of a spoon. Yelling sometimes, or tearing at her own hair.

I return to the stairwell and walk up another flight to the engineering floor. I feel drained from the fight, drained from worry. I'm also famished—it's nearly one and I haven't eaten a thing.

Typically I would be coming back from the soup place or that bánh mì truck on Folsom, or if I'd been feeling ambitious, from eating at Crestwood with Mom. I am not delightful on an empty tank; my direct reports know not to ask my opinion after four-thirty lest my dragon breath singe their code.

Oh well. Hunger will just have to take a number and wait at the back of the line.

On Three, Jim Dawson is addressing the assembled development team. I hear him before I see him, gravel in his voice.

"...checkpoint is missed, there is a consequence," he is saying. "I can tell you from previous training engagements that once an organization begins to fail, the failure snowballs. Timelines compress. Belief in one another erodes. Unless a leader, or leader group, steps forward to right the ship."

He is speaking from Elite's command station, flanked by the doomsday timer, whose value has gone negative. Approaching from behind, I don't see his face.

I see the faces of his audience, though. With the exception of Jared, who sits aggressively unimpressed with fingers laced over his trucker hat, they're petrified. Minosh scribbles notes like every last word is going to be on the test. Prisha's ramrod posture is painful to watch.

I keep my head down to my workstation.

"Miss Bollinger," Dawson says before I make it. "How nice of you to reappear. We've been trying to reach you."

I twist back. "Know what's good for reaching people? Phones. They're handy like that."

A chuckle sounds from a nearby cubicle.

Dawson cocks his head. "What happened to your neck?"

"Hm?"

"Your neck," he says. "There are red marks."

I tug my collar back into place. "Yeah, I was assaulted. Remember? I tried leaving and your guy dragged me through the streets like roadkill?"

"The injuries were primarily to your arms. Your neck did not—"

"The hell it didn't."

And I stalk the rest of the way to my cubicle and plunk down. Dawson eyes me, then—apparently prioritizing the project over a precise accounting of my injuries—resumes lecturing the broader audience.

"When failure does occur, we seek to understand. A root analysis is necessary." On a projector screen, he activates a graphic showing each Blackquest module and its progress. "As one sees, this afternoon's missed checkpoint traces directly to the performance of the algorithm team."

The algorithm team is mine. No kidding we missed deliverables—I was AWOL, off discovering that Elite Development may or may not be an arm of the post-Soviet oligarchy.

But Dawson's glower doesn't settle on me.

It settles on Prisha.

"Miss Agarwal," he says, the name clunky in his accent. "You are second in command on the algorithm module, are you not?"

Prisha's cubicle sits in the middle of her cube farm. This area, occupied by junior programmers, has low borders such that all can see the alarm in her face. I know from speaking with her references during hiring that large-group communication isn't her strength.

She says, "Yes."

Jim Dawson pumps his stress ball. "In Miss Bollinger's absence, you took charge."

"I attempted to."

"Attempted?"

Prisha, seemingly in answer to his tone, rephrases, "Yes, I did take charge."

Jim Dawson paces nowhere for a few strides. His square jaw shifting, he ponders the projector screen—awash in graphs and percentages. The algorithm module is represented by an oblong, red-pulsing rectangle.

"Leadership requires a certain magnetism. A self-assuredness that inspires others." He folds his arms over his yellow polo shirt. "Do you believe you have magnetism, Miss Agarwal?"

It takes every ounce of self-control to not go tackle him.

*Remember: mouth shut, profile low.*

"Perhaps my style is quieter than others," Prisha says. "We did make significant progress on the matrix transforms."

Dawson's pursed lips drip sarcasm. "The American educational system places a high value on creativity. On novel approaches to problem solving. We often find these abilities lacking while working with employees educated overseas. Particularly Southeast Asia, where curriculums focus on rote skills."

"I received my master's from Cal-Berkeley."

"Unfortunately the mindset takes root early, during primary school."

Prisha holds his gaze, but I can see it's a struggle. She keeps touching her keyboard tray, then withdrawing, then touching it again.

A growl starts in my chest. I keep my chin pressed against my shirt as though I can pin it down, forcibly restrain my rage.

Dawson is watching me out the corner of his eye—I'd swear to it.

For the twentieth-eighth time, I remind myself that Cecil and I just stuffed a body in a dumpster.

Graham spots me, seems to perceive my internal strife. He is standing off to one side, fingers tucked into his trim jeans, beside bright-smiling Katie Masterson. Elite's version of Ken and Barbie.

"Miss Agarwal drew a bit of a rotten lot," Graham says. "The early algorithm work is challenging and down one, truly, it—"

"Challenging *by design*," Dawson interrupts. "All projects present adversity. One is either capable of overcoming it, or one is not."

"I'm sure with Deb back in the fold, and the team firing on all cylinders—"

"Miss Agarwal may simply lack the innate abilities required of her post. It happens. Hiring mistakes. The overzealous pursuit of diversity. Let's not sugarcoat facts because we fear saying things which are politically incorrect."

And now he's looking at me straight-on. Not even trying to disguise the fact that he's goading me, that this ethnically tinged cruelty—probably learned at some KGB sleepaway camp—has nothing to do with Prisha.

He wants me. He's drawing me out, punishing me for my absence.

I don't care. He wins.

Flipping a pencil end-over-end in the air, I open my big mouth.

## CHAPTER SEVENTEEN_

"STOP," I SAY, LEAVING MY CUBICLE, APPROACHING THE command station like some gunslinger in a western.

Heads spin—my coworkers', the Elite facilitators'. The office air crackles.

"You want a scapegoat? Right here." I thump my chest. "I'm the one who disappeared. Prisha is my direct report, and you're not going to stand here and bludgeon her with bogus right-wing talking points."

By degrees, Jim Dawson's eyes shift onto me. "Where did you just come from?"

"Bathroom."

"You were gone forty-eight minutes."

"What, you have stopwatches on us all?"

He ignores this. "You couldn't have been in the bathroom forty-eight minutes."

"I got sidetracked, made myself tea up on Ten. The executive floor has those fancy loose teas—oolong. I had an impromptu brainstorm."

"A brainstorm by yourself?"

"Yep."

My stomach growls, and my hip aches from standing. But I'm not about to sit now.

Dawson asks, "Any useful insights?"

"Could be," I say. "I need to catch up with my team, bounce some concepts around."

Mulling this, he fingers his glasses. I have the stray notion he's activating a truth detecting feature, some military-prototype overlay that tells him I'm lying with 97.2 percent certainty.

"Returning to Miss Agarwal," he says. "She is a recent hire, correct?"

"Relatively."

"The hiring decision was yours?"

"Mine and Susan's."

Dawson pulls a faux-thoughtful face. "You believed Miss Agarwal was the best individual for the job?"

"We didn't believe. We knew."

"Best resume? Outperformed all other candidates in interviews?"

The pig says it without saying it: *Did we give her special treatment? Did that second X chromosome get her the job?*

A throat clears behind me. I turn. Paul Gribbe, standing outside his office, gives me a significant look. I remember his advice from before. *Play it cool.* And that was before Cecil and I had our dumpster adventure.

Still.

Gender studies was one of my majors at MIT. Now Jim Dawson is going to smirk like he's won the point, reducing a complex topic and decades of scholarship to schoolyard trash talk?

"Let's discuss your qualifications," I say. "Where was your primary education?"

"Military academies."

*"Explains the fashion,"* I say under my breath, then aloud, "U.S. military academies?"

Dawson smiles into the question, but his face is rigid. Have I gone too far? Tipped that I know about his foreign ties? Would he even care?

Before he can respond, Carter Kotanchek breezes in from the elevators.

"Alrightee, what'd I miss?" One cuff of his linen suitcoat is rolled; one isn't. "We on track? Slayin' it?"

Carter's long-legged strides seem to generate wind. He comes to stand beside me, eyes sweeping the area for takers.

Paul pats his paunch absently. I'm sure not saying a word.

Jim Dawson pipes up, "Checkpoint number three was missed. We have concluded our root-cause analysis, and I was just discussing consequences."

Carter winces like he just shanked his three-iron from the fairway. "And?"

Dawson checks offstage with Katie Masterson, whose lips press together. "Each member of the engineering team will have 10 percent of his, or her"—nodding nastily to me—"Q4 options seized. The next missed checkpoint will mean half."

A groan rolls through the room.

Jared calls, "Everyone, or just the algorithm team?"

"Everyone. You succeed or fail as a unit. Although"— Dawson singles out Prisha with his eyes—"if an individual repeatedly falls short of expectation, further sanctions are possible."

Jared rips off his trucker hat. Prisha looks ready to crawl underneath her chair.

Personally, I am unmoved about the options. There's no way in hell that stands up once Susan gets back. She'll set things right. It's like a Hasbro steering wheel, something for Dawson to twirl and honk and pretend with.

Carter Kotancheck—a richie himself with no need of options—isn't perturbed either. The next Elite news, though, wallops him.

"A second missed checkpoint would place FPP-1 at risk," Dawson says. "Consistent, repeatable work processes are a core requirement of the certification standard."

Carter swears into his armpit. "We gotta get FPP-1, team! Got to."

Watching his head tick back and forth, and watching Dawson *watching* his reaction, I have questions. About a billion.

If Elite Development is not a corporate training outfit, if they're instead an arm of some foreign entity, what does that make Carter Kotanchek? A conduit? A conspirator?

How much of the truth does he know? And what's in it for him? Is this a power grab, Carter using Eastern European heavies to overthrow Susan? The timing fits, Susan off at the World Economic Forum in Davos. Maybe Blackquest 40 is a canard, an impossible project we have no chance of completing, our failure providing the pretext for ousting Susan.

My reptilian brain wants this, that straightforward co-villain to despise alongside Dawson. Logically, though, I can't quite make it fly. I keep going back to the code. That algorithm. The seven-variable matrix.

Purpose.

I felt purpose in the code. It can't be throwaway work. It matters. Somehow.

Carter is mid-lecture. "...realize we're asking a lot, but the market is demanding differentiators. We believe FPP-1 certification can be ours. The building used to be fuller, as you all know. Right? We ran up against some harsh realities in April."

And there it is: the direct reference to layoffs.

The threat.

*It's the monstrosity of Blackquest 40, or your job.*

I cut in, "Say, where'd you guys meet?"

Carter's eyebrows go the way of a stumped dog's. I think I see Jim Dawson flinch, the slightest wariness in his face.

"Just curious," I say. "Tech conference? Karaoke night at some bar?"

Dawson says, "The history of my association with Mr. Kotancheck is unimportant. Recall our previous discussion of *muda*, the quest to remove all inessential—"

"Was it essential we all hear your backwards dogma about diversity? And those rote curriculums in Southeast Asia?"

He has no answer for this.

I press, "Tell us—who cares? Just water cooler chitchat. How'd you meet?"

Again Dawson balks. In the silence, the steady hum of monitors and hard drives seems to swell. It gets awkward. People are looking around sideways—really, why *can't* he answer?

Carter Kotanchek, ever plugged into the social dynamics of a room, offers, "Believe you're right, Deb. Believe it was a conference. Moscone Center. Symposium on the intersection of military and tech. My old general buddy introduced us."

*His old general buddy?*

I ask, "Chum of yours from Carnegie Mellon?"

Carter's eyes betray nothing at all, zip. "That's right."

"Did Paul know him?" I twist around and spot my boss, who studied at Carnegie with Carter and Susan. "Paul, I can picture you in that whole ROTC scene. Friend of yours, too?"

Paul frowns like someone just handed him a McGriddle minus the maple flavoring.

"Frat brother of mine," Carter says. "He and Paul wouldn't have crossed paths."

The sight of CK Slick on his heels like this cheers me.

Adrenaline kicks in, pulling me out of the trough I sank into after the garage-dumpster exertion.

I was planning to do my digging on Elite under the radar, but now I think...*why?* Emotions are running high. Maybe Dawson will slip. Mikhail's body is not well hidden; I could be found out at any time, hauled off in cuffs. This might be my best shot.

I take a stride toward Dawson. "Does Elite still do military trainings?"

"We maintain a diverse client list."

"Gotcha. Wouldn't want to go soft in the middle, huh?"

Dawson allows a smile.

"Ever bring weapons to a training?" I ask.

"Of course."

"*Of course?*"

"We are training you in software and optimizations, we brought computers," Dawson says. "When we train soldiers, we bring weapons."

I nudge Carter. "Wonder if that's all they brought, computers. Was equipment discussed in advance? Are they allowed to have guns on-site?"

This, surely, takes it too far. The engineer who sits next to Minosh—Patton? James?—has shuffled into a corner at the word "guns."

"I—well, I wouldn't know," Carter says. "They're pros, they know the job. I'm sure they bring whatever the exercise requires."

I huff. *Yeah, pros. Pros armed for a minor coup.*

Dawson seems to note my reaction. Face darkening, he transfers his stress ball between hands. "Can we agree these questions have gone beyond water cooler chitchat?"

At this point, I back off. Dawson too dials it down, saying the time has come to look forward and devise a plan to meet checkpoint number four. He invites Jared and me to lead the exercise.

As my pulse slows, I recall his comments about "further sanctions" on "individuals who repeatedly fall short of expectations." I decide it's not fair to place Prisha—in the country on a precarious H-1 visa—and the rest of my team at risk, no matter what beefs I have with Elite.

A dozen of us from Codewise join yellow-shirted coordinators in the Latrine. There I get my first taste of Elite's catering, and I must admit: it is sublime. Salmon cutlets that flake like pastry, artisanal rolls, tabbouleh so bright-tasting my empty belly cheers. It feels bizarre to be assembling sandwiches on a china plate after what happened in the garage. On some level, I know it's illusory—this corporate gentility can't hold.

But gosh, these sandwiches.

I wolf three by the time we've settled on a work plan. I am just dabbing chipotle aioli off my chin when Katie Masterson sidles up to me.

"It does a body good," she says, patting her own flat tummy. "Nutrition matters for productivity. We put serious thought into the menu."

I nod across the room to Dawson. "Your brother should add some fruits and nuts to his diet. Maybe chamomile tea."

Katie chuckles. "You're right, I am his sister. I actually came over so we could chat a bit about him."

"Girl talk? I don't know if it would've made the dossier, but I actually prefer the company of—"

"Jim hasn't benefited from the same communications training I have. Clearly there's a culture gap between you two. I feel like you're talking past each other."

I shrink from this assessment, which Katie has tossed off with a twinky grin.

"He's spewing racist, disrespectful bile at one of my direct reports," I say. "That's no culture gap. That's ignorance and intimidation."

Katie Masterson peers through the dull-yellow office light to her brother, busy with a pair of facilitators. We are standing near the door. Now she slips out to the hall, beckoning me to join.

"Can I be honest with you?" she whispers once we're alone.

I glance around, not trusting this. Is she going to confide in me? Me, who she's known for twelve seconds? Will she tell me about the van arsenal in some sort of preemptive admission?

Does she *know* about the arsenal?

"Please," I say. "Honesty would be greatly appreciated right now."

She checks ahead and behind, confirming the hall is empty. "Elite is not a large operation. We did $500,000 in revenue last year. Codewise did $42 million. My brother and I..."

Her lip stiffens. "We don't come from money. Jim took out loans. He does our parents' taxes by hand. He feels a lot of pressure, this large imbalance between Elite and Codewise, and I suppose he..."

She grimaces at the ceiling, searching for a word.

"Overcompensates?" I say.

"Yes! That's what he does." She clutches my sleeve at our new camaraderie. "That Southeast Asia bit—I am so, so sorry. We know you're a protector. Jim knows he's asking extraordinary things of the team, and he feels like he need to project this overpowering authority to make it happen."

For a moment, I just stand there. Has an employee of Elite Development just told me their leader is full of hot air?

I could absolutely use this against Dawson. I could throw it back in his face, or repeat it to Carter or Susan—if she ever returns from Davos.

*Why is Katie divulging this?* Did she sympathize with

Prisha? Did her brother pinch her mercilessly in childhood and now's her first chance for payback?

Which gets me thinking.

I venture, "Where did the two of you grow up?"

"Outside Columbus, Ohio. Are you familiar with the Westerville area?"

That answer came awfully quick.

I fix Katie Masterson's eyes, wishing I had some truth-detecting overlay of my own. "Did your brother display any, oh, antisocial behavior growing up? Skinning live pigeons, stuff like that?"

She giggles, high-pitched from the top of her nose. She thinks I'm joking.

## CHAPTER EIGHTEEN_

ONCE CHOW TIME IS OVER, WE BREAK TO OUR RESPECTIVE module teams. I find Prisha hate-typing at her workstation. Seeing me, she sniffs and pulls around a second chair.

"Thank you for stopping that," she says. "I—I wasn't sure it was my place to push back."

I sit. "And he was counting on that. Bullies always seek out safe targets." I mime shooing away a fly, then borrow her keyboard to bring up the Blackquest code. "He'll get his. Believe me, when Susan shows up? She'll put him on a train back to the 1950s where he belongs."

I walk Prisha through the new plan, and together we review the remaining pain points.

Generally I'm not a hand-holder, giving my engineers space, not troubling over how they're interpreting my sometimes manic and scatter-shot guidance. But now I go with a softer touch. That matrix of variables won't transform? I can take a crack. Jared's being stubborn? No sweat, I'll pay him a visit and convince him of the error of his ways.

When I say this last, Prisha rears back in her chair and looks beyond me.

Shoot. I've laid it on too thick.

I did the same thing in June when I invited her to my diversity meeting, explaining how important I felt it was that women support each other in the workplace. I talked about being lesbian and an outsider in Corporate America, and refusing to stand for their myths and double-talk.

She leaned slightly away with an expression that said, *Ummm, okay, can you just say which conference room it's in again?*

"Or whatever," I add now. "You can handle Jared yourself. I know, you're—"

"Deb," she interrupts.

Keeping her neck and shoulders perfectly still, she fixes her eyes up the hall. I realize she wasn't responding to my words at all.

She was looking over my head at a group of Elite yellow shirts. "They're talking about you."

It's true. A whole posse is gathered in the hall, pulled together by the corners of whispering mouths, gazing straight at me.

Katie Masterson's grin is marred by a crimp. Graham's fingers are spread in what might be a plea for restraint. Two previously unseen facilitators—on the beefy side, rumpled—are doing most of the talking.

Of the bunch, only Jim Dawson seems unperturbed.

They know. These new goons must've been running an errand to the van and stumbled across the demolition-derby scene in the garage.

"I need to, uh...check in with Paul," I tell Prisha, standing. "You go ahead, get rolling on the code. We'll catch up soon."

I slip away, taking longer strides than usual but keeping my torso slow—as though doing so will dupe Elite into thinking I'm not going anywhere. I watch them for a few steps.

Their focus stays on me, but they don't pursue.

I turn up the hall. Paul's is the corner office, one half visible from this hallway, the other obscured around the corner. I see him hunched over his desk talking to...let's see...gotta go a little farther...okay, now I see who he's with.

Minosh.

I accelerate to the office. "Need to talk, Paul. I have an idea. Just came to me out of the blue."

I've stepped directly between him and Minosh. Minosh scoots his chair sideways to peek around me.

Paul says, "I'll be with you in a moment. We're nearly finished."

"It's urgent, has to be now," I say. "Minosh doesn't mind, right?"

I grip his chair's ridged spine and all but eject Minosh toward the door.

"Not appropriate, Deb." Paul gestures Minosh back to his place. "I realize you've been through the wringer today, but—"

"It's about Li Wei!" I say, spitting the most impactful words I can think of. "Okay? Minosh, how about it? Five minutes."

Paul drags one broad leg up into his lap, suspicious. Minosh squats a few inches above his chair, not sitting but not leaving either, looking between us like a kid caught in the middle of arguing parents.

I goggle my eyes at Paul to communicate that I need to talk him, like, *now*.

"I'm very sorry, Minosh," he says. "Please give us a moment."

Minosh taps a loose paper flush to his notebook, scooting to the hall.

The door claps shut.

"This had better be good." Paul exhales through his nose. "No one employee's time is more important than another's."

I bob my head contritely, glancing back through the door glass to check the Elite yellow shirts. They're harder to discern at this distance, twenty or thirty yards. I think they're still looking my way.

Are they drifting closer?

"Yeah, it's not good," I say. "Actually it's pretty awful."

"How on earth are you in touch with Li Wei? With the data blockade, I haven't spoken—"

"It's not about Li Wei, my God are you literal." I grip the scruff of my neck. "It's about Elite—these thugs who've taken us hostage."

I rock forward on my tiptoes, then back, then forward again. I don't want to tell him. I don't want to tell anybody—the plan was to keep Cecil's and my ordeal secret until I turned up some answers about Blackquest 40. But that ship has sailed.

I need an ally. I need a smokescreen, or magic rabbit—but first off, I need Paul to not go running apoplectic to Carter and Dawson, demanding the police be called in.

Because I'm not ready for cops. Essentially I'm in the same situation I was in the parking garage. Even if the cops had the knowhow to dig into Blackquest 40, they wouldn't. Mom and I used to deal with SFPD. Unlike their movie counterparts, they don't pursue conspiracy theories. Dead guy plus my blood and fingerprints, plus irrefutable evidence of forced entry—those alarm codes sent by Hedgehog Eleanor Roosevelt—equals case closed.

On a wing and a prayer, I launch into a censored account of my joyride in Elite's van. The guns and vials and hypodermic needles, Mikhail's passport, the generator-powered server big enough to power the International Space Station. I gloss over the breaking-in part, admit to "tussling" with Mikhail but say I only knocked him out, and omit Cecil altogether.

Paul's expression degrades over the course of the tale.

Consternation turns to disbelief, which turns to flabbergast. Each time I think his outrage has maxed, another vein goes purple.

Finally he is holding his head in both hands, spreading them over his skull as though fighting to keep stuff inside.

"Deb," he says.

He fits his hands differently over his skull.

"Deb," he says again.

My name seems to physically lock his tongue.

"I know, I know." I peek down the hall. "This is not ideal."

"*Not ideal?*"

"No it's bad, I get that. I do. But listen, all the firepower in that van, and the source code—which they've *definitely* worked on before, I saw the notes. Somebody tried Blackquest 40 and couldn't make it work, and now they've come to us because we're the best. They think we can crack it."

I argue that the underlying function of the code, whatever it is, must be evil. And not I-disagree-with-your-views-on-campaign-finance evil. Criminally evil. Otherwise why go to such great lengths obscuring it?

As I huff on, Paul's attention drifts past me—like Prisha's earlier. I glance back. The same Elite posse is watching, but closer now. One of the new goons reaches for the rear-right of his belt. For handcuffs?

For a gun?

They found Mikhail. They're taking me.

The only question is the location of my jail cell: SFPD, or Jim Dawson's kitchen detention center—if the progress of Blackquest 40 is deemed so important that a small matter like death can't get in its way.

SFPD might be better.

Paul says, "That crate of weapons, maybe it was from a previous job."

"Are you *high?* You don't just forget to take instruments of killing out of your car—like they're your bike helmet or paper towels from the market. And what about the passport?"

"Bulgaria." Paul swirls the word around his jowls. "Unusual, but not unheard of. I hired a Bulgarian contractor a couple years back. Adobe Flash specialist. Bright kid."

"Paul. Seriously."

"And if my recall of geography is correct, Bulgaria wasn't in the USSR. It borders Greece. Actually closer to Turkey than Russia."

I consider going into those VERBAL scraps and Mikhail's feigned muteness, but there's no time. The yellow shirts are advancing. I pop out of my chair and start up the far side of Paul's desk, out of view of the door glass.

"Let's walk and talk, okay? There's more I need to tell you— because when they haul me off, it's all gonna be on you."

"All what?"

"The truth! Figuring out the truth—why we're being locked in a building for forty straight hours. Why I've been brutally assaulted twice. You've lived inside this code, Paul. You know logic and algorithms. This is your bread and butter. Tell me, honestly. Do *you* believe this is corporate training?"

As Paul considers, I take hold of his wheeled chair and start pulling, dragging him to the side of the office Elite can't see. If we can slip out by his other door, then swing a snappy detour, maybe we buy ourselves a few minutes.

Paul neither helps nor hinders me at first. My already sore muscles are suffocating with effort. I strain for leverage, taking backward-chopping steps, accidentally stomping his foot. He glances down, taking the opportunity to leer at my toes.

A bleak thought occurs to me: Paul is not going to help.

He's one of the most risk-averse people I've met, and the risk here is gargantuan. I think of that Sunnyvale mortgage, of his and Li Wei's three children and all the financial obligations they must bring. Probably the family budget depends on those Q4 stock options. Certainly it depends on his continued employment and Codewise paycheck, both of which he imperils by siding with me.

I think of how I have treated Paul Gribbe over the eight months he's managed me. A few kindnesses. Some heartfelt technical discussions. Beyond that, it's not a record I'm proud of. I have not endeavored to know him, or particularly respected him.

Allowing my sandal to slough lower down my foot, I curl my big toe kittenishly underneath my second.

Is it wrong to flaunt my lower extremity assets like this? Cynical, in the context of my anti-Jared crusade?

I don't care. I need a miracle.

CHAPTER NINETEEN_

When Paul's face lifts to mine, it has a new tint: in that same neighborhood as dough, but darker. Golden gray. His eyes aren't judgingly on me, ready to find fault or impertinence. They are focused inward.

It's a look of resignation.

"No," he says. "Blackquest 40 can't be an exercise."

And his palms find his knees, and he's pushing up to his feet, following me out of the office's second door to the hallway.

Relief floods through me. *Yes, he IS a sentient being capable of logic!*

We rush by six or seven occupied offices—a quality-assurance manager leans to look but stays in his chair. We pass a utility closet and bank of printers and kitchenette. I plant my foot at the kitchenette...but decide no, that half-wall won't fly. Paul crashes into me from behind. We pick ourselves up and clamber on.

I just need someplace that'll be safe for five minutes so I can offload my theories and information to Paul. Now that he's bought into the premise, there is hope. Probably I'll be locked up by the time Susan arrives (*when is that Davos flight getting in?*), but he can be whispering in her ear, making sure Dawson and Carter Kotanchek don't pull the wool over her eyes.

The hallway ends at the elevator bank. Three-quarters of the way there is a small conference room whose door is papered over. The paper is from last Friday's staffing discussion—brown, torn off a roll and masking-taped up to guard against busybodies like Jared who try peeking and finding out other people's review grades.

I bolt inside, waving Paul in too, slamming the door after us.

"Port 9009," I say, gripping his shoulder. "That's where you start."

I explain how to circumvent Elite's data blockade. He can send and receive data using port 9009. Start with Bulgaria. The name was "Mikhail Stepanoff." Find his records, figure out what devilry he's done in the past, then look for a link to Jim Dawson.

Paul smears a hand across his mouth. "I disagree."

"Oh, please, we don't have time to—"

"Carter is the key. This whole operation is right out of Carter's playbook."

"Playbook?" I keep peeking at the brown paper, which won't fool anyone for long. "Blackquest 40 seems like once-in-a-generation lunacy to me. Who has something like this in a *playbook?*"

"The ambition of it," Paul says. "The scale. Carter's always working some hustle, each bigger than the last."

"Look, I don't like CK Slick. I'd love to strike a match off that lacquered hairdo and watch him dance—but I have to say, even he seems skittish about where Jim Dawson has taken this. I think Dawson is our Bad Guy Number One-A."

I plant my index finger on the circular table, which houses a desktop computer and standard UFO-looking conference phone. Aeron office chairs are spread about the room like overgrown spiders.

"Dawson is intense," Paul says, "but intense in the service of results. He came to see me when you were missing, you know."

"What, to harass you?"

"No. For my help. He knew we were on track to miss the checkpoint, and he was desperate. It's my sense he's under tremendous pressure himself."

I remember what Katie Masterson said about loans and doing their parents' taxes. "What kind of help?"

"He wanted my opinion on how to bring you on board. How to motivate you."

"Yeah? Did you suggest fewer assaults?"

Paul smiles, leaning a khakied hip into the table. "I told him traditional methods wouldn't work. I told him underneath that tough veneer of yours, all you care about is people. The welfare of others."

I feel a pang of warmth for my boss, whose remark naturally brings to mind Carebnb—which may or may not be revolutionizing the unhoused problem as we speak.

It occurs to me now that Paul knows I spend more time on Carebnb than my contract allows. He may even know I'm running that GPS data through Codewise servers without asking. I see six months of his burbling lips and pained forehead rubs in a new light.

"Where's the pressure coming from?" I say. "And what drove Carter into bed with a ruthless outfit like Elite?"

Paul looks at me frankly.

We speak the word together, the answer to both my questions: "Money."

I feel something in the walls—creaking, swelling. The groan of movement.

Then footsteps. Far off still, but they won't be for long.

Elite is coming for me—and Paul and I are nowhere near settled on a post-my-incarceration plan. I peek again to the paper covering the door glass. If Dawson thinks about it for more than two seconds, he'll know exactly where we are.

I scan the room, spotting the PC. "These conference room machines all have multi-card readers, right?"

Paul has wobbled back into a corner. "M—most do."

I simultaneously knock the mouse to deactivate the screensaver and dive under the table to the computer console. It's dark, and I have to check for a card reader by feel.

*Slick case...optical drive, no help...wait, go back...there, some slits!*

The face of a multi-card reader. From my pants pocket I produce my SIM card—the one I fished out of my phone before slinging it at Dawson—and wedge the pinkie nail-sized media into a slit.

Computer innards stir. An indicator flickers green. I hop back above the tabletop to check the monitor, and am ecstatic to see the contents of my SIM card on-screen.

I cruise past cellphone pics and videos and downloaded files to what I need right now: Raven commands.

There are more than a hundred. The subset fitting on the screen ranges from FIND_SUN to FOLLOW_AND_FILM_-JARED. As I scroll the list, both elbows and half my chest urge over the table.

Paul asks what I'm doing.

"Buying us time," I say.

"How?"

"Raven's going to draw them away." I find and click on REMOTE_CONTROL_MODE. A new window appears containing the drone's livestream and graphical joystick control. "I'll have her pretend she's tracking my GPS signal. Maybe she can lead them down to the garage."

"Why would they follow her?"

"Because they think she knows where I am."

"What's going to make them think that?"

I squeeze my entire face at Paul's stickler questions—the plan makes perfect sense in my head and I'm busy watching the livestream, dragging controls, navigating Raven up the hall—before realizing he's right.

I slump back from the keyboard, leaving Raven in a hover outside Paul's office.

"Grr. Yeah, we need her to vocalize the command. 'FINDING DEB GPS,' something like that."

Paul asks whether Raven usually vocalizes commands.

"No, but they don't know that." Struck with an idea, I replace my fingers on keys and mouse. "An audio file! We can record one here and sent it to her. She can play it out her speakers, I'll crank the volume."

On the livestream, Elite yellow shirts are approaching Paul's office. The group has shrunk, no more Katie Masterson. Apparently girls are unwelcome in their vigilante roundups.

The remaining hard guys lean through the doorway, heads quick, looking up-down-left-right.

The fine-coiffed head of Graham turns Jim Dawson's way. He seems to be dissuading Dawson from entering Paul's office. They argue, then Dawson thumps Graham in the chest—whoa! —and powers inside. He stalks about briefly before finding the second door and motioning the others to follow.

I pull the PC microphone near and speak into it, "*Locate Deb GPS.*"

After I click the *Stop* rectangle, an audio file appears on the desktop. I drag it onto Raven's icon. It uploads in a half-second. I am about to issue the PLAY command when Paul objects again.

"Won't they recognize your voice?"

Double *grr*. He's right again.

I shove the microphone across the table. "It's gotta be you, Paul. Here, say the command."

He recoils as if the mic—black, goosenecked—could strike him. "They've heard my voice too."

"No offense—because I mean this in the best possible way? But your voice has a natural robo-synthesized quality. It's perfect."

He puckers his mouth, but does speak the command.

I zap the audio file up to Raven, then check her livestream.

I have to pan around to find Elite—they have left Paul's office and started down our hall. Using a feather touch on the mouse, I guide Raven in pursuit. She hums along eighteen inches below the ceiling, straight (she's able to auto-course-correct finger slips), gaining ground.

When the yellow shirts are directly underneath, I instruct Raven to surrender altitude. She runs so quiet they might not notice her up high.

Paul whispers, "That's us!"

His eyes bug at the livestream. Off Elite's left side, the very next door shows glass covered in brown paper.

It's now or never: Jim Dawson's square jaw has paused, fixed in the direction of our door. He still hasn't noticed Raven overhead. I click back to her commands from my SIM card and run COUGH_LOUD.

Raven performs a series of hardware restarts—fan, hard disk —that makes a few seconds of mechanical scratch. She is so close I hear through the wall.

On the livestream, four faces whip up.

Paul and I look at each other. We whisper at once, "*Now!*"

I issue the command to play the audio file. A beat later, the voice of Paul—hollow but clear enough from Raven's speaker— says, "Locate Deb GPS."

Jim Dawson's eyes remain centered in the screen, staring up my girl's skirt. He does not blink.

Next I engage Raven's autopilot, providing her the GPS

coordinates for the parking garage. She begins traipsing ahead for the elevators. Her livestream shows nothing but clear hallway now, the yellow shirts behind her.

*Did they buy it?*

*Are they going to follow?*

I'm not hearing footsteps.

Across the table, Paul's half donut-bald head is sinking. I am confused. Those Aeron chairs aren't losing height again, are they? Moments later, a ripple passes through the carpet. I look underneath the table.

Paul is hiding. Lowering himself quietly as possible, contacting his knees in succession, then butt cheeks, then arms with wrists joined gingerly. He finishes on his side like a felled bowling pin. Full cheeks tell me he's holding his breath.

I think I'll join him.

## CHAPTER TWENTY_

WE STARE AT EACH OTHER TEN ENDLESS SECONDS, LYING stock-still on our sides. My left hip bone is made of pain. My scrapes and open cuts itch. Our ears prick at any noise—a faraway door, air through overhead ducts.

Finally, we hear a footstep in the hall. Then another. I brace for Elite to burst in, for some thug's arm to jerk me to my feet...but the door stays shut.

I roll painstakingly to my knees and peer over the tabletop to the monitor, which shows Raven's livestream.

"They went!" I whisper.

The yellow shirts are boarding the elevator with the drone, wedging themselves into the car. "It worked. They're following her to the garage."

Paul picks himself up off the carpet to confirm. "It's only four floors."

"I know, not much time. Okay—so assuming Carter Kotanchek is the mastermind, what're we looking at? What is he capable of?"

"Hard to say."

"Criminal stuff? You were at Carnegie with him, did he have a record?"

"None that I'm aware of."

"Hazing? Some date rape-ish thing?"

Paul shakes his head. "The key is to think big. In the grandest imaginable terms. When he pitched Susan and I on the Cray supercomputer, he predicted we'd solve global warming. He thought we could box the problem algorithmically and then blast scenarios until we licked it."

"And you *bought* that? He just wanted a shiny toy."

"No." Paul pushes his lip forward. "He had a vision. He believed in that vision. When it didn't pan out, he dreamed up another—he thought the Cray would be great for reality TV. 'Geek Versus Machine.' He actually found some producer-type to shoot a pilot. It almost worked. The network backed out last second, but for a while there it looked like they'd buy it out from under us."

"Instead it's collecting dust up on Twelve."

"Right. Sixteen million dollars' worth."

On the livestream, Raven leads the yellow shirts off the elevator. She floats along, hugging the parking-garage ceiling. By default she will fly to the geometric center of the room and wait. I decide that might seem suspicious, like she's stumped or malfunctioning, and so dash off a RANDOM_CRUISE 15 command. This will keep her wandering in a fifteen-foot radius of that point.

Paul adds, "I don't believe Susan would've sided with him about the Cray under different circumstances. She and Carter were...well, closer then."

His words contain a tiny sulk. I can't believe he's making this allusion now, of all times.

Huge triangle dynamics exist between the Codewise

founders. Jared dished some of it to me when I started, before my aversion to workplace skeeze turned us into enemies. Does it nauseate me that Carter and Susan briefly dated, in the lean days before she was a tech mogul-trailblazer? Yes. Still, imagining Paul as some jealous third wheel—brooding, huffing around the office kneading his hands—is nearly as gag-inducing. I'll pass.

"Let's forget the Cray, that's ancient history," I say. "If Blackquest 40 is Carter's baby, it goes back to money. Just how brutal are the numbers? He told me something about 'swimming upstream,' said we were getting squeezed on price?"

"My understanding was things had improved." Paul raises a shoulder, befuddled. "The April layoff was painful, but suddenly in June Carter had budget room to hire all that new sales staff."

"Yeah, I remember June—they started taking out the trash again." Janitorial had temporarily gone to an every-other-week pickup schedule, which did not mesh well with my Greek yogurt obsession. "Something changed in the middle. In May. What?"

Paul has no idea.

"And why didn't it last?" I continue. "Why does he suddenly need Blackquest 40 and FPP-1, or whatever else this entails, if things were better?"

We brainstorm—talking fast, thinking fast, an eye on Raven's livestream. How might Codewise profit from this scheme? Can Carter's claim that FPP-1 is essential to compete over the long haul be taken at face value? What counterbalancing benefits to Blackquest 40's surely exorbitant cost could there be? Neither Paul nor I really dig balance sheets, but we bumble along as best we can.

"I wonder if it isn't some backdoor equity play," Paul says. "Maybe Carter negotiated us taking an ownership stake in Elite. He's always wanted to diversify. It helps explain the options penalty—if we're all under the same fiduciary tent, transferring options from us to them would be easier."

"So Codewise gets into the corporate training biz?"

"Maybe. Maybe Carter covets the military contacts."

"And then you've got these brutes coming to company barbecues? We're supposed to stand around playing cornhole with Jim Dawson?"

Paul shrugs.

None of this is getting us closer to the truth. My thoughts are gunked up. All this money talk has dragged a slime across my brain—I'd rather be exploring Carter's probable betrayal of Susan, or how Blackquest will help Elite subjugate the masses.

I bite my cheek and growl and check Raven's livestream. I don't see yellow shirts.

*What happened to the yellow shirts?*

I pan around, using the joystick controls to swivel Raven's camera. On the third sweep I spot Elite.

Jim Dawson has led them to the alley exit, near where the van crashed. He and three goons face the wreckage. Their fifth member, Graham, stands palming one elbow, fingering his thermal undershirt. He twists to peek back at Raven's camera.

He can't be smirking.

What are they saying? Anything? No one is rushing into the van or banging on windows for Mikhail, or whipping out his phone to dial 911—which seems to confirm what I thought earlier, that they already discovered this.

Did they discover the dumpster too?

I tap out instructions for Raven to creep closer, hoping her mic can pick up their conversation. She's just started moving when Dawson whirls and leads his team directly at her.

He is angry. Maybe he's wise to my deception. The chunky glasses sit on his nose at a crazy skew he doesn't bother correcting. Forget that stress ball of his—Dawson looks like he might take a running jump and rip Raven down by a rotor blade, start slamming her into a concrete pillar.

There's no time for evasive maneuvers. My jaw goes weak thinking about my pal of several years and dozens of loving makeovers. I recall the early days, feathering pink highlights onto her case even though I hate pink, because I was sick of people calling her "he." The first time she ran off 100 percent solar. I brace for her plastic and silicone guts to rain down on the parking garage.

But Jim Dawson keeps going. He zips by underneath, vanishing from the livestream. The rest of the yellow shirts, Graham pulling up the rear, do likewise. I rotate Raven's camera to track them.

They are shrinking. Soon they've reached the elevators.

I take the keyboard urgently. "If an equity stake is coming back to Codewise, there must be a record. You have top-level access to the financials, right?"

This conference room PC has badly cluttered menus. Annoyed, I squint through icons for the accounting database. I've just found it and am clicking through login dialogs when Paul responds.

"No," he says. "Not top-level. Only Carter and Susan can see everything."

I growl more and spin the mouse around, a full 360 on its pad.

*Argh.*

The more I consider it, the more convinced I am we need to see that balance sheet. To dive into those cash flows, see whether Codewise invoiced anything from Russia or Bulgaria—when, how much, who authorized the transfers.

I think I need to be on the loose a bit longer.

"Hey, what if I could get onto Carter's machine?"

Paul stares at me like my yellow spikes just turned fuchsia. "Up on the executive wing? Tenth floor?"

"I just saw him down here, I'll bet he never logs off. All I need to do is to slip into his office. My badge won't work on E-wing but yours would."

Paul claps both hands over his badge as though I'm mugging him. "Every badge-in is tracked. Elite would know immediately what was going on."

"Not necessarily," I say. "If anybody's checking the badge log—which you know they totally *are not*—all they'll think is that you're upstairs looking for Carter. Or putting a paper on Susan's chair, or finding her office professional, whatever."

His hands stay on his badge. The lanyard, stretched taut, divides his palm into two pink patties.

"Let's step back," he says. "I—I think we should go through proper channels. Carter is the CFO, after all. Breaking into—"

"Screw proper channels! Don't go soft on me now. Carter sold us out! He forfeited his rights."

Paul's mouth folds into itself. My pulse is galloping.

We both look to Raven's livestream. Down in the parking garage, the elevator car has arrived. The doors split. Yellow shirts step on. Jim Dawson thrusts his index finger at a button. Behind him, Graham flops his head back, hinge-like, in what I read as a pose of submission. The doors close.

Suddenly, I know what to say.

"Look, if this is illegal—guns, the white collar financial piece, any of it—then we're on the hook too. You especially. You're an exec."

"How?" Paul says. "I've done nothing but my job."

"Right." I drum my fingers pertly on the tabletop. "How'd that work out for Bernie Madoff's people? Or Enron?"

The threat of legal jeopardy has the desired effect. Paul's eyes pinch to dots, then swell, then pinch again. He cocks his head as though preparing to object but thinks better. His whole torso lifts in a trembling inhalation. Is he about to sneeze?

He unclips his badge from the lanyard.

"Please, Deb."

I accept the badge across the table, waiting for more. He's either unwilling or incapable of elaborating.

"Of course, absolutely," I say, off to the hall.

I sprint for the staircase, two halls away. Pivoting at the first corner, I twist back and see Paul emerging from the small conference room. I guess he'll just...return to his office? What will he say if Jim Dawson comes to question (interrogate) him? Maybe he can keep Elite busy for a while, buy me a few extra minutes.

I flash a thumbs up. Paul nods. He looks green.

He never would have given me his badge if he'd known what happened to Mikhail, the full extent of the garage incident. I feel bad deceiving him. He's been a prince—if I was at my desk, I would flip Polarity of the Universe from *Evil* back to *Amoral*. Still, Paul will thank me after I turn up proof Carter's in bed with these oligarchs—proof we can share with Susan to get this nightmare shut down.

Won't he?

## CHAPTER TWENTY-ONE

Much as I want to, I can't sprint the stairs. Starting at Two, they leave their dim fire-exit confines and become focal to a towering, tiered balcony overlooking the Codewise lobby. Cinder steps yield to pine, the switchback slopes turn gentle, and parallels of sleek metal twine demark the shaft.

I approach the first pine step with panther stealth.

I see the lobby—and the lobby sees me—through a minimalist glass balustrade that always strikes me as disturbingly low. Below, mounted flat-screens play static rather than their typical CNN—a consequence of the data blockade. Security Kyle mans the badge reader. Forward of him, an Elite yellow shirt paces before double doors. Over this entrance hangs a three-foot-high banner:

CODEWISE SOLUTIONS IS CURRENTLY CLOSED FOR A TRAINING EXERCISE.

Neither Kyle nor Elite's bouncer notice me creeping upstairs. I'm grateful for *Sempiternity*, a commissioned water statue whose gurgle masks any clacks from my sandals. The statue, together with a pearly water wall that opposes it from the west end of the lobby, gives the air a greenhouse tinge—a humid lick against my skin.

Winding my way to Ten, I wonder if any outsiders have been turned away. Few clients come to Codewise for on-site pitches. The most likely visitors would be delivery companies—these, I'm guessing, would've been allowed in to drop their packages. What would it take to arouse suspicion? Smoke alarm? Busted-out window?

I think of Bruce Willis in *Die Hard*, chucking that terrorist's body from the fiftieth floor out onto a cop's windshield.

By the time I've climbed the eight flights, my quads burn from keeping my footfalls soft. I lay Paul's badge against the reader and slip into the Executive Wing.

There is nothing wet or remotely organic about the air on E-wing. You're awash in moneyed comfort. Car coats, silk scarves. No stacks of programming reference tomes spiraling out of cubicles here. Workspaces are orderly, filled by ski portraits and bric-a-brac arranged for impromptu client or manager visits—that indispensable face time—rather than...well, work.

Besides executives, E-wing is home to Sales, Marketing, Business Development (you say "BizDev" with jazz hands), Corporate Strategy, and whatever management consultants are currently feeding off the host organism.

I cut between a man laughing, thumbs tucked easily in chinos, and a woman bobbing her tea infuser in a porcelain mug.

My blood boils reflexively. Where are *their* doomsday countdown timers? Elite must've decided this part of the organization is above cattle prodding, or at least not worth troubling over. What did Paul say they were tasked with, some random business plan?

On sheer outrage, I'm ready to whirl on the pair, who're surely trading raised eyebrows over my warzone appearance, when I hear the cheery voice of Katie Masterson ahead.

I stoop-walk nearer. Probably I should skedaddle by to Carter's office. I can't remember whether Katie was still on Two when Brother Jim began his witch-hunt for me. Even if not, he could have broadcast a message to all Elite personnel.

If she spots me, I'm toast.

I cruise behind a file cabinet—as good a cover as I'm going to find in this open-plan workspace. Pulling out a drawer absently, I begin fingering through paperwork and tune my ears forward.

In fact, Katie's voice is not cheery.

"...mood is all wrong," she is saying. "The imagery is so wispy. Why this soft blue sky? Where's our dark, mysterious outer space? And doves? *Doves?* This could be feminine hygiene ad copy."

I risk telescoping my neck beyond the file cabinet. Katie Masterson is gesturing at a poster board print that shows an aircraft, sized between a 747 and NASA shuttle, soaring over a lushly rendered earth. The title reads in unassuming sans-serif, "Join Our Stewardship of the Final Frontier."

"The doves symbolize openness," explains a Codewise employee I don't know, thirty-something with a shaggy hipster beard. "We wanted to create a warm, inclusive feel. Welcoming. Safe."

"Safe, yes. Safe makes sense. But why *stewardship?* The business plan you've been assigned is private space flight. This sounds like some NGO consortium."

"We—er, were hoping to capitalize on the preexisting good-will capital."

Katie Masterson looks between Shaggy and his team's concept art, vexed.

Shaggy goes on, "OurSpace has such overwhelmingly posi-tive brand identification. The commitment to sustainability, the great transparency with test flights. If we play off this image, revenues—"

"What does OurSpace have to do with anything?"

"Well, if we—that is, if we're going to model their business, we have to account for how—"

"You *aren't* modeling their business," Katie says. "You're modeling the business of a generic private space flight company."

Shaggy stops talking. "Oh."

Exasperated, Katie accepts his apology. Shaggy explains his team has spent the last six hours devising a plan specifically tailored to OurSpace, the Bay Area firm featured in the article Carter chose off the front page of *SF Chronicle* at the kick-off meeting.

OurSpace is a cool company—I actually interviewed with them before taking the Codewise job. Oren Andreassen, their founder, is a major open-source booster and runs all their software through the cloud: launch and nav systems, everything. He took me for a spin around San Mateo in his driverless car, resplendent in silk bodysuit, gushing his philosophy of code ecosystems and interoperability.

Katie Masterson is clearly not feeling the coolness. It's her own fault. Apparently this is Elite's first trip upstairs—they've been busy tormenting us engineers. These sorts of definitional confusions plague every project. If they wanted their phony business plan nailed, they should've paid more attention.

As Katie pivots from the poster board, my chest seizes. *Did she spot me?* I jerk back behind the file cabinet.

A moment later, I hear her reengage with Shaggy.

I hustle away to the next hall, around a corner to the C-level offices. I've dallied too much. Elite could be questioning Paul right now, grilling him for my whereabouts. They could be telling him their version of the truth about Mikhail—that he's marinating in a dumpster, that I did it.

Hearing that, would Paul keep protecting me? I hope. It's no slam dunk.

The first office I encounter is Susan's. Dark—but the door is cracked. I catch a whiff of her space, the crispness of the damask couch, after-scents of a cashmere trench coat. My strides slow unconsciously. A burn passes through my body—a good, restorative burn. I yearn to dive into her office like a defector hurtling an embassy fence, to shelter there.

Soon.

My ex once accused me of having a crush on Susan. I don't. I'm fully cognizant that the Susan Wright of my imagination is not real. Real Susan can be a tad officious. Real Susan wears foundation at times, and once glossed over an office mold concern during a town hall, which irked me.

But I refuse to nitpick her. That's what happens to women in power—theirs flaws go under the magnifying glass instead of being subsumed by gestalt.

Not My Susan. My Susan is non-perfectly perfect, and I'll hammer anyone who says otherwise.

I pull myself away from her office. The next gleaming brass nameplate I encounter reads *CARTER KOTANCHEK, CHIEF FINANCIAL OFFICER*. Lights blazing, door wide open. There's no sign of CK Slick.

His office professional, though, stands just outside the door, frowning at the clasp of a manila envelope. She doesn't see me.

## CHAPTER TWENTY-TWO_

THE WOMAN IS NEW, PART OF CARTER'S RECENT HIRING binge, and fits the feng shui of E-wing. Six foot. Voluminous roan hair. A cream suit that belongs on a mannequin rather than a real person knitting her brow, standing right where I need her not to be standing.

Before her eyes lift from the stubborn clasp, I sidestep to the desk of one of the office professionals—possibly hers—and grab a paper stack. Any stack. The top page reads *Regional Network Opt Proposal: Giga Telecom*.

It'll do.

I saunter back toward Carter's office. The woman is still finagling her clasp. I croak idly from my throat until she looks up.

"Oh. Can I—" She breaks off seeing the state of my face. "—er, assist you with something?"

I fill my lungs with air, hoping the floor's management essence will seep its way to the bullcrap-generating region of my brain.

I need a story. *But what?* She didn't use my name. She does not seem awed or on-guard, the two most common responses my presence invokes here. I don't think she recognizes me.

"Sorry about the gorefest." I touch my lump. "I'm new, from the mailroom—they had me bike halfway across town to get this for Carter. Pothole on Folsom Street one, me zero. At least I got here. Now I just need to leave this on his chair."

I wag the papers, mopping my brow.

The woman looks downhill at me. "I'm new as well, relatively. Ashley Thimms."

"Hiya Ashley, Zaya," I say, recycling the name of my old Harvard grad-housing roommate.

Ashley initiates a handshake. "You said you biked? Isn't campus sealed?"

"That's the official story, but this Giga Telco thing is so important Carter said we could." I cup my hands around my lips. "I'm not supposed to tell anybody they let me through. Hypocrisy and all."

She accepts this without flinching, which I take as proof hypocrisy is king here on E-wing.

I continue, "So...right then, I'll just leave this on his chair."

"Oh, I can do that." Ashley offers her slim-fingered hand, palm up.

"No I'm good, thanks, you keep working that clasp." I crimp my face apologetically. "We have this sadist down in mail? He takes pleasure in overwrapping those till they're literally impossible to open. I report him, nothing happens."

With all the self-assuredness I can muster, I breeze past to Carter's office.

I've been here before for Susan meetings. The space is showy and over-prosperous. Armless blue velvet chairs preen. An art deco chandelier looms over a tulipwood table. He's all set for Annie Leibovitz and *Vogue* to show up.

I go straight for Carter's desk. A glass top and spare, drawer-less design do me no favors: Ashley will see exactly what I'm up to if she hangs around. I don't look over, not wanting to appear furtive if she is keeping tabs.

I need a few minutes. The "leave it on his chair" ruse has gotten me inside, but it won't explain me sitting here typing furiously at Carter's machine for any length of time.

Hmm.

I drop my pilfered packet on Carter's chair. I watch it land, then cock my head. I gnaw my lip. I glance quizzically to the hall—confirming that yes, Ashley is watching the performance—then manufacture a few more gestures to show my distress.

From the hall, Ashley asks what's wrong.

"Wrong version," I say. "Downstairs they handed Carter the Q3 proposal to compare with this, what Giga marked up. But Giga actually gave me Q4. The slides don't match. He won't know what he's looking at."

"Should you...call Giga? Could they courier over the Q3 proposal?"

I mime walls around us. "Can't call out. And I want no part of another bike ride."

Ashley looks all about for solutions, wincing up the hall, patting her blazer pockets. Office professionals are either like this, taking up the cause of whoever's in need, or else putting every last non-bigwig petitioner in her or his place, zealously enforcing the boundaries of their duty. I'm lucky Ashley is the first kind.

"Can we print out the other version?" she asks. "The Q4?"

"That's *exactly* what we can do." I stop myself from smiling. "Where's your print station?"

She points past Susan's office.

"Great, lemme just hop on"—gesturing to Carter's machine —"and find the file."

This dents Ashley's helpfulness. As she watches my fingers

slide to the CFO's keyboard, her neck straightens. "I—I really can't let you use Carter's computer."

"Oh, I'll use my own credentials—see, bossman here isn't even logged in." Actually he is. "See, I'm just using the terminal. His files and stuff are all totally secure, totally siloed."

As I'm saying them, I realize these terms are too sophisticated for a mailroom employee. Still, Ashley seems to accept the explanation. Must be the yellow-spiked hair, which is murder with hats but dandy for exuding generation-appropriate tech savvy.

I tell her I'll send Q4 to the printer as soon as I find the file. Few minutes, tops.

She leaves.

I bang keys. Carter's desktop has a shortcut to the financials database, which I click. A staid interface unfurls—tables, charts, some cheesy speedometer gauge depicting current annual revenue versus the same period last year.

The speedometer is in the green. Dark green. Denoting "slow."

I navigate to *Cashflow Dashboard*, which confirms Paul's and my earlier discussion. The beginning of the year was rough; the April layoffs slashed cost but didn't improve incoming revenues; May was a mixed bag; in June, the coin came roaring in.

I drill into detail views to see what's behind the topline numbers, annoyed at these cutesy sports car loading animations —which bog the software down. I make a mental note to hack in later and swap in that internet graphic of a turtle stroking her chin.

I investigate any large credit or debit. Each month shows a similarly-sized red block representing a hunk of cost. I click one. The sports car materializes on-screen, spinning its tires.

*Yeah, look at you motoring.*

Eventually the debit's name appears: CRAY XK7 DEPRE-CIATION. Makes sense. The Cray will probably haunt Codewise's balance sheet for another five or ten years.

I'm squinting around May to see what changed when Ashley returns.

"I haven't seen any print jobs come out," she says, then begins spelling out the printer's network ID, benignly assuming that's the holdup.

"Thanks, but it's the file I can't find," I tell her. "I think I'm finally in the right directory, though. I can shoot it over in one sec."

I hunch back to the financials, hoping Ashley will disappear again to the print station.

She doesn't.

"You strike me as an honest person, but—" Her almond-shaped eyes squinch. "But I'm not comfortable with you being on Mr. Kotanchek's machine like this. I need to get his consent."

"Yes, do." Without cellphones, it'll take her some time to track him down. "I just saw him near Paul Gribbe's office. Extension B2381."

She leaves for her workspace. Without a cell, it's the only place she can call from.

I refocus on the screen. Working two fingertips into my temple, willing myself back to accountant mode. My brain feels shrink-wrapped. All these dollar signs make Microsoft Windows look greasy.

It's odd seeing projects I've led represented like this, in terms of pure monetary contribution. Big healthy blocks of green from Universal Studios for my buggy dragonflies. A sickly sliver for that mind-blowing AI routing bot I wrote for Portland's department of urban planning. My level of effort and enthusiasm, I realize, bears zero relation to these projects' actual value to the company.

I return to May. Okay, first two weeks...look terrible.

The Boeing gig dropped out—that's right, I remember now, Paul and I walked them through final output at an April thirty-first meeting.

The joint project with Dynamix scaled way back, the spend level falling by 75 percent. We were getting paid *that much* to consult on basic neural-net architecture? I wonder if they got wise half the information could be had free off Wikipedia.

The bosses must've been panicking. They had tried layoffs but were still bleeding cash. Did Codewise have some emergency line of credit? They would've struggled just meeting payroll, paying for the juice to keep water pumping through *Sempiternity*.

What was *I* doing in May? Perfecting the Carebnb user interface? Dreaming up a costume for Bay to Breakers? My girlfriend at the time wanted me to be ketchup—she was going as mustard—but I stuck with Mitch McConnell. I choose my own costumes.

On May seventeenth, a giant green mass appears. It occupies a full third of the screen's vertical rise, blowing away the *Revenues* scale. On the strength of this entry alone, May goes from unmitigated disaster to middle-of-the-road profitability.

I expand the date range to June and find two more blocks of identical size, making it the company's best month of the year. Of the last two years. Looks like these bonanza payoffs appear every other week, starting that seventeenth of May and ending...

Not ending.

The last one credited Tuesday.

## CHAPTER TWENTY-THREE_

THIS IS IT. NO DOUBT.

I know the engineering queue backwards and forwards, and *nothing* started around May seventeenth. Somehow that money involves Elite.

I stare at these big honking chart segments and they taunt me, morphing into servers and fifteen-passenger vans with death black sides, and Jim Dawson is there too, his face grumping out from within green pixels.

It's them.

I click into the first box. Up pops the label JOURNAL ENTRY DEPOSIT.

I click the June boxes, the July, the August, all of them, and get the same result.

JOURNAL ENTRY DEPOSIT.

I double-click for the detailed record, which 99 percent of the time would show me the full company name, billing address, and designated contact person.

But it won't now. Instead, the cornball sports car returns—right, *vroom, vroom*—and moments later, a new login screen appears.

Username and password. Neither is pre-populated with Carter's credentials.

Grr.

Journal entries are like money that got stuffed into the cash register between normal transactions. They don't arise from our regular billing flow, which means the details aren't captured—or at least not captured here in the main financials system.

The details exist, but they live in their own separate reporting database.

Which requires its own login.

I slam my fists on either side of the keyboard, rattling the glass desktop. A framed picture of Carter at Pebble Beach, holding a flagstick with Phil Mickelson, splats flat.

I have to get in. I have to filch his password. I hunt around his space hungrily, drawers, sticky pads, the bottom of his stapler.

I *know* Carter has a password cheatsheet somewhere. The Great IT Push Toward Password Security—change every two weeks, must include alphanumerics and at least one Farsi character—is great for foiling hackers on all seven continents, but makes it impossible for anybody to memorize their own.

His pen cup. Underneath his mousepad.

*Damn.*

I check his virtual desktop. Fairly clean. A few stray document icons scattered around his background image of pink-orange sunrise over a vineyard.

Wait! What's over there in the corner? Between those last two rows of grapes, off on its own?

A plain white rectangle. Text file.

I highlight the icon, causing its title to turn bold: **groceries.txt**.

Grocery list?

Oh Carter, you dog you.

I double-click and sure enough, here's the motherlode: credentials for email, Skype, online banking, and two dozen more.

I scan down to the line beginning "Journal Ent DB" and copy-paste the username and password. The software accepts them without a hitch and gives me a report screen. In the upper-right, account options under the heading *Hello Carter K.* Navigation tools in the left and top nav bars.

I am expecting details for that May seventeenth entry to unfurl like gold doubloons in the middle.

But what pops up is not details, or doubloons.

PAYER/DETAILS REDACTED.

You're kidding.

I click every last pixel of that phrase to get more info, but nothing leads out. The dollar amount is there, $425,334, but that's it. No company name. No contact phone or address. Zip.

I switch over to the first database and try the next big green block in the series, and the one after, and the one after that. My finger weakens with each hopeless click.

They're all redacted. Someone wiped the data.

A pregnant crackle fills the office. I have a flash fear Elite is deploying some futuristic weapon, vaporizing me over Wi-Fi or delivering infrared pain-daggers through the screen, before recognizing the pre-hiccup of the public address system.

"*All engineers, return to the third floor immediately.*" The voice is Jim Dawson's, harried, booming. "*Return to your work-stations at once.*"

I glance to the hall. Ashley doesn't know I'm an engineer, but this unusual broadcast—the PA has been used maybe two, three times in the entirety of my Codewise tenure—might set her on guard.

I open one of Carter's random desktop documents and shoot

a print job to the LaserJet, then lean into the hall. "Okay, found it! Can you check and let me know if it's coming out?"

Ashley's hair crests a monitor, then the rest of her. She nods brightly and disappears up the hall. I wave thanks and point back at Carter's computer, like some refrigerator repairman just gathering up their screwdrivers.

I pull the door closed, depress its push-button lock, and dash back to the keyboard. Ashley will think it's weird when she finds me locked inside, but I don't care. I'll deal with the consequences.

I am figuring this out. Now.

Whoever's behind this shady money can weasel it in by journal entry, they can redact, hell maybe they incinerated whatever paperwork accompanied the cash too, but they can't destroy data.

There is an underlying record, some primordial string of zeros and ones their money-stinking fingers can obscure but not remove.

I stare at the screen. *How deep do I start?* It depends how extensive the cover-up of these payments is. Has the finance team merely slapped a "Redacted" tag on these records but left the source database alone? Carter and his near-underlings could've pulled this off by themselves. If so, a simple database query will cough up what I need.

But what if Carter involved the database engineers? Waltzed into the techies' space fuming aftershave like some morality-twisting mist and made them zap the relevant rows from the table?

That'd be hardcore.

Up to this point, everything about Blackquest 40 has been hardcore.

I obtain a command prompt and navigate to the absolute

bowels of the Codewise data world: the A server, which stores flat origin files.

Every application, from email to reporting to Jared's *3D Putt-Putt Golf*, has its incoming data stashed here before being prettied up with tabs and column headings and various formatting. This data is pure ASCII gobbledygook, primordial as it gets.

Even directory names are nonsense. /wfeoi_2. /3332iEV. I scan for something that might correspond to the journal entry database. I read and tap-tap-tap with dizzy abandon, opening files, glaring at datum, pulling at my yellow spikes. Numbers and letters and out-of-context punctuation waterfall down the screen. My eyes pinch for silver flashes, for some fish to snatch.

Nothing.

I need a key, some unique sequence to orient me in the gobbledygook.

I return to the PAYER/DETAILS REDACTED screen and pour over it. They haven't left me a client name or ID. The amount, $425,334, reeks of rounding—I could try matching, but I don't like my odds.

Then I see. At the bottom of the screen, grayed-out to near invisibility in the status bar, an ID passed in from the financials database.

994kSiofwe!__32.

Now *that* is unique.

I highlight and copy the string, zip back to the command prompt. Paste. Perform a quick string-matching search...wait...down on Two, the A server spins into action...an actuator arm traverses a disk platter, reading microscopic bytes...tens of thousands of data comparisons are made...more bytes are read...more comparisons...

Finally, my search returns.

*Displaying      1      of      1      result(s):      994k-*

Siofwe!__32|5|17|2017|425333.3333|ELITE_DEVELOP-
MENT_LLC|6235|np.ТруДа|Voronezh|Russia|394036

My heart gulps. My toes burrow deeper in their recycled rubber footbeds. I could move the text into Microsoft Word and un-chunk it for readability, but there's no need.

Russia.

Mikhail was no outlier. The headquarters for Elite Development is in Russia. I have no idea where Voronezh is. It doesn't matter.

They're Russians, and they've turned my workplace into a gulag.

And they are paying us. A lot. I count nine of these murky payments, nearly four million dollars altogether. And as of this Tuesday, they were still coming.

Could there be an even bigger payment in store, some whopper lump sum if we complete the software?

Seeing the transactions in detail, I dismiss Paul's equity stake theory. You can't buy another company under the table. The government—the SEC or whoever—requires filings up the wazoo. These backdoor payments wouldn't withstand any sort of rigorous investigation.

No: we're being paid to *do* something.

I allow my eyes to close. I meld back into the algorithm—the Blackquest algorithm, its loops and slippery seven-variable matrix. Floating through the logic pathways, I am pricked by thorns and thrown by hairpins and seized with a confining, all-over severity. And again, always, I feel purpose. Only now I know more about that purpose. I know it's worth four million dollars. At least.

When my eyes open, I find an alert box on the screen.

CARTER K., YOUR ACCESS PRIVILEGES HAVE BEEN REVOKED. PLEASE CONTACT IT@CODE-WISE.COM FOR REINSTATEMENT.

## CHAPTER TWENTY-FOUR_

THE GAME'S UP. IF ELITE KNOWS THE *CARTER K.* ACCOUNT is accessing raw journal entry data, they'll know which machine the access is occurring from too.

It's a blessing they revoked his privileges first instead of coming up here and catching me in the act. Probably they were hoping to close off the spigot before somebody figured out their big red secret.

Too late.

I leave Carter's office and walk swiftly through E-wing, head down. Is Katie Masterson still here on Ten? I don't know. I'm not about to go looking.

I fortunately miss Ashley Thimms too. Maybe she's still at the printer. I have no clue how big that document was—she could be waiting out two hundred pages of a transistor parts catalog.

I reach the stairs. Ten stories below, through the low glass balustrade, I see Security Kyle and the Elite guard patrolling idly. I tiptoe down one flight of stairs and am swinging around to the next, handrail twine skimming through my palm, when a *clink* sounds below.

Door handle. Several floors lower, judging by its faintness.

I let go of the twine and backpedal to the entrance of Nine —another floor that's mostly empty after layoffs. I press Paul's badge against the reader. I baby the latch, pull the door gently, and hustle through.

I'm buzzing as I find the first lockable door and shut myself inside. Office? Utility closet? Secret torture chamber? I'm not choosy.

It turns out to be another bathroom. I sink to the tile, my back flat to the wall, legs straight out. These belligerently-white LEDs overhead unnerve me.

*Okay.*

*Think.*

They know about the van. Mostly likely they know about Mikhail. They know I have been digging around the money trail, and if they know that...if they think I know about Voronezh...

Then I'm a threat. They can't hand me over to SFPD for Mikhail's death: I might blab about the Russia connection.

I should run. Where? How? I'd have to bust out a window on a lower floor, or else overpower one of their entry-exit sentries. Could Raven alert the authorities somehow? Doubtful —after the parking garage ruse, she'll be about as conspicuous as I am.

Can I just bury my face in my knees and cry until Blackquest 40 ends?

The sheer hopelessness of the situation brings to mind Carebnb. Cecil, Wanda, people I've squatted beside over sewer grates and talked into wearing my wristbands. I think about their dangers. Hunger. Addiction. Ruthless predators—not the kind in polo shirts, the ones who'll settle for children if they have to, who'll tear off an ear for its metal stud.

The dangers Mom and I used to face.

And actually, I don't think I will cry. Or stay here one minute longer.

I rise to a knee, then stand. I leave the bathroom and walk to the elevator bank—no more slogging it on the stairs. The handful of employees on Nine, back office types, gape at my wounds.

I walk on. With a stiff middle finger, I press *Down*. I board an empty car. I ride it to Three.

Disembarking, I head directly to my cube. Brows raise in my periphery. Conversations pause. I push my chest out, loose-wristed, sucking in all the air and attention the office cares to give me.

I'm done cowering. I just am. Knowledge is power, and I know plenty. If Elite wants to lock me in a conference room, fine. I'll scream through the glass. I'll scream until they put me in a straightjacket and cinch the straps so tight my windpipe closes.

Nobody stops me.

The whole floor feels neutered, hushed. Nobody else is up and about. The prattle of keys is furious, but it's not the happy, progress-making industry of a bank of typists. It's brittle. No sighs, no humming, no thumbs tapping denim.

Once I'm at my cubicle, Jared kick-wheels his chair over.

He looks to either side and whispers, "*Where were you?*"

"Away."

"I can't test my module until you check your code into the repository."

"I'll get right on that," I say. "Did you need coffee with that? Glazed donut?"

Jared lifts off his trucker hat but finds nowhere to throw it. "We can't miss another checkpoint. These guys are insane."

"You're only now realizing?"

"Well I didn't—er, these restrictions just...and someone said there was a crate of *needles?* Like, to inject us."

"With what?"

He shudders, gripping the rumpled cuffs of a sweatshirt. "I dunno."

I tell him we'll try to check some code in soon.

As he grumbles back to his own workspace, I punch up the Blackquest interfaces and consider them fresh. The seven recurring variables in bold. The cursor blinking off its even, sinister beat.

In light of Voronezh, I try to imagine what we're being whipped into building. Russia loves meddling in U.S. politics, but so far its preferred methods have been low-tech social media manipulations. You don't need Codewise engineers if all you're doing is blanketing social media with phony xenophobic news.

Are they upping the ante? Looking for more direct control over results, perhaps some means of infiltrating vote tabulations? That injection module of Jared's could conceivably wriggle itself into a city or state's software, then my piece would—I guess, extrapolating the scheme out—replace the correct vote totals with fake ones. But how would the seven-variable matrix figure in?

Also, the next presidential election is three years away. They wouldn't bother rigging a measly midterm, would they? Voting software might be completely different by then anyway.

The bigger rub, in this and any other scenario, is why Russia needs to go five thousand miles fishing for black-hat engineers. Hacking is right up there with borscht and vodka in the Eastern Euro/Russo wheelhouse. My Google friend Arkady regularly perused the sealed minutes of Mountain View zoning board meetings—and swore he was the dimmest of seven siblings.

So why outsource?

I'm still pondering the question five minutes later when

Prisha calls via office land-line. She says she just wants to confirm some subroutine logic, no big deal, but her voice sounds hollow. She must be feeling the same heat Jared is.

"Let's take a look together," I say. "I'm walking your way."

"But—can you?"

"Oh sure, I can spare the time."

She falters more, but I assure her it's no trouble and hang up.

I scoop up a notebook and, issuing a FIND_SUN command to Raven—all my shenanigans have run her battery down to 14 percent—start Prisha's way.

My strides have softened since my initial fire-stomp into Three. Astoundingly, it seems I've escaped Elite's wrath again. Yellow shirt facilitators have been around. I think I even heard Jim Dawson's flyover drawl in passing.

Like the kid who steals a swipe of frosting, then three fingers' worth off the edge, then finally decides it's safe to plunge mouth-first into the cake's broadside, I keep gaining nerve. How am I getting away with all this?

I busted into the CFO's computer and found his stash of dirty-money porn. I slipped the thugs' dragnet with a choice Raven fakeout. I stuffed one of them *in a San Francisco municipal dumpster*—even though it wasn't my fault and I felt awful.

Yet here I am.

*"Back to your workstation!"*

The voice shatters my mental strut. I turn to find a yellow shirt, one of the beefy facilitators who joined Jim Dawson's search posse.

I never got a good look at him on Raven's livestream, but I see now he's a bruiser all right. Snarling. Shoulders like cantaloupes. Flattop ears you can't see without wondering what the hell happened. He has a scar like Dawson's, but instead of the temple, his zags from a snub nose across one cheek.

But that's not the scary part.

The scary part, which I spot in the distance behind this man, is that Paul Gribbe is sitting alone in the kitchenette. Two lengths of duct tape span a closed door. Paul has neither papers nor laptop. He's watching his thumbs twist.

They put Paul in jail.

## CHAPTER TWENTY-FIVE_

I START FOR PAUL'S KITCHENETTE, BUT THIS NEW enforcer is blotting out the hall. He stands bowlegged, the insteps of his boots open challengingly. His ears are little shelves of hard, pink flesh.

"The project has reached Code Orange," he says. "Employees on this floor aren't permitted to leave their workstations until the progress is repaired."

Now that I know these guys cash their paychecks against the Bank of Lenin, their word choices and accents are glaring— the missed r's, long vowels clipped at the roof of the mouth.

"No *moving around?*" I say. "For a Snickers bar? To stretch our legs?"

He grunts in the affirmative and thrusts a finger back where I came from.

"Well, that's absurd. But I do need to get past this impromptu roadblock of yours so I can talk to one of my people."

Being let by to see Prisha seems more likely than for prisoner Paul.

The enforcer negs me anyway, explaining that all Code Orange collaborations must occur by phone.

Now I understand the communal anxiety from before—furtive Jared, Prisha stressed about me coming over.

Jim Dawson, ever-present as the cockroach, overhears the exchange and approaches. To this point, Dawson has struck me as tough—but tough within corporate bounds. Maybe naturally built, or a lunchtime lifter-type. Beside the new enforcer, though, his guise is slipping. The his-and-his scars. Their musclebound stances.

They're starting to resemble a unit.

"Miss Bollinger," Dawson says. "Back in the fold again, good."

His lips are dead level, but I sense them aching to curl at the corners—whether up or down I can't tell.

"Not good," I say. "I'm trying to get work done, and this bizarre cubicle house-arrest policy is stopping me."

"Quite the contrary—it is a productivity measure. We're ten hours into Blackquest 40, and quarter-mark objectives remain unmet. To continue on the same track is to invite failure."

"And I heard you brought needles? Didn't figure you for a drug pusher."

Dawson sends the enforcer off with a head flick, then halves the distance between us with one step.

"Supplements," he says, just above a whisper, "may be introduced at Code Orange. Not every worker is blessed with your natural gifts."

"So you...what, shoot them up with some IQ serum?"

His eyes harden as he says, "Amphetamines."

Up and down my spine, something like teaming, furry-foot centipedes begin crawling.

Dawson explains, "Progress has slipped to such an extent

that we don't believe the required timelines are feasible without external enhancement."

After the day I've had, I didn't think shock was still possible. But forced amphetamine injections?

It reminds me of Crestwood Psychiatric, where I'll be coaxing Mom into eating some boiled potatoes and see an orderly jamming a hundred and fifty ccs of happy juice into some uncooperative resident's IV. They aren't authorized to medicate Mom beyond her regular lithium except in cases of "agitation so extreme that harm to self or others appears likely." I often wonder how liberally they apply that criterion.

I tell Dawson that's beyond warped. "You have no way of predicting how that affects some random person, running a live wire into their brain chemistry."

"We've obtained full medical histories," he says. "Any employee with a confirmed diagnosis that conflicts with our prescribed—"

"I can't," I cut in. "The doublespeak, man, the lies upon lies —it's toxic. Where's Carter? Carter!" My voice cracks through the office, lightning in a bleak sky. "This is beyond rogue. *Carter!*"

Things are bad when I, Deb Bollinger, am screaming for an audience with Carter Kotancheck. But Susan is still en route from Davos—I'm starting to imagine an unplanned stopover in Moscow—and the third founder is in kitchenette-jail.

I'm loud and angry for long enough that, despite Dawson's jaw-gnashing demands for calm, Carter does turn up. He breezes into we engineers' domain with sandy brow raised, like he's been called in to settle his kid nephews' squabble over action figures.

"Deb Deb Deb, ho now," he says. "Where's the fire?"

"Did you authorize this, injections? Forced amphetamine injections?"

I glower between them. Dawson's stress ball is pooching out from between two knuckles. Did he really expect me to preserve his secret?

Carter's mouth hangs open, those pearly gleamers flashing. "Well, as you're aware, I'm no micromanager. I said before—these guys are pros, I leave motivation to them."

"You know where else had pros? Abu Ghraib. I bet the officers in charge—"

"The doses are conservative," Jim Dawson says. "At the levels we are talking about, there are no long-term health impacts."

"Says who?"

"The World Health Organization."

I make a few hyperventilating starts before facing Carter again. "Are you *hearing* this? The W.H.O.? Do you realize that the guy you brought in is on intimate terms with international torture protocols? I bet they know him by sight at the Hague."

"Granted," Carter says, "Blackquest 40 is extending all our comfort zones. Video game industry—hey, those guys have their crunch periods, mandatory hundred-hour weeks. Could be this is where ours is heading."

This meets with airless silence.

I say, "Pretty sure the coders who made Grand Theft Auto never got shot up with amphetamines."

Our CFO, well-practiced at adopting and quickly discarding arguments: "Maybe the injections can be, uh—I dunno, delayed. Maybe we find some wiggle room on timing."

He peeks at Jim Dawson. Dawson inhales at length, then exhales—a respiration that smacks of some anger-management technique.

"Carter, snap out of it." I pass my fingers to and fro before his face. "Shut this trainwreck down. I have no clue who or what forced you into bed with these devils, but consider the facts. They're *sizing up our veins to shoot us up with illegal drugs!*"

It's no use. Although Carter winces some and his complexion seems a little piqued, he's not budging from his support of Elite. FPP-1 is the way forward, he insists. The status quo isn't getting the job done. Blackquest is a bear, sure, but think how strong we'll come out the other end.

I consider hitting him over the head with Voronezh, those whopper cash deposits. Why not? It's right here underneath the surface already. Elite detected my access; they likely know that I know. Carter knows. Jim Dawson knows.

Some danger sensor in my brain stops me. The entire floor is listening to us. If I pull back the curtain with a flourish, exposing the fiction of Blackquest 40 being a pure training exercise, everyone here becomes party to it. Jared. Prisha. Minosh. Minosh's neighbor Patton. Or James.

For all of them, I think the charade needs to continue.

"Fine. You want to ride this out, all the way down? Fine." I slice between Carter and Jim Dawson, brushing the latter's stiff shoulder. "I'm going to see Paul now. Just try stopping me."

## CHAPTER TWENTY-SIX_

Jim Dawson does try, explaining that Paul's timeout is meant to simulate "full removal from the project, military-grade incarceration." When I explain back that I *can* do what needs doing without consulting Paul, it just might take an extra two hours of guesswork, Dawson relents.

I rip the duct tape from the jamb and blow into the kitchenette.

It's grim. Paul's wrists are zip-tied to the table. Plastic chords looped through AV cutouts allow just enough space for him to twist his hands perpendicular, but no further. The pantry and sink areas are tarped-off, limiting him—if he were free to walk around—to maybe an eight-by-five-foot area. The lighting feels cruelly yellow. The only item in sight is a stapler, jaws open, vaguely menacing with its springy guts exposed.

I bite the corner of my lip. "Paul, oy. You're in here because of me, right? The badge. They blamed you for accessing the journal entry data—"

"We can still make the next checkpoint," Paul interrupts, louder than necessary.

I squint. He angles his half donut-bald head toward a corner of the room, where a dark lens peers down from a silver box.

He beckons me closer. There are no other chairs so I hop up onto the table, legs dangling over. Then I shuffle around, Paul directing me with small gestures, until my back blocks both our faces from the lens.

I whisper, "I'm so sorry, Paul. I should have been quicker."

"Don't apologize. It was my decision to take the heat." He looks down at his wrists, chapped from the zip-ties. "We can't build this software without you. You see what they're doing—injections, stock options. Who knows what else."

Finishing, he drops his gaze to my toes—which are apparently too close to resist, even under the circumstances.

"How'd they even believe you?" I ask. "You were on Three the whole time."

"I'm not sure they do," Paul says. "They may be turning a blind eye for the same reason: they know if you were here instead, the project would have virtually no chance of success."

He recounts the last hour on the engineering front. While I was digging through the accounting labyrinth, the team was treading water. Jared's module is stuck at 25 percent test compliance. Half his interfaces don't have a single line of code written. To Paul's knowledge, the prototype hasn't escaped its sandbox—the overriding goal of that piece of the program —once.

I ask how Prisha is doing on our optimization piece.

"Little better," Paul says. "But Elite wants 80 percent compliance by tonight, and she'll need a giant leap to get there."

I push my tongue high up my cheek.

He continues, "Our Q4 options vanish at seven o'clock. They start borrowing against Q1 at midnight. That money, I—if that goes away, I probably have to switch my daughters to another school."

His face crinkles at the thought. I feel bad for him, but I also think we've wandered off the main point.

"This outfit is controlled by Russian interests," I say, and briefly explain what I discovered in Carter's office. "Whatever they're doing here—whatever *we* are doing *for* them—is in the service of a hostile foreign entity."

My eyes burn with zeal while his, once again, fall to my feet.

Really? Paul's been great today, but come on already. We're discussing the seizing of our company by armed oligarchs and he can't muster the willpower to suppress his fetish?

I say, "Could you just not stare at my feet? For two minutes? I get that workplace harassment issues aren't top of mind right at this moment, but please. It creeps me out."

His whole body stiffens. His eyes snap forward like he's been hit by a wave of ice water.

"I—er, no it isn't your, um, feet..."

I wait for him to elaborate. Paul stutters and cycles through a range of pukish expressions.

"...sometimes you, well, it can be very hard to look at you. At your eyes. They get so, oh, intense I suppose, and I've never liked managing anyway, and—but...I guess I developed this habit of looking down, which you've been interpreting as...harassing...gosh, Deb, I apologize."

I cross my ankles and avert my eyes, which feel weaponized. Some balloon in my chest is deflating, fizzling out.

I feel sick. Besides landing this man in pseudo-jail, I have been ascribing the worst proclivities of a gender to him when all he's guilty of is struggling with eye contact.

"That's cool, Paul—my bad. I'll get over myself," I say. "So what should I do here? What do you want me to do?"

He takes another moment composing himself—this type of allegation packs a punch in the modern workplace. When he seems recovered, he looks out the door glass. In the distance, Minosh is peeking over his sit-stand monitor at us.

"Pull us through." Paul nods to the workers. "That's our team out there. The two of us, we're responsible. I know you try to help people. Carebnb. Your mom. These engineers—they aren't homeless or destitute, but they need help. They really do."

This curbs my warm and fuzzy mood toward Paul. I know nothing of his politics, but this statement has a whiff of something. I hope he isn't aligned with Jared's man rights cohorts, who—Raven has observed on reconnaissance runs—whine on message boards about reverse discrimination in Silicon Valley.

The possibility revs my outrage motor. But I stop myself.

No. No wasting time down moot intellectual paths. No impulsive moral quests, or therapeutic popping off. No conflagrations.

I tell Paul I'll do what I can and return to the cubicles. I veer toward Prisha's, thinking to make a plan with the module leaders, but Flattop Ears falls in beside me like some bailiff escorting me to a cell.

I allow it.

I'm committed to no conflagrations.

Once Flattop leaves, I hike up onto my desk. My hip screams and I stagger, knocking my bin of droid-Hot Wheels. I punch the spot, which relieves or at least distracts me from the pain.

I manage to stand fully upright, my monitor at knee height. I test the cubicle border.

Feels sturdy. The borders are two-ply, my neighbor and I each have one. There's a little flex, but it should take my weight.

Using various Java and LISP manuals for a step, I climb up. Raven and I are at eye-level now. She winks. (Closing her camera's aperture, then opening back up at quarter-speed.) From this vantage-point, I command all three cube farms.

"Eyes and ears please!" I begin. "We're not allowed to gather in the Latrine, so this'll have to do. Look, I don't wanna be here, you don't wanna be here—so let's build this software and send these joyless jerks on their way."

Maintaining a wide stance, I do check-ins with each module leader. Minosh's small piece is furthest along. We discuss tweaking the memory usage, then I slap my hands and tell him to run with it.

Prisha next. I bend low and turn my head upside-down to check UnitTracker; she's only at 47 percent. An associate engineer, two levels down, has the promising idea to adjust our lead coefficient based on previous outcomes. I talk it forward with him. Why just the lead? Let's adjust them all, dynamically, with exponential smoothing. Prisha thinks it'll get us most of the way there.

Next up is the injection module.

Jared.

"All right, so for unit compliance we're seeing..." I bend again to confirm what I already know from Paul. "Twenty-five percent. And we need eighty by seven o'clock. That's a big gap. How're we going to close it?"

Jared, slumped in the adjacent cubicle, murmurs indistinctly.

I say, "*What?*"

From up here, I can see the button on top of his trucker hat, brown with grime.

He says, "I have some ideas."

"Good ones?"

He shrugs.

"Have you checked these ideas into the repository?" I begin

lowering myself yet again—if he's checked in code, I can read it on my machine.

But Jared hasn't. "I've just been bouncing stuff around, subroutine here and there."

"On your laptop or desktop?"

"Laptop."

I flit my fingers. "Here, pass it up."

"You can't just take my laptop," he scoffs.

"If you're not doing anything useful with it? I sure can."

I motion again for Jared to give it over. He frumps his arms closed.

I stalk along the cubicle border, crossing from mine to his. Mom never signed me up for gymnastics, but skateboarding gave me decent balance. Nearby engineers gasp as the panels rattle underneath me.

Graham appears from the direction of the elevator bank. He stops short.

"You can't take my laptop," Jared repeats. "You think just because you made yourself a bunch of flying toaster-gizmos, and you're like this demographic unicorn who's everybody's darling, that you get whatever you want?"

I'm standing over him now. The whole third floor is silent, excepting the ambient hum of monitors and overhead lights. The unicorn crack—which he'll undoubtedly share with his oppressed online brethren once the data blockade lifts—bothers me less than the juxtaposition of Raven with a kitchen appliance.

I lower myself down his cubicle border. My sandal kicks over the Slurpee cup he keeps his code highlighters in.

"Do you remember those needles you were just pooping your pants about? If this injection module of yours doesn't start injecting? Quickly, like it's supposed to?" I mime pushing a plunger. "Yeah. That."

This could be construed as conflagration, I realize.

Jared passes me his laptop.

I carry it back along the cube borders to my workspace, plunk down, and read what he's got. Reviewing code while others are waiting can be nerve wracking, but I do it quickly, tracking his logic, silently cursing his non-uniform tabs. A border intersection makes a passable seat; I sit with a butt cheek on two of the four radiating panels, feet on the remaining two, laptop on my knees.

Graham ambles over. "Unconventional spot for peer review."

"Is this verboten?" I call down. "Nobody said anything about the workspace-tether policy having a vertical component."

"I'll give you a pass." He fingers his turned-up collar. "Progress good? Anywhere I can assist?"

I consider Graham over the laptop. The tenor of our interactions so far has been conspiratorial, Graham the understanding, laid-back uncle to Jim Dawson's taskmaster dad. I've seen Dawson reprimand him—thump his chest when they were pursuing me.

Is this dynamic real, though? Or does every word I say to Graham end up repeated back to Dawson in some backroom debrief?

"If you're offering, yeah." I tap my fingernail on Jared's code. "This sandbox we're breaking into. It searches for all files with a .bl extension and runs them. Why? What sort of system does that?"

"It's an emerging architecture," Graham says. "Much in vogue now among military and utilities programmers. It allows for multiple deployments in a single system. Frequently, as here, it's coupled with randomly algorithmic gatekeeping, which stops Trojan files from gaining access. The systems are rarely penetrated."

Behind me, Jared brags, "I did. I got through once."

Graham chuckles. "'Once' being the operative word. The Blackquest requirement is one hundred percent-repeatable success."

His warm eyes return to me. He's ready to forget the slovenly slacker, but I stay on Jared.

"Wait," I say. "Tell us how you got through. What happened?"

"I threw a bunch of parameters at it. Varied the header strings."

"How many headers are there?"

"Fourteen."

"You varied each of them? That must've taken forever."

"Yeah, three hours. One at a time. You have to do it like a thousand times to find the right combo, and then it changes."

Graham brushes his windswept hair with a disdainful air. "As I explained. This strategy has no chance in a live system."

But I'm not so sure.

I curl into a pensive ball, rocking in place, letting Jared's solution rattle around my brain. I imagine it working...see it knifing through filters...attaching itself to the main thread...handing off its payload...

"Much as it pains me to say this." I turn to Jared. "You're right." My mouth tastes ashen from the admission. "You do it a thousand times."

Jared clearly distrusts this, face pulled sideways. Graham too—everyone on Three, in fact—is looking at me like I'm about to twist-honk their noses.

I hop off my perch and dash over to the whiteboard in Elite's command center. Flattop Ears makes a move to stop me, but Graham motions to allow it.

I start sketching. My hand arcs and darts and drills. Symbols coalesce to a flowchart. Forests are sprouting inside me. Data leafs up around my bones and between tendons.

People ditch their cubicles to come watch. Faces change from blank to curious, to confused, to hopeful, to stunned, and finally to awed.

My algorithm uses a single file that stamps out versions of itself, each with different header strings, each capable of replicating itself in turn, the net effect being to bombard the host system with .bl files until one works.

Jared's looking at me, stupefied. "That's...yeah. Yeah."

He turns around to face his grinning module-mates. The approach is clear as Twin Peaks after the fog burns off. Parallelism. It's audacious and elegant in the way of the best computer science solutions.

"Let's do it," one says.

Another reaches in his pocket to snap a cellphone pic of the whiteboard, but of course his phone is gone—Elite took it.

"Nah, we're good." Jared taps his head. "I got this."

Watching their confidence, I feel the day's first glimmer of hope. Up to now, it's been all gloom and doom. Maybe Blackquest is doable. Maybe we can keep raising our game, jump through every hoop and sail right past Voronezh.

Part of me knows this is mere post-epiphany euphoria, but other parts are telling it to just shut up and live in the moment.

Graham gives an impressed nod. "I never expected you to get there."

I don't cap my whiteboard marker, knowing I still need to make some magic for my own module—the optimization piece. "Get where?"

"Out of the sandbox," he says. "I'd started to believe it was unbeatable."

"No security is unbeatable."

"Apparently."

Graham sighs, palming the back of his great hair. He looks sad.

"Cheer up," I say as we walk a few paces together, back toward my cubicle. "You're our liaison—aren't you supposed to be rooting for us? Why do you care if we beat this dumb sandbox?"

He glances behind him, twice, then answers, "Because I built it."

## CHAPTER TWENTY-SEVEN

I STOP WALKING. GRAHAM KEEPS MOVING AND, WITH A casual shirk of the head, disappears around a corner.

*He built it?*

I'm disoriented for a moment, hearing an echo of myself telling Jim Dawson earlier about my role with the Google phone. I'd all but concluded Blackquest 40 was a live hack, an operational system someplace we were designing a picklock for. Otherwise why pay us? Presumably if you can build it in-house, you can solve it in-house.

But maybe not. I think back to that incomplete answer key, or whatever it was I found in the van.

Maybe they can't solve it. Maybe Graham activated some next-generation safe nobody can crack. If they manage the system, though, there must be a way to circumvent the security more straight-forwardly. Deploy a fresh sandbox. Flip some configuration to *Easy Mode*.

Pull the lousy plug.

Underlying all this is a central question: where does this system reside? The real McCoy—not the replica running on those behemoth servers they brought. In Russia? In Langley, Virginia? Some Bitcoin server in Uzbekistan?

We do make our seven o'clock checkpoint. The workspace-tether policy is lifted. The threat of amphetamine injections seems to wane. We eat scrumptious plates of baked halibut, couscous, broccoli, and all the blueberries we want. *"Brain food,"* someone whispers in the mess line.

Then it's back to work. Things are oddly normal for a few hours, a bit like the Boeing job where we worked late for a solid week nailing down tweaks. Prisha has her own Eureka moment on the optimization piece, putting us on track for the next checkpoint there. Minosh complains of lumbar pain and switches his workstation to *stand*.

It's still creepy seeing Paul zip-tied to a table every time I pass the kitchenette. I ask Graham when he'll be up for parole, and Graham says if the midnight checkpoints are met, he'll likely be allowed to sleep with the rest of us on cots.

Cots.

Actually a cot doesn't sound bad right about now. It's 11:15 p.m., and my head feels wrapped in gauzes of fear and exhaustion and memories I barely believe. Blackquest 40—at about its halfway point—has grown from annoying makework into an eclipse, blotting out all previous concerns.

What was I thinking about this morning, rushing from my apartment for the thirty-four bus? Mom. Carebnb. Whether or not the rumor Kim Nalley is playing Fillmore Jazz was true.

Everything runs together, Cecil and Wanda and the seven-variable matrix, Graham's thermal undersleeves, the purr of Raven in low-power mode.

Unsteadily, I wander to the window overlooking Second Avenue. South of Market is asleep, the metered lot across the street empty but for red cage-lights, grates down on the taqueria and Thai joint. In front of El Farolito is a shape that might be a sleeping bag.

I wonder...how many spare beds are being used tonight? Did my Carebnb wristbands help users navigate to hosts? Did they cooperate and make it work? Or did I overlook some critical X factor and the whole thing flopped?

A dark sedan passes through my sightline, obscuring El Farolito and the sleeping bag. It slows passing Howard. My wilting eyes follow. At the main Codewise entrance, the sedan pulls up to the curb. Its motor cuts.

A man in a driver's brimmed hat emerges and starts for the right-rear door, which springs open before he reaches the handle.

A high-heeled shoe plants on the sidewalk. Its owner rises swiftly, her knee parting the skirt of a cashmere trench coat. The driver fumbles for her purse and laptop bag, which she accepts onto an outstretched arm.

I can't see her expression this far off, but I perceive resolve in her gaze—which moves smartly up the building's face.

Susan.

# PART THREE_

## CHAPTER TWENTY-EIGHT_

THE RELIEF THAT SWEEPS THROUGH ME IS WATER THROUGH a burning home. Muscles I didn't know I had unclench—inside my knee, between ribs. My brain's gray matter has gained another quarter-inch of space on all sides. I inhale deeply, taking in changed air.

Susan Wright has the type of presence that bends the space-time continuum. Hosts forget reservation lists at the crook of her eyebrow. Crotchety financial journalists become fawning lapdogs under the spell of her silky answers. When I only knew her from TV, I figured her power was strongest over men, but I've since seen it wielded over employees' daughters, female publicists, Uber drivers.

Anyone and everyone.

That morning we first talked at *du Soleil*, I'd been having second thoughts about leaving Google. They were giving me carte blanche to choose my next project, after all—were my grievances imaginary? Was I just itching for change?

But Susan distilled my thoughts perfectly. "They're Google, they're amazing," she told me. "They have a blueprint for how they run projects, and that blueprint works. You can't help but excel there. Of course, for some—and I've known many, folks who've left to do their own thing—the framework becomes stifling..."

My fatigue is gone. I start running. Through the cube farms, quaking their borders with my clomping strides. People look. Graham cuts short a manly stretch to crane his neck.

I pay no attention. I pop the doors to the lobby balcony with taut wrists and hit the stairs in stride, three at a time, racing toward Susan like a magnet after its mate.

I've reached the bottom of the staircase at One when Jim Dawson appears at the balustrade.

"Stop!" he calls down. "Your progress is admirable, but the midnight checkpoint..."

I don't hear the rest, running, rushing.

Susan is through the lobby double doors. The sedan she arrived in motors off. Elite's doorman blips out of a walkie-talkie conversation to greet Susan with hands professionally over his belt buckle.

They confer. Susan is average height, but the cashmere coat, purse, and laptop bag lend her an outfitted heft that dwarfs the yellow shirt.

Her eyes bore into his face. The toe of his boot turns submissively out. He breaks his hands to fidget an earlobe.

She's finishing with him as my front sandal hits the lobby hardwood. Our eyes lock. She's been on a plane for twelve hours, but there's not a trace of blear in hers, orbs of flawless green seaglass.

I bound past Security Kyle, knowing I'm headed for a cheesy hug and not caring.

Susan drops her bags and spreads her arms wide.

"I got your messages, every last one," she says, her mouth somewhere in my yellow spikes.

I grope back in memory for when I would've left her phone

messages. Oh right—this morning before the kickoff, about a hundred years ago.

"It's a coup d'etat—they're Russian, the money comes from Russia!" As we separate, my head is light and warm. "Nobody knows what we're building but it's evil, I know evil code and this is seriously evil."

Words are tumbling backwards out of my mouth, landing on each other.

Susan brushes the welt under my temple. "Who's Russian?"

"The trainers!" I say. "Elite Development, it's a front. They're paying us. Carter—I think Carter's funneling their money in on the sly."

She leads me by the hand to the bench near *Sempiternity*. Beside the gurgling water statue, I tell my story. Stretched like a squirrel-pelt over a server rack. Jim Dawson reciting my bio, shoving his box in my face. Trying to leave and being dragged back inside. The weapons cache in the van—once again, I omit Mikhail and the dumpster. The redacted journal entries. Amphetamines. Paul and the kitchenette.

Susan listens with evident revulsion. She leans forward over crossed legs, head cocking a few degrees more with each disclosure—until at last it's nearly parallel to the floor.

Jim Dawson has made his way downstairs. "Miss Wright, I assure you whatever Miss Bollinger is telling you is—"

"Deb is speaking now," Susan says. "Which means you shouldn't be."

Dawson passes his stress ball between hands. "Certainly. But perhaps you should hear a range of perspecti—"

"Perhaps you should start gathering your things." The CEO's voice resounds through the upper reaches of the lobby. "Given what I'm hearing from Deb, I think it's likely this exercise is over. I'll be around shortly to evaluate, but you might get a head start."

She dispatches him with a sniff. Dawson visibly fights his own body—his shoulders flex and cheeks flush. The stress ball disappears in his fist. I have an urge to tug Susan's sleeve and explain this singular weirdness, but it's a detail she doesn't need.

Finally, like a dog giving up a beg, Dawson retreats.

Susan turns back to me. "I cannot express enough sorrow for all you've been subjected to, Deb. I signed off on this training. Carter said it would be tough—he told me about the forty hours, said this company had the logistics nailed and everyone would be comfortable. Clearly he was wrong. *I* was wrong. I should've insisted on being here for the duration, to prevent these..."

She glances around the building as though considering a foreign planet—rather than this company she shepherded from startup to global powerhouse.

"Abuses," she finishes. "I...there's just no other word for it."

*Sempiternity* burbles on. The bench feels warm underneath me, Susan's heartbreak seeming to flow through it to my body.

I ask, "What're we going to do?"

She smiles at my use of *we*. "First, gather information. Once we understand the full extent of the situation—and Carter will have to be central to that effort—we'll see about next steps. From what you've said, it sounds like the authorities will need to be involved."

Susan shrugs out of her coat and doubles it over her arm, starting for the elevator bank. "Deb?"

I linger at the water statue. Now might be the time to come clean about Mikhail, while we're bandying about atrocities. I raise up on tiptoes to tell her...

Then stop. I can't. She is such a steamroller right now, and I refuse to diminish her power. Going up against Jim Dawson, with all he has riding on the success of Blackquest 40, she's going to need it.

I follow Susan to the elevators. She presses *Up*. We wait for the car, eyes hungry.

"Well," Susan says. "Ready to right some wrongs?"

I'm flying out of my sandals. It's 1789 and we're coming for the Bastille. "Absolutely."

We ride to the third floor. Susan is fuming before the elevator doors have fully receded, blasting inside, hips jutting. Every eye whips our way. A plant bounces in her wake. The overhead lights—I swear to this—dim like power is being siphoned off by her passing aura.

Jim Dawson steps in her path. I have a premonition of them colliding, destroying one another in a supernova.

Susan speaks from ten yards out. "Paul Gribbe, where is he?"

"Mr. Gribbe engaged in behavior detrimental to the project," Dawson says. "He was placed in detention. His term ends in thirty—"

"*Where.*" Her lips build the word up from its letters, one sound at a time.

Dawson scratches furiously at his side, a jerky cross-body move. His mouth works several moments without sound. Finally, he points to the kitchenette.

We go there. Before Susan showed up, preparations were beginning for bed. A wheeled platform of cots appeared. Several people untucked shirts or took off shoes.

Now, there is none of that. All activity has frozen, a kind of hopeful paralysis settling over the office. *Is this it? Can she end it?*

*Are we about to go home?*

"Abominable," Susan mutters, catching sight of Paul. She walks in, sliding a hand down her face.

Paul looks beat.

"What's wrong with your elbows?" she says. "Why are you sitting..."

She trails off as Paul turns his wrists against the zip ties, showing her the red seams sawed into his skin.

"This is barbaric. Deb—" She hoods her eyes with one hand as though unable to look, makes a snipping gesture with the other. "Can you, please?"

I find scissors at the nearest engineer's desk and cut Paul free. He rubs his wrists, then stands too quickly and has to sit again.

Susan swivels around with hands on hips. She considers in turn the tarps on the windows, the walled-off pantry and sink areas, the stapler.

She squints at its springs and jaw. "Did they—was this *used* in some way?"

Paul shakes his head.

The answer only seems to confuse Susan, who begins pivoting in circles as though deciding where to start, or what to hit.

"*How did this happen?*"

I can't tell if she's addressing me or Paul, or just the world.

Before either of us answers, I hear the thud of Jim Dawson's boots. He approaches the kitchenette with a cardboard box.

The box.

The box is back.

Dawson says, "Our man at the door should have collected your phone, Miss Wright."

Susan blinks a few times, then shifts the orientation of her head and blinks more. "You expect me to surrender my phone?"

"These are the terms of—"

"To *you*?" The word drips contempt.

Jim Dawson raises his box. "These are the terms of participation. We find that when upper management adopts a behavior, it filters down. Compliance is contagious."

Susan plows past out of the kitchenette, into view of the cube farms. She stops and faces him. "Tell me exactly what sort of corporate trainers you are."

"Extreme Readiness. We prepare organizations with the most grueling, most demanding—"

"I don't care," she cuts in. "I just wanted to confirm you weren't communications or body language trainers. Because if you were?" An airy note comes into her voice. "You would realize how moronic it is, asking me for one damn thing right now."

She asks Minosh if she can use his desk, then climbs up to survey the whole floor—like I did before, only without needing to risk life and limb standing on a border. Blond billows of hair sway as she scans the outlying workspaces.

It's gotten ragged. Printer trays gaping open. Chairs toppled, their legs jumbled together. Hairdos matted and smushed. I only notice now, possibly in contrast to Susan's lovely scent, that the place stinks like the bottom of a Doritos bag.

After several seconds, Susan spins on Jim Dawson. She is barely recognizable—rage twists her face. For a moment I think she'll lunge at him.

Instead, she stands tall again.

"From the bottom of my heart," her voice rings out, "I apologize. I apologize on behalf of management. I apologize on behalf of myself. This is ghastly. None of this should have been allowed, but we're fixing it.

"I—I mean, have you been offered showers?" she wonders aloud. "Any of you? Or a change of clothes?"

Silence answers her. Susan turns questioningly to me and Paul.

I say, "No. Nothing like that."

"It's close to midnight. Have you spoken with your families? Spouses? Reassured them you're not lying in a ditch somewhere?"

Around the room, chins fall. Nobody mentions Elite's auto-responses, which are supposedly answering all incoming texts and emails. If Dawson wasn't lying.

A collective gloom settles over the team as Susan further articulates the horrors of Blackquest 40, but also a glint of hope. Because finally somebody—somebody who's part of the corporate regime instead of a marauding outsider like me—is acknowledging the truth. Spoken aloud like this, it cannot continue. It can only end. My heart feels this.

My eyes, though, see yellow shirts massing in the periphery.

## CHAPTER TWENTY-NINE

AFTER ASSURING EVERYBODY "THINGS WILL BE SET RIGHT," Susan leads me and Paul to her office. If she notices the yellow shirts frowning like a band of grumpy shepherds, she doesn't let on. Her skirt whips, and her fingernails dig into the crisp cuffs of her blazer.

Following to the elevators, I cut my eyes to Jim Dawson. His expression is prickly, but neither he nor any of his stooges move to stop us.

I must say I'm enjoying having somebody else carry water for the rebellion. Susan commands attention like a warlord cantering through her domain on horseback. I love it. I walk happily in her wake.

Onto the elevator car, Susan punches the button for Ten. The doors sigh shut.

"Ubb." She knuckles the corners of her eyes. "This is not how I was planning to beat jetlag."

I ask if her plane got delayed. She says it was.

"The clean itinerary had me in at noon, just a few hours into Blackquest 40. None of this creepshow stuff should've gotten off the ground."

The elevator dings. Entering E-Wing, I stride forward...and land short. It's dark. Nearly pitch-black once the elevator's dome light dims. Paul stops altogether. Susan and I edge ahead. Every floor has the same layout near the shaft; I move by memory muscle into space.

Paul asks, "Did they go home?"

Susan scouts forward using her cellphone flashlight. From the interior of the floor, I hear a noise.

Judging by her grimace, I gather Susan hears too.

I whisper, "A cough?"

Susan beckons me on. We pad forward shoulder-to-shoulder, crouched low, peeking in offices. Paul lumbers to catch up before we turn the corner.

I feel the bodies' heat before I see them. Muggy, a staleness in my jaw.

Forty or fifty people on cots. By some pale glow in the middle—a corporate night light?—the forms resemble lumpy potato sacks. Katie Masterson, who I recognize by her Elite polo shirt, sleeps slightly apart; otherwise the rows are perfect.

The sight is raw and wrong and incongruous. It feels like Neo's first glimpse of the human battery-farm in the Matrix.

Susan gasps.

I say, "Are we gonna, I guess, wake them up?"

For a moment, Susan can only shake her head. "I—we need to get our heads around this first. Let's talk in my office."

As we leave them behind, I feel weirdly jealous toward the snoozing biz-siders. Clearly all checkpoints have been satisfied here. There's no sign hypodermic needles were brandished, and I'll bet if I go check the kitchenette, I won't find it transformed Guantanamo Bay-style. The faux-business plan must be coming along swimmingly.

Were they grilled about color palettes for the logo? Did Jim

Dawson poke his finger in somebody's face about customer segmentations or ten-year revenue projections?

At her office, Susan flicks on lights and sits. Her navy suit looks regal against the couch's silver floral pattern.

"Please." She gestures for us to join her.

I take a spot that gives me a view up the hall. Paul collapses wherever, massaging one wrist with the opposite thumb.

"I've heard Deb's angle," Susan starts. "Paul, now I want your take. How far off the rails has this thing run?"

This momentarily stings—*she thinks I'm lying?*—but Paul backs me up 100 percent. He portrays Elite as the aggressors in my failed attempt to leave, using words like "criminal" and "assault," and describes their draconian motivation techniques, including the options grab I forgot to mention in the lobby.

Paul's testimony is winding down—and it does feel like testimony, him sweating and paining over memories—when the global intercom blips on.

We listen to irregular static for a few seconds, then it blips off.

I wonder if this could be disorder on Elite's part. Are they contemplating some hostile move against Susan? A seizure? Could they *do that?*

The rest of us are guppies, but Susan is a minor-to-midrange celebrity. She just got back from pressing the flesh with sheiks and technocrats in Davos. Can you seize a person like that?

"Talking this through—Elite is claiming they've taken ownership of stock options," Susan says, raising a finger, "but over the last several months, *they've* been wiring *us* money? Through some shady backchannel?"

Paul says, "If what Deb saw reflects reality."

"Oh, it reflects," I snap. "The Voronezh money was something like 60 percent of our revenue in June. Carter was making his bacon off it."

Susan taps her curvy lips. "He told us it was the new aero-space dollars, plus the growth in biomedical. That was his justi-fication for the hiring push."

Paul slumps back into his cushion. He was against hiring all Carter's slicksters from the start, but doesn't gloat now.

"Where is Carter?" Susan asks. "I haven't seen him yet."

I look to Paul. Paul looks to me. With a shiver, I realize I haven't seen our CFO for hours. Not since I told him to shut this trainwreck down and cut his losses.

Uh-oh.

What if he tried?

CHAPTER THIRTY_

What if Carter had a crisis of conscience? What if Elite soft-pedaled the more wacko elements of their program and his doubts had been mounting all day, and finally my challenge nudged him over the edge? What if he walked into Jim Dawson's lair—I assume he has a lair someplace—and said he wasn't doing it anymore? Forget the cash, forget the whole deal. He wanted out.

What if Dawson said no?

What if he's crammed into that dumpster with Mikhail?

I ask Paul, "Have *you* seen him lately?"

Paul shakes his head.

I ask if Carter was involved in the decision to lock him up in the kitchenette. Paul says he wasn't.

"Okay. That makes a few hours unaccounted for." I gulp. "We should find him."

"Agreed," Susan says. "If he wants to keep his job, he's going to need some very good answers for me."

It's mildly encouraging that she's talking about Carter keeping or losing his job, as though such issues will be important in a post-Elite world. To Susan, fresh off lecturing corporate titans about New Economy innovation, all things are manageable.

I tell myself she's right. Of course Susan is right. Blackquest 40 is a blip. A big, scary, dictatorial blip, but a blip. Next week we'll be back to dreading meetings and arguing Java versus C++.

Won't we?

Carter's office is a stone's throw away. Susan leads. His lights are off and she nearly walks right by.

"*Stop!*" I whisper. "Something moved in there."

I peer into the shadows behind his desk, pulling Susan back by the sleeve. She and Paul wedge in beside me to look through his door, which is cracked. The dim outlines of a figure rise and fall above the glass-pane desktop. I hear a sniffle.

Susan calls, "Carter?"

She pushes inside and flicks the light switch. Carter looks up, and he is a shambles. The blue eyes crunch up in sobs. The Gatsby slickback is all mats and flyaways.

I've caught hints of his stress throughout the day, but this is different. This is meltdown.

Nothing in Susan's manner suggests sympathy.

She says, "Did you pad your sales numbers with money from these people?"

Carter nods.

"Is it actually a training exercise?" Susan's arms extend straight from either side, elbows perfect right angles. "Or are we building software for them?"

Carter snivels and nods again.

"*Which one?*" Susan says, adding an expletive.

"B—building. It's a deliverable. We have to deliver."

"Or?"

Carter glances dismally to the hall. "We should close the door."

"No! I don't care what these hoodlums hear. What're the

terms of this deal? Why did you have to sneak the cash in through journal entries?"

His neck snaps straight. "Wh—how do you know about the journal entries?"

I worry that he seems not to know about my database snooping. It means they didn't tell him, which points to a relationship with Elite that's less collaborative—and more antagonistic—than I was figuring.

"Doesn't matter." Susan's calves are flexed, a pair of tightly strung harps. "I'm responsible for the welfare and safety of each and every employee in this building. I need to know what's going on—and I need to know *now*."

Carter splutters a moment without forming a sentence, eyes flitting between his lapels and the hallway.

"Oh, close the damn door," Susan says, and Paul moves for it. "Now talk."

Carter waits for the door to clap shut.

"It was...I mean, the upside was enormous," he begins, "and I was seeing this gaping hole in the budget, and so...y'know, it—it becomes one of these impossible choices..."

Much as I've loved watching Carter squirm in the past, I don't enjoy this. His thumb is white against the glass desktop. A folded cot leans against one of his blue-velvet chairs, and somehow this—skuzzy green canvas encroaching upon his prized luxury—drives home the extent and dizzying speed of his fall.

"...and the thing mushrooms," he goes on, "and Dawson's taking heat himself and passing it down the chain...and for that kinda money? It just got...I—I got in over my head—"

"How?" Susan says. "Over your head in what respect?"

"I don't even know where to start."

"The truth. Start there."

Through several non-answers, Susan thunders away, advancing on Carter until she is literally shouting in his face.

Paul steps in like a referee. "Okay, all right—we'll get everything squared away." He ushers Susan back, then turns to their former classmate. "How about a glass of water?"

Carter coughs his appreciation. Given the history between these three—the lowball buyout, the icky love triangle—it's fairly astonishing Paul is the one coming to Carter's aid.

Susan is taking the situation fresh, outraged, wanting scalps, whereas he and I have lived under Elite's yoke for eighteen hours. Indignation and shock have been whipped out of us. We just want it to stop.

Before Carter gets his glass of water, the door opens.

The action is brisk—displaced air ripples through the spikes of my hair—and isn't preceded by a knock, or knuckle, or hesitant query from the hall.

Jim Dawson enters, trailed by Katie Masterson and the flat-top-eared goon. They walk several paces inside, then stop in a perfect triangle that makes me think of fighter jet formations. Their energy is different. Dawson isn't smiling, quite, but the consternation that seemed to dog him after Susan arrived is gone.

"Excuse me," Susan says. "When an office door is closed, it means you knock. Or go away and come back later."

Dawson gives a low, possibly sarcastic murmur. "Is that so?"

"Yes. This isn't your company, regardless of the arrangement you made with Carter here. Please wait outside, Mr. Dawson."

The man flips his stress ball from one hand to the other. "The time for artifice has passed, wouldn't you agree?"

Saying this, he allows his voice to change—a faint shift from Midwestern neutral to Slavic sharp, his words gaining barbs and studs.

## CHAPTER THIRTY-ONE

DAWSON CONFIRMS MY WORST FEARS: HE, HIS SISTER KATIE (whose name contains the hint of a third syllable now, *Katya?*), and flattop-eared "Fedor" represent the Russia government. Blackquest 40 is software commissioned by and for the Kremlin. If the project is not completed prior to the deadline, all payments shall be returned.

Fedor flares his nostrils as he's being introduced—or reintroduced, whatever.

I feel queasy. I have a sudden urge to shrink or drop through the floor. In a random flash, I'm thankful for Crestwood Psychiatric's strict confidentiality policy—which has hopefully kept Mom's whereabouts out of Elite's dossier on me.

Susan bolts from the couch. "Right here, right now," she says, "someone tell me what in holy hell we're building."

Dawson looks to Carter with arms folded, like a mistress with no remorse.

The CFO snivels, "We had to get creative, they—er, the client had to be secret, and with this tight timeframe, it, you know...Jim and I put our heads together and came up with 'extreme training.'"

"*Put your heads together?*" I say. In this moment, I just can't abide the lingo. "You turned this place into a forced labor camp, Carter. The engineers—we do the work, you know? We basically *are* the product you jet-set all around the world selling. And you cut these ghouls loose on us."

Dawson says, "Our techniques are tough but proven."

"Proven on who, enemy combatants? Mercenaries? What's your real background? What's your real *name*—it can't be Jim Dawson."

The man answers none of my questions.

I say, "Come on, 'the time for artifice has passed.' Tell us about the crate of weapons in the van downstairs."

His face stiffens. "This crate of weapons—you found it when you killed Mikhail?"

The bosses' heads snap my way. Paul looks like a chunk of McGriddle is lodged in his windpipe.

"He attacked me," I say. "It was self-defense."

"Our logs indicate the van's security measures were defeated using spoofed disarm codes."

"So?"

"So you broke in. When Mikhail discovered you, you killed him."

"No—when Mikhail discovered me and *tried his darnedest to strangle me*, then I killed him. Like I said, self-defense."

The truth is more complicated, but there's no way I'm touching on Cecil's part.

Dawson shrugs, either granting the point or crediting my brutality—I can't tell. "How did you get him to the dumpster? Mikhail weighs nearly a hundred kilos. This is not possible for a female of your size."

Susan jumps in with a different objection than I expect. "There's a dead body in the dumpster on Second Avenue? A municipal dumpster, which anybody off the street could stumble across?"

"The body has been recovered," Dawson says. "Nothing on police frequencies indicates it was reported or otherwise detected."

I can't be sure—my senses are oversampling wildly in this standoff—but does a flicker of relief enter Susan's face?

Paul huffs from the side. "I still haven't heard an answer for what my team is building. Is it part of a weapons system? Some hacking operation?"

Susan piles on further questions. Why the time pressure? We've worked for governments before—how is this different?

As two co-founders lay into the third, I have a vision of them back at Carnegie Mellon, spitballing in the grad student lounge about what their theoretical company might do. Academic consults? Pure software? B2B or consumer? One of those giddy discussions where all answers are right, every conceivable path is golden. You're picking flavors of champagne.

How far wrong it's gone.

Jim Dawson offers, "It is no weapon. One could call it a hack, partly."

"Bag the twenty questions," I say. "Tell me what I built—or started building."

The office feels like a dark accomplice. It's after midnight and the streetlights on Howard blink red, their after-smear in the windows a mute, bleeding alarm.

Jim Dawson looks out these same windows. "There exists a nuclear power plant near the Russian border with Ukraine. Although it is physically in Ukraine, it was designed by Soviet engineers in 1988 using state-of-the-art technology. The mistakes made at Chernobyl were corrected; indeed the plant, known as Vlast, was constructed to replace the output lost by the closure of Chernobyl. It was a marvel—is a marvel—of the Soviet mind.

"In 1991, when the Soviet Union disbanded and Ukraine declared its independence"—Dawson grunts his dismay—"control of Vlast ceded to the new Ukrainian leadership. Two Chernobyl reactors continued producing power after the accident, but were being phased out due to international pressure. Ukraine boosted output levels for Vlast to compensate. Within five years, core heat readings exceeded the maximums established by the plant's Soviet architects. My government warned the Ukrainians. If another meltdown occurred, the fallout would be catastrophic for both countries.

"For a time, Ukraine moderated its demands upon Vlast. The filthy *khokhols* began stealing Russian gas from the pipelines that run under their soil, and this relieved energy demands. Often they were stupid and stole too brazenly. When we or their European neighbors caught them, they were forced to stop siphoning and lean harder on Vlast.

"During these periods, our satellites detected heat blooms indicating production far beyond safe levels. Again, we warned Ukraine. We offered to send experts, which the Ukrainians dismissed as attempted espionage. A minor incident occurred in 2013—press coverage was effectively suppressed."

Dawson smirks inwardly. I wonder which handiwork is his, the incident or media suppression.

"This scared the Ukrainians for a time, but their economic stresses have only worsened. Starting in January of next year, Russia will export no more gas through Ukraine. With Yamal—Europe and Nord Stream both operational, the *khokhols* can..." He spits a Russian phrase that makes Fedor chuckle. "Now the pressure on Vlast is even greater. We have recorded unprecedented heat blooms this month. If Ukraine is not stopped, Vlast will meltdown. This is imminent. Their politicians will destroy thousands of Russian and Ukrainian lives in pursuit of prosperity."

As he's telling the tale, the puzzle pieces fall into their grim spots. The injection piece of Blackquest 40, Jared's, hacks into the controlling software. My optimization alters Vlast's output subtly, without being detected.

It is the truest nightmare I've known. My head chugs against fatigue; my hip sings with pain; my heart is sick about Cecil and Carebnb and Mom eating dinner alone—and now I learn I've been drafted onto Team Red Square?

Susan sat down at some point in a velvet chair. Now she's leaned back with a kind of gallows whimsy, one calf rubbing the opposite knee.

"This is how you saved us, Carter? Drop us into the middle of a geopolitical, geo-*environmental* conflict?"

Carter drops his head, digging a finger in his lacquered hair. "Look, I realize communications-wise I made mistakes, big mistakes. But we have been talking expansion. This is the type of project we discussed explor—"

"*You* discussed," Paul says, eyes flaming. "Russian agents? Nuclear power plants? We would've never gone in for this."

The founders hurl recriminations back and forth. Carter sticks to his argument Blackquest 40 was a valid, necessary step toward keeping Codewise competitive. Paul's speechless at this. Susan demands details about the software. Why does it need to be done in forty hours?

When Carter can't answer, she rounds on Dawson. "Don't tell me you can predict this meltdown at that level of time specificity—that's preposterous. So why the hurry? Why the rush job?"

Dawson answers vaguely that the timeframe comes from his superiors.

"I'm not given every detail," he says. "The Kremlin may have an operational plan with a precise window of execution."

"The Kremlin." Susan squeezes her eyes. "We are a private company. We do software and robotics and algorithms. A modest-sized group of people who get together five or six days a week to meet in conference rooms, to bitch if the machine in the breakroom spits out weak coffee. That's it. No more, no less."

Oddly, Dawson's face brightens at the characterization. He begins nodding along. When she finishes, the Russian faces me with an expression like he just found that hundred-dollar bill I lost.

"Perhaps we should all think of Blackquest 40 as an opportunity." He tries grinning, but his lips only make an ugly crimp. "An opportunity to do more. To do good."

## CHAPTER THIRTY-TWO

DAWSON'S EYES TWINKLE. HE'S DELIGHTED ABOUT THIS moral conundrum he thinks he just boxed me into. Preventing a mushroom cloud, saving thousands of lives—*how could I refuse?*

Here's how: I don't buy it.

I don't buy a squad of Russian paramilitaries flying over the Pacific, cooking up passports, collaborating with Carter on this bogus corporate training scenario—with its yellow polo shirts and motivational packets and elaborate phony business plan— all to cover up an essentially benevolent mission.

I step to the fore of the Codewise group. "Russia's full of black-hat hackers. Why do you need us?"

"We have tried others," Dawson says. "Unfortunately the security apparatus was designed and implemented by, well, by a quite brilliant engineer." His face curdles as if that was hard to say. "The best of Russia cannot crack it."

Now I think of Graham's comment, "Because I built it." So he used to work for the Ukrainians? Why would he have switched sides? Is he a hostage too? Also—if this Vlast was designed in 1988, he seems way too young. What is he, thirty?

Nothing is adding up.

"This sandbox we're trying to circumvent," I say, "these randomly algorithmic security measures? Nobody was doing that in the eighties. Or nineties. Or even five years ago."

"True," Dawson concedes. "The security was added last winter. We attempted to regain control of the plant previously, without success. We played our hand too soon."

I'm reeling. The nuclear stuff is scary and wild, but for some reason the implied revelations about Graham pack an even greater wallop.

Is he some cyber-mercenary? The hostility between him and the rest of Elite Development has been clear. What are the terms of his employment? Is he getting paid megabucks too? Seems likely.

I think I hate the world a little bit more.

"What was the point of Blackquest 40?" I ask. "You could've just hired us."

Dawson gives his stress ball a pump. "My country's involvement cannot be known. If word leaks of our new effort, Ukraine will lock down Vlast completely."

I mull his answers. In isolation, they seem logical enough. But taken altogether, given all I've lived through today, they are impossible to accept as genuine.

Katie watches beside her brother. Puffy eyes remind me that she was just asleep with the E-Wingers, but she's alert now, feet staggered, watching our movements. Fedor has the self-satisfied look of the baddest bruiser in the room.

I can't see the three Codewise founders behind me. Where are *their* heads? Is anyone else going to question Dawson's fantastical tale, or is it all on me? Susan has explained to me before that in the corporate world there's benefit to "listening more in the first half, talking in the second."

Maybe that's her strategy now.

Me, I hate football metaphors. "Here's my issue. Let's

assume we make this software work and manage to secretly limit Vlast's production. Can't they measure how much juice is coming out? Aren't they just going to sniff it out?"

Dawson seethes at the challenge. He takes a lumbering step closer, that very male move of emphasizing one's physical size. "The aftermath is none of your concern."

"Humor me."

"We aren't here for humor." He pivots to Fedor, who underscores the point by flexing his muscle-corded neck. "To complete your module, you don't need to know my country's long-range plan for combating Ukrainian aggression."

I close the gap between us even a bit more, two quick strides that set Dawson on his heels.

"The 'aggression' seems mostly Russian. And I'm not asking because I need help completing my module. I'm asking because I am deciding *whether* to complete my module. Whether this Vlast deal is real or another fat lie."

Dawson glares down at me. We're so close that my chest brushes his polo shirt at the level of his ribs. That scar near his temple is shiny, boiled pink.

"Your job is building software. Not assessing my truthfulness."

I consciously do not control my spittle in saying, "We already played this tune. I don't work on projects I don't believe in. And I'm not hearing enough now to believe."

Reflected in Dawson's chunky glasses, I see Paul start forward to intervene. Susan catches him by the arm. She's watching closely, clearly wanting the same answers I want.

Susan trusts me. She knows I don't need protecting—not now, not ever.

In a grudging manner, Dawson begins, "Belarus has similar energy problems. If a portion of Vlast output disappears...and certain Ukrainian officials are discovered corresponding electronically with certain embassy personnel of Belarus...a different conclusion may be reached."

The scheme slithers from his mouth, easy and—I have to admit—plausible.

"Oh joy, we start an international conflict," I say. "The hits keep on coming."

His teeth compress. "We are talking about heading off thermonuclear disaster, and you joke."

"I'm not joking. I'm calling BS. There is a difference."

Dawson drops his voice so only I can hear. "*Your talents are tantalizing*"—he inhales, a lascivious sucking of air like he's taking my body smells by force—"*but you are immature. You would benefit from time under me.*"

He blinks, and I hear the eyelashes join and separate.

These last words ignite me. The condescension, the lewdness of "under me"—I can't pinpoint the exact trigger, but it fires. Rage starts in the soles of my feet, flattens my kneecaps and turns liquid black in my gut. My jaw coils back like a viper preparing to strike.

I headbutt Dawson.

"Jesus, Deb!" Paul cries, rushing in with the others.

I'm lifted up by the armpits and spun parallel to the floor, and squeezed, and have fistfuls of yellow polo shirt myself. As he grapples, Dawson emits an extended "*Gggnnnnn*" that reminds me of mute Mikhail.

We claw at each other a few moments before Fedor bounces us apart. Susan wraps her arms around me, her blazer ripped up the seam.

Katie shoves her brother roughly to a corner. A nob appears over his brow, red and swelling. She tells him something in Russian. *Nyet!* he answers, then faces us.

"You will do your jobs!" He stabs his index finger between

us. "All of you will do your jobs! My government has paid a tremendous sum of money, and we do not take betrayal lightly."

The top of my head feels warm, and I wonder if my platinum spikes will be bloody in a mirror. Susan is rubbing my neck, smoothing down from the base of my ears.

Paul has lost a shoe.

Carter is hotfooting in place between the two groups, muttering.

"Everybody relax, *relax*." Susan says, continuing her buttery touches. "We'll get through this. We will find a way."

## CHAPTER THIRTY-THREE_

THE COT IS STIFF AND SCRATCHY. THE BLANKET SMELLS like it's been moldering in some rusty crevice of the Bay Bridge. I buck and flop and rearrange myself, and stay uncomfortable. My toes poke past the covers. The blanket's stitching chafes my cheek. I'm nauseous. Also hungry. It's possible I have a fever.

How good would a bath feel? My arms and legs floating up off the porcelain...a sprinkle of those lemongrass-rosemary salts my ex gave me last Valentine's Day...

Prisha's cot is beside mine—our unsleeping eyes keep meeting. Jared is above me, his feet by my head, and Minosh below. Through the office white noise, I'm besieged by an assortment of nasal squeaks, fizzes, and honks.

I peer up the aisle. Silhouetted by a faint glow from the elevators, hunched on a stool, sits Fedor. His hands rest in a joined fist atop his knees.

Prisha whispers, "Deb, you're awake right?"

I squirm up from my pillow, which crinkles like newspaper. "Very much so."

"That bump on your head, did you—was there another fight?"

I glance around and confirm nobody's eavesdropping. How much should I say?

After the blowup in Carter's office, Susan and Jim Dawson came to the third floor and issued a joint statement. Susan apologized again and announced "significant modifications" to Blackquest 40. For the next thirty minutes, people were free to email friends or family from the fourth-floor breakroom. A pair of showers on Ten would be made available in the morning. An Elite facilitator had gone out for toiletries and fresh undergarments for all.

*Nobody*—Susan growled the word—would be injected against their will.

Jared shouted, "What about our stock options?"

Susan looked at Dawson, who was sporting his own bump from my headbutt.

"Options are still TBD," she said, dialing cheer into her voice. "Let's sleep on it. Everything improves with sleep. This training has suffered missteps. Carter, myself, Jim here—everyone acknowledges that. But we'll come out the other end stronger. That's a promise."

Then they left. People filed up to Four to email their families—with Dawson and Katie Masterson monitoring—as Fedor snapped open cots.

Rumors raced through the weary workforce. *Carter got fired...Elite barred Susan's entry to the building but Kyle let her in...The Blackquest deadlines are getting reset, that's why the countdown timers went dark...*

Susan was playing along. Up in Carter's office, she had smoothed things over after the headbutt, agreeing to keep the training sham in place overnight in exchange for concessions—email, showers, et cetera. She and Dawson hadn't discussed whether Blackquest 40 would be canceled in the morning, or its true purpose revealed. Or who was actually in charge. Each side had just retreated to a corner.

Did Susan have a plan? As Paul and I had left for Three, she'd given me a look, eyes large in her still face. She had wanted to communicate something, but what?

A warning? A wink to not take her future actions at face value? I had watched those luminous green pupils as long as I dared. Did she want me to attempt escape? Come find her later, once we were both clear of Elite? Or just get some sleep?

I had no clue.

Now I find Prisha in the dark, her blanket balled under her chin.

She asked me if there was another fight.

I answer, "Not a major one."

"The Elite guy, Dawson, he had a mark." She points to her own head. "Did you make that?"

"He and I are, uh...not meshing. Interpersonally."

Prisha does not crack a smile. "Did you talk to Susan? What does she think of Blackquest 40?"

"She knows it's nuts, she gets it. She'll shut this thing down."

I hope.

I waste the next hour trying to sleep. Adrenaline and exhaustion wrestle over my head. Every time I start drowsing, I catch sight of the unfamiliar carpet, or ceiling tile, or Jared's fleshy soles, and wig. It's simply weird—surrendering consciousness in this bland, antiseptic office. I feel like I'll wake up made of Formica. I want my apartment.

As a kid, I could sleep anywhere. You have no choice when you're unhoused. I wonder how my Carebnb users are doing. If all went according to plan, they should all be matched up with hosts and sound asleep.

Did they mind the disposable bed liners? I had a few hosts stressed about bed bugs and so distributed liners "for the safety of all Carebnb participants." I worried this could offend users, but Cecil convinced me it was no problem.

*You're giving people a bed? They won't care. They'll sleep on tinfoil.*

But maybe Cecil was wrong. Maybe my users took one look at those liners—the hosts watching superiorly from the doorway —and beat it. Maybe I overshot my "walkable radius" assumption and some users didn't even make it to their assigned host. It occurs to me that I made no allowance for disabled users. Really, Walkable Radius should vary based on a user's mobility rather than being this fixed, monolithic value.

Needless to say, I'm still awake.

I reach underneath my cot for Hedgehog Eleanor Roosevelt. Everyone got an allotment of personal items for their sleep space. She just did fit inside the facilitator's airport security-style bin.

I catch a rubber quill between my fingers, lift her, and check the time.

3:37 a.m.

Prisha is dozing. Jared's feet, mercifully covered now, have been stationary a while. From the near office, Paul's, I hear rattling snores—he relaxed visibly after sending and quickly receiving email back from Li Wei.

If you'd asked me yesterday where "becoming intricately aware of coworkers' sleep habits" belonged on my scale of dreads, I would've rated it near the top.

Now? Middle of the pack.

I know it's a terrible idea to start another day without sleep —doubly terrible given my family mental health history—but there's nothing to be done for it.

I lower a foot to the ground, then ease off my covers. I tuck Hedgehog Eleanor Roosevelt into my pocket. Slip on sandals. Tiptoe to the end of the aisle.

"You require assistance with something?" says a low voice.

Fedor. I thought he might've fallen asleep, as Katie did with her E-wing charges, but no such luck.

I say, "Just hitting the restroom."

He straightens on his stool, scar glinting by the elevators' light. "Sixty-four workers on this floor, and you are the one who needs to go. One out of sixty-four. These numbers interest me."

"Odds aren't as long as you think," I say. "It's actually a sanitary situation that only applies to seven of us. I can go into more detail if you want. If that *interests* you."

Fedor either clears his throats or chokes on snot, then stands aside.

I slip past. The restroom is a ways up the hall, but not so far Fedor can't see. Luckily the door opens out. I pull until it hangs perfectly perpendicular to the wall, blocking half the hallway. With a tiny push back toward the cots, I start race-walking ahead. The door's hinges hiss shut as I'm whipping around the corner.

I don't know if I made it—if Fedor thinks I'm in the bathroom or saw me sneak off. Either way, my play is forward. I walk to the stairwell and feather open the door, exit, feather it closed.

Beyond the glass balustrade, the lobby is dark. I hear *Sempiternity* and see the Elite guard by the mounted television's static. He is slumped on a cot. I'm surprised Dawson would allow his guard to sleep—if indeed he's sleeping and not lying in wait—until I notice small boxes blipping red at either side of the entrance.

Sensors.

If that beam of light breaks, the whole building gets an earful.

How many other sensors are spread around? A set for every unattended first-floor window, I'll bet. For both parking garage levels. It's savvy use of tech. Guarding entry-exit points with sensors lets Elite seem mellow manpower-wise, like they're only bunking down next to us, rather than maintaining a max-security perimeter at all times.

Climbing stairs, I glimpse into each floor to assess. Four, Five, Six, and Nine have significant numbers of employees. Two of these floors have cots visible through the door glass. I count seven more guards. Adding this number to Dawson, Katie, Fedor, and Graham—who's been ominously absent—yields eleven. Factoring in locations I just didn't see, I peg their force between fifteen and twenty.

I reach the E-wing badge reader. Fortunately I never gave back Paul's badge, and use it now to enter. I creep down the main hall. The biz-siders are sleeping as before, Katie now joined by her brother at the head of the sleepover.

All quiet.

I pass Carter's office. He is sprawled on the floor—none of his modernistic furniture accommodates a prone human—with belt undone, one elbow torqued behind the opposite ear.

Here is Susan's door. Should I jostle her awake? Hang out in her office, wait for her eyes to flutter open and find me? Will that spook her? I am generally anti-spooking people, but under the circumstances maybe it's excusable.

My calculations turn out to be moot: Susan is awake at her desk.

"Oh," I say.

She gives a groggy smile. "Can you believe anyone can sleep with all this going on?" She rolls her head languorously, freeing her hair to bounce in lazy spirals. "How did lights-out go downstairs? People all right?"

"More or less. Considering."

"Right."

She's kicked off her shoes and sits with stockinged feet tucked underneath, now rubbing her instep, now yawning wide.

I feel weird watching this. Not because she's sexy as sin—which she is—but because it's too conventional. Too relaxed.

How long do I have before Fedor realizes he's fallen for the easiest lady trick in the book and comes hunting?

Whatever is going to happen here, it needs to get happening.

To get the ball rolling, I say, "I kept the whole Vlast situation quiet."

"Good, I don't think we want it out. It would only alarm people."

Again I feel a disconnect. If ever there was a time for alarm, surely that time is now. "Who did you tell up here on E-wing?"

"Nobody," Susan says. "They're already asleep. I tried getting them sent home altogether—seems silly to keep a bunch of sales reps and ACs around for this private space business plan if all they want is software. Dawson wouldn't go for it. He thinks it breaks the cover story."

I place my hands at various points about my neck and throat, making sure my head is still fastened.

If Susan tried getting the business side sent home, doesn't that imply the engineers are *not* going home?

"Just—let's just reset," I say. "I got here by dicey means—that guy with the ears could be in pursuit—so we should start planning. Step one is getting the word out, right? I found a backdoor through their data-block earlier. If I can use your machine ten minutes, I can slip a message through to SFPD. Now whether or not they believe—"

"A message saying what?" Her tone is mild, genuinely confused.

"One possible opening line might be '*Save us, we're being forced to do the bidding of armed Russians.*'"

I don't say this with snark—like I would to literally any other person on the planet—but unspool it word by word, gauging Susan's reaction.

It's not positive. She's not leaping into action.

I say, "We are putting the kibosh on this, right?"

At my pique, Susan stands and starts around her desk. "Deb, I know this is tough because you've been personally—"

"Hijacking a nuclear power plant on a different continent can't be legal." I heard where she was heading and refuse to accept it. "It's dishonest. It's repugnant and immoral. And I only 60 to 70 percent believe it's true."

Susan waits to make sure I'm done. "I hear all of that. I do. I agree with everything you just said."

We are standing nose to nose. More like nose to chin.

"But?" I say.

Her face is pure anguish. "I just don't see a way out."

I struggle keeping it together. Inside, pressure seals are swelling and gear-teeth grind.

Susan notices. "A way that doesn't burn Codewise Solutions to the ground. We don't have millions of dollars sitting in the bank to pay Elite back. If they call us on non-delivery? We're sunk."

"But it's fraud! The whole thing was a fraud—isn't the contract null and void?"

Her chest sinks. "Carter entered into it. Of course I'd have to see the language in the document, but given our employee was involved...I doubt a court would void it."

"Screw the contract. And screw the money—we just back out. You heard Dawson: the Russians can't reveal their involvement. They won't go after us in U.S. courts."

"That may be," Susan says. "But that doesn't mean they wouldn't go after us."

I have no answer. It's late and sinister and I look around the office and it's thick with terror—trench coats, tossed dresser drawers, sudden-onset radiation poisoning.

She says, "Of course I want to poke Dawson in the eye." Though she doesn't add *like you would*, it's there. "But I have to think about our 317 employees. Their families, their livelihoods. I can't do this on emotion."

In the face of her capitulation, I am nothing but emotion. I'm shriveling. I'm tearing apart.

"So we're building the software. That's what you're saying?"

Susan takes my hand. She lays her palm flat to mine, squeezing, passing her heat into me.

## CHAPTER THIRTY-FOUR

SHE TALKS MORE, GUSHING APOLOGIES AND ASSURANCES and *never agains*. The only thing stopping me from closing off, from dismissing these rationalizations and tossing her in a bin with Carter and Dawson, is the touch.

Our hands stay joined. She isn't caressing, exactly, but there is intimacy in how her fingers permit mine. I feel the bind she's in, how this surrender kills her—is leaching the life-force from her bones.

I think of my graduate adviser at Harvard, who'd wanted me to stick it out in academic robotics. He never told me not to accept Google's offer, but he did say, "Corporate research is fundamentally different. It may feel the same. Perhaps you're in some progressive environment that obscures the primordial motor driving the beast. There will come a moment, though, when you see it. And you won't be able to unsee it, and you won't be able to delude yourself again."

At the time, I wrote him off as stuffy and jealous.

I leave Susan in a haze. My feet drift of their own accord, taking me left instead of right, the direction of Carter's office and the stairwell. This is the sleepy side of Ten, housing only a few office professionals like Ashley Thimms, and a specialized wing of Accounting that exists solely to produce reports for outside investors. All are relocated to cots for the night.

I walk distractedly through this unfamiliar turf. I'm just registering the navigational mistake when a rustle sounds ahead.

I snap to. In an instant, I process where I've wandered—and the fact that nobody here should be awake and rustling.

I slip inside a vacant office. I crouch behind the door, listening.

The noise grows beyond a rustle. Now it contains scraping, thudding, rattling. Snipping?

I cup a hand to my ear. It isn't much—certainly not enough to wake those sleeping on cots. I crawl to the doorway and peek out, exposing a sliver of my face.

I see a ladder. Ten yards away at the end of the hall. Halfway up the rungs is a pair of military lace-up boots. Their owner's head and torso are obscured by the ceiling, but a small penlight illuminates a yellow shirttail. Laid against the wall below is an air duct cover, a panel of concentric-square vents.

They're in the HVAC.

Are they installing surveillance? Monitoring Susan's cooperation with Blackquest 40? Or Carter's? Maybe longer-term surveillance, keeping tabs after the fact so they'll know if we're about to squeal on them?

But...would a microphone work this far from the executive offices? Doubtful. They'd need to crawl way back through the ductwork and plant it in the right ceiling panel, possibly even gouge a hole.

I hold my position, watching. The pain in my hip radiates clear to my ribs, and my sleep-deprived brain suffers from a constant seashell-over-the-ear thrum.

After a few minutes in the ducts, the Elite guy descends. It is a guy—trim brown beard, slighter than Fedor but with comparable biceps. He replaces the duct cover, then collapses the ladder noiselessly and sets a softball-sized box in a sack. Tucks the ladder under one arm and starts toward me.

I scramble behind the door. The man's boots drill the office carpet. As they pound closer, I hold my breath.

He comes level with the doorway. I note grease on his hands and forearms, and get a decent look at his sack, which bulges in a way suggestive of many softball-sized boxes inside.

Signal boosters? Frequency blockers? Are they beefing up the data blockade? Maybe they detected packets slipping through.

I don't think so. I brainstorm a few other theories. None feel right.

I need to get into that duct, but the entrance is twelve feet up—and the ladder just took off.

Once the man is safely gone, I cruise the nearby workspaces. In one I find a rolling cart of binders, reams of paperwork loading down its upper and lower decks. I move all the binders to the bottom and drag the cart underneath the duct vent. I grab a letter opener from a different cube, then hike up by the lower deck. The cart wobbles but stays upright.

I pause to let my heart restart, then boost myself to the top deck.

I can just reach the vent. Using the letter opener on each of four flathead bolts, I nudge the vent up into its duct. The metallic *thunk* is agonizingly loud, but I keep going. I feel around.

My fingertips brush something thin and plastic. A cord? Wires?

I don't know what it could be, and whether or not Elite placed it. All manner of electric or coaxial line might run overhead, but would they run through the ducts?

I could wave Hedgehog Eleanor Roosevelt's screen around up there for light, but I don't think it would do much for me.

I need to see from inside.

With a jittery breath, I dip my knees and jump. My elbows clear the adjacent panel and I slam my forearms down, palms smacking cold metal, the impact echoing up the duct. Some sharp edge pierces my skin. I ignore the prick and snagged-on-a-fishhook sensation, gripping, fighting, like a third grader struggling on her pull-up test in gym.

I manage to hoist my head and chest into the dark duct, then tumble the rest of me inside.

The noise is tin cans off the back of a *Just Married* car.

I cough at the foul air. Dust lodges in my eyes and arm hair. It feels muggy up here, like some basement sauna gone to seed.

I hasten my feet up into the duct so as not to hang down—though with the cart below, I'm not fooling anyone. I pull Hedgehog Eleanor Roosevelt from my pocket for light.

That thin, plastic thing is wire. White and slack—not pinned along a seam like you would expect of a permanent installation. I follow the wire one way until it terminates to a compact, hinged antenna.

The design is unfamiliar, but its function is clear enough: a transmitter. For communicating with some central data service. Surveillance, signal interference, field amplification—any number of purposes fit a transmitter.

I squint the other way along the wire, angling Hedgehog Eleanor Roosevelt, casting her screen's glow down the duct. It's a seven-foot wire and I have to crawl deeper. I move as gently as I can, but each knee strike is still a minor thunderclap. I can only hope that's because I'm confined up here—that the noise doesn't reach the cots.

My periphery constricts. Claustrophobia starts in the corners of my mind. I follow the wire on.

Finally, in the near total darkness, a light.

Blinking.

Red.

When my tensed, shivering hand gets there with Hedgehog Eleanor Roosevelt, I see that the wire connects to the source of the light: a small black cube.

Just the right dimensions for those softball-sized boxes.

My nose twitches. That smell. What *is* that smell? It's chalky and dry on the roof of my mouth. My face takes on that reflexively humorous expression you get trying to place an everyday scent. *Oh, what is it? I know it, it's right on the tip of my tongue...*

When it finally does come, I can't breathe.

Almonds.

# CHAPTER THIRTY-FIVE_

I CAN'T REMEMBER IF IT'S CYANIDE OR EXPLOSIVES OR sarin gas, but the scent of almonds means something.

Something bad.

Maybe this would move Susan, the possibility of her 317 employees being blown up or drowned in their own seizure-induced saliva, but I'm not stopping to find out.

It's yank-the-fire-alarm time. I have to get word outside.

How? Earlier I had the idea of using that Carebnb backdoor to slip a message through the data-block, but that requires specific computers—computers with the same database access the servers on Two have.

The straightest line between here and police cruisers roaring up Second Avenue, I think, is to physically escape the data-block. Depending on their antennas' strength, the block could extend anywhere from five to ten feet outside the building perimeter. Beyond there, I can broadcast a message to the San Francisco police, fire department, the FBI, Drudge Report, *The New York Times*—the full cavalry.

The ground floors will be guarded. Even assuming I can break a window on a higher floor, how do I get sufficiently far from the building? Hedgehog Eleanor Roosevelt has the ability to transmit, but my arms aren't ten feet long.

I could throw her. Set a timer, rig a message to send two or three seconds after I activate the job from her keyboard. Then hope she gets the message off before crashing to Earth.

This feels like a loser. I could knuckle down and do the requisite deceleration calculations, but off the top of my head, it's doubtful.

No, I need something that can gain those ten feet of space and stay operational. Either by surviving a fall, or...

Or not falling.

I lower myself out of the duct, leaving the vent panel askew, and step down by the rolling cart. I take the long route to the stairwell exit so as to avoid Jim Dawson and the sleeping biz-siders.

Raven could rendezvous with me by riding the elevator or bumping handicap-access push buttons, but neither option is quiet—I'll need to let her out myself at Three. Then we can relocate to an emptier floor and try our SOS.

I slip out of Ten and begin tapping on Hedgehog Eleanor Roosevelt. My fingers keep striking between her keys—I'm still recovering from the shock of those almonds—but eventually I get the command issued for Raven to go to the stairwell and hang tight.

I walk down eight flights. When I nudge open the door, my girl is hovering at forehead-height like a spare brain.

"*You rock,*" I whisper.

The least-populated floors are Three and Eight. Deciding Eight is better, the transmission having a better chance away from street-level interference, I lead us back upstairs. Raven follows in EXTREME_QUIET mode, using only two propellers, virtually silent with *Sempiternity* for a backdrop.

On Eight, we walk to the far east edge of the building. This floor used to house Graphic Design before it got outsourced. A few giant monitors and easel-style displays dot the area, left behind after the furniture got reclaimed—dinosaurs after the layoff meteor.

Hedgehog Eleanor Roosevelt pegs the time at 4:57. If I remember correctly, Elite was planning to wake us at 5:30.

Thirty-three minutes is a decent chunk of time, but it's not forever. To pull off her distress cry, Raven will need custom logic. She needs the text of her message. She needs recipients. She needs fly and repeat logic—if the SOS doesn't go at ten feet, I want her beaming it again at ten-point-one feet, at ten-point-two feet, at ten-point-three feet...

The first decision is where. Which window. We cruise this east hall, gauging thicknesses and surroundings. I find a usefully-eroded stretch of caulk in one corner office, but the neighboring building is too close and might hamper transmission. In theory Raven could pathfind around it, but she's been an indoor cat for years now and I don't trust her maneuvering around such large objects.

The center windows are better, overlooking that thirty-five dollar in-out parking lot. Soaring above this, Raven could spray data-packets at will.

Sold.

I prop myself cross-legged on a folding table, power Raven down to save battery, and set about writing her logic. Coding on Hedgehog Eleanor Roosevelt is brutal on the wrists, but it's not like I need to rewrite iTunes. (Which someone does need to do.) I create a simple executable command called SAVE_US.

*SOS_message = "Russian terrorists with guns and explosives have taken over 235 Second Ave. Building locked down. Employees held hostage. NEED HELP NOW.";*

```
recipients = {tips@fbi.gov, info@fbi.gov, info@sfpd.gov, tips@ny-
times.com, text_to_phone("911")};

fly(DIRECTION.east, SPEED.medium);

success_or_fail = transmit(SOS_message, recipients);

If(success==TRUE)
fly(DIRECTION.west, SPEED.fast)
end
else
loop;
```

I pour over the monochrome screen for typos. Hedgehog
Eleanor Roosevelt doesn't do autocorrect, and it would suck if a
misplaced semicolon left Raven burping out syntax errors, hung
out to dry 800 feet over Folsom Street.

My head feels furry and slow and sore, but the code looks
clean.

I press Raven's ON button, right at the neck of her frame,
and zap her the file. She accepts with a grateful *bleep-bloo*.

Next I scout about for something to shatter glass. The few
remaining chairs here are upholstered and without sharp edges.
Those giant LCDs are nice and angular, but heavy. I'd never
muster the velocity to pierce a window.

The time is 5:21. Rise and shine in nine minutes, assuming
the Elite facilitators haven't beaten their alarm clocks up.

I keep scouting. The kitchenette is a husk. The breakroom
barren. The bathroom stocked with soap and toilet paper, still
on the janitorial sweep apparently, but nothing pointy.

Should I try another floor? What else is there to find? The
item that keeps returning to my brain is a claw hammer—those
flat, juicy edges—but I'm not going to find one of those.

5:25.

I am rushing, yawning, three-quarters asleep when I stumble onto a copy nook. The copier itself is long gone, but various accoutrements remain. Loose staples, notebook dividers, a labeler with tape dangling from its mouth.

Tucked in a corner is a broad black object. An inch high maybe. I think paper cutter at first but, upon closer inspection, find no blade—just jaws and three evenly-spaced teeth.

A hole punch.

Sturdy-gauge metal. Two sharp edges. Weighty, but when I grip it one-handed and rear back, my arc rips the air.

"Start warming up your pipes!" I tell Raven, trotting to our window. "It's time to sing."

The clock flips 5:29 as I reach the window. The sun hasn't peeked out yet, but a murky luminescence coats the cables of the Bay Bridge.

I check Raven's logic over one last time—*yep, fly until transmit success, then scoot right back*—then put her in a hover six feet from the window. I can't have some stray shard lodging in her motor.

"Okay, partner. It's your time to be a hero."

I raise the hole punch. It feels eager in my hand, heavy but lithe, pulling for the window.

The glass begins forty inches off the floor and stops at the ceiling. Single pane. Rubberized eighth-inch caulk. No tint that I can see.

Structural engineering was never my favorite, but I can plot a load map when I have to. The glass's center is its strongest point. I want to hit near an edge. I want to lead with this right-angled bottom and cleave the material. If I strike true, there's a chance it shatters.

And if it doesn't? I'll whack again, and again, and again.

I expel a hard, hot breath. I square my feet and settle weight in my hips. With Hedgehog Eleanor Roosevelt in my left hand, I grip the hole punch with my right and draw it back, then—marshaling every ill, ugly urge from the last twenty-four hours—swing forward.

The impact deadens my arm. Numbness sweeps from wrist to shoulder to chest.

I expect to feel air rushing in. Why isn't air rushing in?

The window didn't shatter. It only spidered. I gaze through the fractal pattern at the parking lot below, oddly segmented by cracks.

Grunting, I shake out my arm and set down Hedgehog Eleanor Roosevelt to use both hands, and chuck the hole punch viciously into the heart of the web.

The crunch is tremendous. Glass cascades out into the sky, busting a three-foot void, the hole punch soaring through.

I grab Hedgehog Eleanor Roosevelt and tap out "SAVE_US."

Raven blips green; all four rotors whir and she bolts forward. She flies through the heart of the hole—collision avoidance working like a charm—and out into the black-gray morning.

The air is bright and sweet, and seeing Raven in it cheers me. She is a drone, after all, a mechanical bird—if for no other reason than to freshen her intake filter, I really should be getting her out more.

I flip Hedgehog Eleanor Roosevelt and type *Status*, then flip back over to see the screen.

*Transmit FAIL.*

Raven must've sent the first SOS message too quickly, before escaping Elite's data block. That's fine. That's why I used a loop: she'll keep resending until it works.

No worries. The message will definitely get through on her second or third—or, at the very worst, fourth—try.

I look outside to see how far away she's gotten, but my drone is not there.

A fiery ball is.

## CHAPTER THIRTY-SIX_

RAVEN'S PARTS FALL AT A DIFFERENT SPEEDS, PROPELLER blades fluttering, smoking innards knifing straight down. Heat licks my face. I pull back from the glass.

Raven's greatest hits are flashing through my mind: her inaugural self-nav flight through a hula hoop maze at Google, the pilfering of a Confederate flag off my caveman-neighbor's pickup truck, yesterday morning's water cooler knockout...

I hear pattering and think for one zany instant it's applause. People must be cheering Raven, right? Remembering these same triumphs?

It's not applause.

The stairwell door is on the opposite side of the floor from me—a blessing. I hear two or possibly three sets of boots. Harsh voices. I grab Hedgehog Eleanor Roosevelt and run. First left, three strides toward the elevators. Then back right when the voices seem louder.

I stop in my tracks. The boot-claps seem to come from everywhere, through the walls and floor and air.

I dash to the copy nook. My eyes zip along baseboards and between counters and up a center beam to the ceiling.

A vent! HVAC runs straight over the top. I start patting my pockets for that letter opener before realizing that even if I have it—which I don't appear to—these pounding boots are too close. No way can I dislodge four bolts, boost myself into the duct, and push the vent cover passably into place before they arrive.

My gaze moves on. In a corner of the room is a shred cabinet, an opaque panel with a wide mouth for dropping documents through. These panels typically hide bins that catch the documents, but this one hasn't been operational for months: four square feet of empty, gloriously hidden space.

I open the panel and dive inside.

Darkness envelops me. Squatting, I pull the panel closed. The odor is stale and musty—a stamp collector's attic. My sandals slip on a loose pile of documents. I push them aside and hug myself small.

"I have the left hall!" calls a voice.

"Every cubicle—every one," another says. "I have the offices!"

I hear them hunting my side of the floor, doors whipped open, drawers rammed shut. *They think I fit inside drawers?*

Through the cabinet's wide mouth, I can observe a sliver of the hall—that stretch where Raven and I tried our SOS. A man in Elite yellow stops to peer through the hole in the window.

He inches closer to the gaping glass. His hair is buzzed, razor burn on his neck. He looks down as though contemplating whether I followed Raven in some Romeo and Juliet nosedive.

I keep still, looking out. My eyes begin to water.

Creaaaa—

The panel! My panel is drifting open—I'm so exhausted I must have let go as I was concentrating. I pull it closed, but too late. The man at the window whirls and shouts to the others.

Up the hall, running boots. They're coming. They know I'm

somewhere in the interior. I hear them search the adjacent room, barking to each other.

Still hugging my knees, I rock myself to the back of my cabinet. I will myself smaller. I'm so compact my heartbeat seems everywhere at once, pulsing in my shins and elbows.

Fedor is first into the nook—I glimpse those ears through the cabinet's mouth. I spot a flash of black too, between his knuckles.

A gun? They've dropped all pretenses now.

Fedor stalks the room's perimeter, a deliberate right-to-left sweep, upsetting papers and folders.

He'll check my cabinet. I know he will. The cabinet has a locking mechanism, but of course I don't have a key and couldn't risk reaching outside to lock it anyway.

Working by feel in the dark, I find the lock's metal tab. When engaged, the tab rises above the cabinet door and prevents its opening. I rotate the tab from horizontal to vertical —a faint click is lost in Fedor's boots—and hold it firm with my thumb.

In seconds, Fedor reaches the cabinet. I struggle to remain flat against the wall and maintain pressure on the tab. The whites of his eyes flash through the wide mouth, quickly replaced by fingertips and five angry knuckles.

He grips the door by its mouth—nearly brushing my thumb —and yanks.

Concentrating all my strength in that one thumb, I stop the metal tab from moving. The cabinet and wall behind Fedor rattle from the impact of his pull.

But the door stays shut.

Fedor moves on. In another moment, he's onto the next space.

I let my head flop onto my shoulder. Hedgehog Eleanor

Roosevelt's quills are in my fist, I realize. When I release her, my palm is a bloodless white.

I haven't actually bought much time, I realize. I'm still trapped. My SOS didn't go—unless Raven sneaked her second transmission through in the nick of time, then got blasted before transmitting confirmation back to me.

Possible?

Sure.

Likely?

I'd sooner bet on a gay president coming out of the next election.

After several minutes searching the floor, the pair of Elite thugs returns to the broken window.

A walkie-talkie crackles. "*No*. But she must be here. She cannot escape."

A blip, then more crackling. Then another blip.

"Confirm, holding position," Fedor says. "We have Piotr on the door on Eight. Call when you arrive—he will let you in."

Then nothing. No receding footsteps, or popping pulltabs accompanied by sighs of "Ahhh, it's Miller time."

They are staying.

This shred cabinet—my new home—seems to shrink by the second. The way I'm sitting forces my sandal strap into my blister, and the cumulative effect of all these bruises and lacerations is a kind of starchy, all-body ache.

Soon I hear another crackle, followed by Fedor dispatching Piotr to the stairwell door.

To let more in.

They are going to re-sweep. They are going to turn over every stapler and mouse pad and rip up carpet if that's what it takes to find me. Fedor gave the cabinet door a single yank. Whoever covers this print nook next time won't stop at a yank. He'll insist on seeing inside.

My options? With Piotr gone, I have a window of time here where Fedor and I are one-versus-one. Could I sneak up on him? Overpower him?

Maybe.

I need a distraction, but my go-to distraction maker was just blown to smithereens. Could one of my other little pals rise to the occasion? My droid-Hot Wheels are quick and clever, but they're sitting in a bin at my cubicle. It's possible if I revved a bunch simultaneously, they could generate enough force to topple the bin.

So...let's say half land with wheels down, such that they could drive...maybe they path-find to the elevators or stair-well...but even then, assuming all that success, a Hot Wheel can't physically board an elevator or climb steps.

You know who could, though?

My dragonflies. My buggy dragonflies, who suck at flying.

Loathe as I am to count on those stinkers for anything mission-critical, I think they're my only chance.

I hole up with Hedgehog Eleanor Roosevelt, obscuring her screen light with my body as best I can, and confirm the dragon-flies are online. I navigate through network folders to DEBS_STUFF.

Yep, BAILEYS_BUZZY_GROUP is there. I touch the icon and type "check status." After a three-second delay, during which my girls should be waking and running diagnostics, the screen returns "43 BAILEYS BUZZY DRAGONFLIES AVAILABLE."

Me likes.

At noise outside, I hunch tighter around Hedgehog Eleanor Roosevelt. I start the dragonflies' logic script, babying each keystroke down to the circuitboard, then keeping finger pressure back up to avoid clacks.

Challenge number one is getting them to the eighth floor.

They could take the stairs. People should be awake, and after the ruckus of Raven exploding, I wouldn't sweat the noise of activating a handicap pushbutton. But could they, physically?

Those pushbuttons are firm, and the dragonflies are light. Two-point-seven ounces, soaking wet. I might need fifteen or twenty striking simultaneously, which means coordination logic. Even if I get that logic right, the plan could fail anyway if the impacts are too diffuse across the button.

So. Elevator.

I play that scenario forward. The dragonflies call a car from Three...ride it up to Eight...at the ding, the yellow shirts rush to the elevator bank, assuming I summoned a car for escape...they scour the surrounding areas looking for me...the doors split and my swarm of freaky mechanical crazoids goes at them.

By the time they know what's what, I'm long gone to the stairwell.

It's perfect. If my dragonflies had brains, they could do it.

But they don't have brains—yet.

CHAPTER THIRTY-SEVEN_

I GET CRACKING, HEAVILY MOTIVATED BY THE LARGER ELITE force now searching the floor.

The dragonflies' navigation is specifically tailored to the 3,000-square-foot theater where Universal Studios is putting *Bailey's Buzzy World*, which means they have nothing like Raven's or even the droid-Hot Wheels' freeform path-finding. I can't feed them GPS coordinates for the elevators and trust they'll get there. They won't. They'll say, "Um, two numbers that are almost 37 and -122" and buzz stupidly in place.

Fortunately, they are durable. One of Universal's use cases called for interaction with kids—and whenever kids are in spec, the requirement is indestructibility.

I write some bare-bones logic to route them to the elevators. No turning, no collision avoidance. They're going to do a lot of slamming into walls, but that's okay. As long as they keep trying, keep vectoring—and this is the beauty of programming loops— they will eventually make it.

What's next? Finding the *Up* button, boarding the car, pushing the button for Eight—each component problem has its own pitfalls. The dragonflies' "eyes" are awful, definitely not capable of identifying numbers. I run my fingers over Hedgehog Eleanor Roosevelt's quills, thinking. Now shapes...shapes they could manage. Also colors.

I know! They can build a list of all round objects of a given size, say one-inch radius, that aren't red (i.e. the alarm button) and press the top one. Should work.

Two problems solved.

I am just considering what they should do off the elevator at Eight when the search becomes suddenly boisterous—Elite is in my hallway.

Deciding there's no time for elegance, I dash out the first logic I imagine might work. The dragonflies will crudely measure the movement of all objects in their field of vision, and the first they identify that's not stationary, they'll zoom at—no questions asked.

I upload the command to BAILEYS_BUZZY_GROUP.

Elite clambers outside. Their heat and crosstalk fill the air. Boots and belt buckles jangle. I think I smell Fedor, a vinegary tang that returns to me from our confrontations on Three.

*"The cabinet."*

The voice is close, maybe at the threshold of the copy nook. Now quick feet. Two pair? I inch back as far as possible and hike my knees out of sight of the mouth, making my hamstrings scream.

I stay like this for sixty seconds.

*Ding.*

The elevator chime cuts the tension. There is a brief confusion. Heads snapping around? Guns being drawn?

"Nobody works on this floor!" Fedor says. "She must have called it—she is going for the elevator."

He and the others ramble off.

I give it two seconds, no more—I need the cover of their loud boots—then sprint from the nook, around the corner, whizzing through cold air from the busted-out window and Raven's acrid fumes.

I round another corner and make the stairwell door.

It's unguarded. *Yes!* Everybody ran to the elevators. I blow through to the lobby overlook.

What's my plan? Where can I go? My best hope is for the lobby guard to have joined the chase. If he's at the elevator bank getting bombarded by pesky dragonflies too, maybe I can book it down eight flights and escape outside. Maybe the bánh mì man is prepping his cart for breakfast and I'll grab his cellphone from his apron pocket and dial 911.

I skip three steps down, pre-smelling coriander and pickled carrots.

It'll have to wait.

Because here is the lobby guard, rushing up, at Six now and charging higher. He sees me. He slows to shout in his walkie-talkie, then speeds up again. From Six to Seven, fists pumping at his sides.

I remember being thirteen and running from attackers with mom up a fire escape. I can't think why now—maybe we'd squatted in the wrong building—but that feeling of pursuit, of men devouring steps, closing the gap, was identical. We raced up and up and up, then finally running out of space, held each other on the roof until they took us.

I'm not running out of space now. I'm not going up either. Twenty-seven-year-old Deb knows physics. I have only one advantage over this guy, but it's substantial: altitude.

He's halfway up the flight below, I gauge by sound. I stutter-step, timing my approach. I take the fifth and seventh stairs in stride, skip down eight, then launch myself—feet leading like the tip of a lance—toward the landing.

The guard turns the corner just as my body goes parallel with the stairs. My sandals drill his chest. I've sailed six feet in the air and been accelerated by gravity, which gives my kick great force. My body snaps like a ripcord on impact.

All my momentum transfers to the guard, who somersaults backward.

As I land in a jumble he keeps rolling, boots over head a second time, gaining velocity rather than losing it. His body whips down the last step to the landing, and he tries standing immediately.

It's too fast.

He gains his feet, but his torso is still in motion. His thighs hit the glass balustrade and suddenly I'm watching the soles of his boots as he tips forward.

He shrieks. The noise dissipates as he topples over. I don't see the fall, but I hear the sickening crash-splat at its end: seven stories down into *Semperinity*.

CHAPTER THIRTY-EIGHT_

I RISE AND GRIP HEDGEHOG ELEANOR ROOSEVELT AND start down, not stopping to see what grisly sight accompanies the grisly sound.

My left ankle is a starburst of pain at every other stride. That side's hip is refusing to participate in locomotion, locked, dead-weight calcium.

Still, I'm hurtling downstairs at speed. The main entrance is free and clear, and I'm going for it.

At Four, I hear a telltale click below. It came from Three, the engineering floor. I skid to a halt at the balustrade above.

Two yellow shirts emerge. The first, dark-complexioned and bald, rushes out to the stairwell on stocky legs. I don't wait around to ID the second, planting a foot and reversing direction. Halfway up the flight, though, my step hangs in the air.

The balustrade.

I could hurdle it. Soar three stories, hopefully missing *Semperinity*, then pop up and run—or at least hobble hurriedly —through the lobby, collapsing into the arms of a cop or bus driver or my favorite bánh mì food-cart operator.

I lean back that way, but my legs revolt. Tiny weaknesses

pip at me from deep within, from the marrow of my bones—which apparently aren't keen on being shattered.

I race up instead. The yellow shirts thunder after me from below, calling out, walkie-talkies crackling. I have a flight and a half lead, but I'm lame.

"Deb!" I hear from far below. "Deb, are you cool up there?"

It's the faintly dopey voice of Security Kyle, crouched at *Semperinity*, looking up skittishly from the body of the Elite guard.

There is nobody between him and the double-doors.

"No, definitely not cool!" I scream without breaking stride. *"Go get the cops!"*

I lose sight of Kyle swinging past the entrance to Six, then glimpse him halfway to Seven from the balustrade. He's out of his crouch, wavering toward the entrance.

"Go, man—*GO!*" I shout.

This breaks his deer-in-the-headlights stare. He jumps up. As I pass Eight heading to Nine, I think we're in business.

A blast punctures the air. I peek down and see a gun extended past the balustrade—a gun and a dark arm, which is attached to a yellow shirtsleeve.

Kyle is back on his knees, a quivering lump.

Just a warning shot, I think. It worked.

I keep running. The last thing I need is more ominous noises, but that's just what I get passing Eight: *clinky* banging, a *thunk*, then a second, more pronounced *thunk*.

The dragonflies must be putting up a fight. I optimistically imagine them swarming Fedor, dogging him down the hall, stabbing with their indigo tails.

How many are still kicking? The initial status ping reported forty-three responsive. Say a dozen missed the elevator. Say another half-dozen didn't make it off. How many would've died fighting Elite?

Sandals slapping pine, I pass the balustrade at Nine. The yellow shirts have gained. Before they were staggered by a half-flight, not visible, but now I see them at every turn.

The gap is one flight.

Now those noises at Eight give way to another door click. Seconds later, a silver and indigo swarm flashes forth like sparks from a firework, shooting past the balustrade and out into the lobby's high canopy.

The dragonflies stabilize in place, a sort of rocking shimmy-shake that's the bane of my existence because it looks nothing like the graceful hover of real dragonflies, no matter how I futz with their flight logic.

There are fifteen or so. *Not bad.* A few dive for the lobby floor, possibly detecting the skulking of Security Kyle. Half boomerang right back the way they came, presumably to open another can of whoop-ass on Elite.

The rest happen to raise their digital eyes and—searching, searching, slaves to the loop I programmed into them—zoom after me.

I head higher. Below, Fedor is barking instructions. He seems to notice the dragonflies noticing me and joins the other yellow shirts' headed up. His face shows erratic red streaks—I guess my stinkers found their mark.

And now they've marked me. Slidey-scratchy noises must be them bouncing up the glass balustrade. Next I hear their distinctive hiss growing louder, and soon after feel a prick in my butt.

Then another. The dragonfly rams me repeatedly, stabbing her antennae through my pants' fabric. Their antennae are exaggerated—real dragonflies' antennae are tiny—for cosmetic and functional purposes, articulated prongs that're doing a decent dagger impression right about now.

I grab back blindly for her. My third try, I snag her by the thorax. Another dragonfly pelts my shoulder blades. I grab her too. They keep hissing in my hands, their silicon-wafer wings slicking wildly, tickling my palms.

At Ten, I pause at the balustrade. Looking over, I spot the yellow shirts—four altogether now—swinging around a corner. I give it a three count to be sure the stinkers get clear looks at my tormentors' faces, then throw them as hard as I can.

The dragonflies plummet fifteen feet before their wings reclaim control. They stabilize in midair, then after a moment reacquiring, bolt toward the stairs.

I don't see them engage Elite, but I hear strangled cries and one "Damn it, *again*?"

Smiling, I scramble up two more flights to the top floor: Twelve. Twelve is more empty space, the Cray supercomputer being the only item of interest there. I rush inside, hoping the stinkers are buying me time. With luck, the yellow shirts won't know which floor I've disappeared to. Maybe they'll split up, each taking a floor between Nine and Twelve. Maybe I'll get somebody one-on-one.

Then what?

I don't know. Something.

I put distance between myself and the stairwell. My eyes dart about. Walls, ceiling, beige carpet—the office has never felt more generic than it does now.

I haven't found a hiding spot when the stairwell door clicks. It whines open, followed by the dread sound of boots.

Again, there's no time for some elaborate ruse involving bolts or vent panels. I hurry along a hall past bathrooms and empty offices.

*He will have heard me. He'll know which side of the floor I'm on.*

My body wants to quit. My heart is pumping out adrenaline, but it's a detached sort of adrenaline—like the buzz of too much coffee.

I keep looking. I'm not finding a shred cabinet or trap door or invisibility token. I'm struck by no great inspiration.

The door opens again. A new voice, loud but gentler than Fedor's, calls, "*Where?* Did you see her?"

"Take left!" answers a different voice. "I have right."

They come from both directions. My buffer is shrinking.

Behind me is the small room containing the Cray supercomputer: a seven-foot-high hollow cylinder, surrounded by burnt-orange benches and open in back. Depending on your frame of reference, it resembles either a teleport station or 1970s furniture.

The boots are getting louder. Time's up. I need to get hidden.

The only spot that occurs to me is inside the Cray's cylindrical body—which is obvious, the first place anyone would look.

I have no choice.

I hustle around the orange benches and inside. It would be hot here if the Cray were on, but it hasn't run since well before my hiring. Translucent panels reveal circuit boards, green organs, copper veins. I press myself up against one side, but it doesn't obscure much. A glance from any angle will betray me.

I'll be found. The Cray is literally the only thing on Twelve, and I'm in it.

I need a weapon. Hedgehog Eleanor Roosevelt is feckless. How about these metal strips along the Cray's segment borders? A few are pulling away from their panels. Could I pry one off?

I scan the vertical strips and find one that's already lost a screw. Wedging my fingernails underneath, I tug. The remaining screw creaks. A sliver of its shaft emerges. I drop all weight into my hips and rock it back and forth, revealing more of the shaft, yanking, grunting, yanking, until finally the screw breaks.

I stumble to the ground, the strip in my hands. It's maybe thirty inches high and two wide, with a sharp lip. A thin, unwieldy bat. Better than nothing.

Muffled voices penetrate the walls. The yellow shirts must've met in the hall. Probably devising a strategy to canvas the floor.

In another minute, footsteps stall outside my room. Somebody has seen the Cray. Of course he has. He may not know what a mid-2000s supercomputer looks like, but a cursory glance will tell him this bulky, C-shaped contraption hides a cavity that happens to be perfectly-sized for a human body.

The footsteps resume.

A walkie-talkie blips. I catch only snatches of a murmured exchange.

The footsteps stop, which I take not as the Elite henchman leaving, but as his strides going light and stealthy.

I spread my feet and poise the metal strip at my shoulder, waiting.

One second.

Two.

A dark forehead appears in the Cray's opening—an inch of scalp, the side of an ear. I don't wait for more.

I swing—an upstroke, leading with the strip's sharp lip. I crack him good and rush out.

The man collapses to one knee. His hand goes for a holster, but I whack him below the elbow first. He groans and pinches his eyes. I kick him in the groin and beat him more with the strip and straddle him.

It's the bald man from the stairs. As I batter his dark-complexioned skin, I conjure a backstory—Dawson plucked him out of unlawful detention, he's some Eurasian Mumia Abu-

Jamal. It's wild and simplistic and surely wrong. All that's clear is that he's large—large and strong—and is budging me, forcing my knees off his chest.

I punch his eye. As his hands move up to defend, I go for his gun. I have two clear seconds but can't get the thing out of its holster—the barrel snags in a twist of leather.

In the next moment, he has me in a vice grip.

I lunge to free myself but only manage to flip us over. Now Eurasian Mumia is on top of me, his weight oppressive, face contorted and gross. I lose a sandal. My shin is pinned against the burnt-orange bench seat.

I snap my head and neck but can't get loose. When his hand passes near my mouth, I bite the webbing of his thumb. He curses, but his knees stay in my armpits.

He sits up taller. He's pulverizing my chest.

"Too much trouble," he says, shaking the hand I bit. "If you would've listened. If you would've done your job. You would be safe."

I barely have air in my lungs to speak but manage, "Says the people wiring the building with explosives."

His eyes narrow. Does he not know? Is Dawson keeping the truth from his own men?

I take advantage of the disorientation to slip a fist free and jack him again. He keeps hold of my other arm.

"*Bitch!*" Blood spurts from his nose. "That's your last mistake."

"I don't think so," I say, back in his grasp. "Without me, you don't get control of that nuclear power plant. And you know it."

Again the man seems confused, but this time doesn't let down his guard. He stays on top. I see up his nostrils.

"Think I care anything about some software?" He slips the gun from its holster. "I am paid regardless."

Now I'm seeing up the barrel of a gun.

"But he—I mean Dawson," I stutter, "if you kill me, he won't be—"

"I had no choice. You had a gun. You would not be subdued."

Relentlessly, the muzzle tracks my face. I can't believe it. This guy is rogue. He's going to pull the trigger. I fight him, but it's just too many pounds and too much force.

My eyes roll up and across the Cray's circuitry, its weird and wonderful guts, wasted up here because of Carter Kotanchek's whim. Maybe it's poetic justice that I expire here too, in a bland floor of a bland office.

Another bad fit. Another corporate casualty.

I can only hope Carebnb lives on as some weak legacy. Who could take it over? Minosh has the right programming skills, but he's too squeamish to deal with the unhoused. Prisha is single and busy. She can't take on a side project. Paul doesn't code anymore. Jared...yeah, no.

Maybe it just dies. Ambitious projects like Carebnb hit snags—big, complex snags—and it takes a true believer to drive through. Nobody working out of pity or memorial is going to realistically overcome what needs overcoming.

I could've finished Carebnb a year ago. If I had just quit Google outright, if I'd done it full time.

A bloodied hand wraps my throat. The forefinger of the man's other hand loops the trigger. His face is exhilaration incarnate.

"You can't," I try. *"They're going to know!"*

He shakes his head. "You refused to surrender. It's your known character."

I pinwheel my legs and spit and scream and buck my abs. Nothing helps. The black muzzle stays on me.

The air shatters around me—the loudest, most violent noise

imaginable. I recoil instinctively and twist away...but feel nothing.

*Why don't I feel? What happened?*

When I look again, Eurasian Mumia is missing half his head. His weight still pins me, but inertly—I twitch my hips and he rolls off.

The office carpet is turning from beige to black in slow, wet waves.

In the doorway, looking all wrong with a weapon in his hands, stands Graham.

## CHAPTER THIRTY-NINE_

I'M NOT SURE WHOSE FACE IS PALER. I FEEL BLOOD LEAVING mine, but Graham looks like he just put down the family dog. He holds the gun so hard I think his knuckles might switch places, and his right eye—typically a pool of easy, ironic hazel—won't stop twitching.

In what capacity did he just shoot Eurasian Mumia? There's a gushy, hopping-up-and-down part of me saying he did it to protect me, but that old street part of me thinks it was on Dawson's behalf—the prevention of a murder detrimental to the cause.

Graham thumbs his walkie-talkie and says into the bottom, "The Bollinger woman shot Misha. I'm in pursuit."

The walkie-talkie clicks off, and our eyes lock. The hopping-up-and-downers inside me are hopping, but there's only so much celebrating you can do beside a dripping corpse—and with a team of mercenaries still on your trail.

Graham steps inside and picks Eurasian Mumia's gun off the ground, replacing it with his own. He offers me a hand up.

I take it.

"You were in the ducts before," he says as we move away

from the Cray supercomputer. "The ducts are good, we should get you back up there."

He stops at the first HVAC vent we come to in the ceiling. From a pocket he produces a screwdriver and begins loosening the panel.

"Wait," I say. "If they know I was in the ducts, won't that be the first place they look?"

He grimaces at a stubborn bolt. "You aren't trafficking in good options. Our men are too large to maneuver through the vents."

The walkie-talkie at his waist chirps intermittently, followed by garbled questions from Dawson or Fedor about Graham's position and sightings of me.

Graham ignores them.

He keeps loading the removed bolts and nuts into one hand. When one drops, I pick it off the carpet and offer to hold the others so he can focus on getting the vent off. As he hands them over, our eyes lock again.

"Just to confirm," I say, "you're helping me because you've come to the realization your side is evil. Right?"

Graham spares a half second to chuckle. "I'm helping because I'm a captive worker, same as you." His gaze moves down my body, every inch of which is bruised or scratched. "Not quite the same, perhaps."

As he finishes removing the vent and boosts me up to the HVAC duct—no time for gallantry, his palm right in my crotch —he explains how he came to work for Elite.

He was at a stag party. Some back room of a gentleman's club in Las Vegas. The girl insisted he close his eyes—ah, what an idiot he was. When he opened them back up, her throat was slit and the knife in his hands. The first ski-masked man bagged the bloody weapon. The second told Graham that in two weeks he would receive a job offer from a company called Elite Development. He should accept this offer.

"They threatened to frame you? But how could they swing that? Strip joints have cameras—"

"They can swing quite a lot."

I have my knees underneath me in the duct now, looking down. Graham gestures for the bolts back, and I pass them through the missing ceiling panel.

"So...you built that randomized security scheme in Ukraine," I say. "To keep the Russians out."

He starts an answer, then stops, then re-poising his lips, says, "It was the best work of my career."

Resignation wilts his face—and it's a handsome one, not easily wilted.

I have known this feeling myself. When Paul told me Boeing didn't care about real-time thrust balancing, a feature I'd spent hundreds of hours perfecting, or that Vancouver thought my trash-sniffing fly prototypes had no use cases. You throw yourself recklessly at a thing, you achieve what you set out to achieve, and it doesn't matter. Outside circumstances negate your work.

I say, "It's standout software. It sucks they did this to you."

Graham's expression turns obtuse as he says, "We are all compromised."

His walkie-talkie crackles.

A voice says, "*I am sending men to help on Twelve. Is she there?*"

Now Graham does answer. "Don't bother. I've been all over Twelve, she must have slipped out. Send them to Eleven instead."

He clicks off the walkie-talkie. I shift to relieve my knees from the hard duct floor and confirm I have Hedgehog Eleanor Roosevelt.

I ask, "Is Vegas a common spot for Ukrainian stag parties?"

His hazel eyes flatten. "They will probably flush you out."

"No, they won't. Like you said, these ducts are small, I can shimmy—"

"Dawson is relentless." Graham is holding the vent steady in the ceiling, inserting the first bolt through its hole. "He has a way of bending people to his requirements. You won't win."

This bugs me—even if Graham is trying to be helpful and did just save my life. As he holds the vent in place, I keep thinking about Vegas. About that San Francisco driver's license I glimpsed yesterday in the van.

"You aren't telling me everything," I say as the duct's darkness becomes complete. "Why? What else is there?"

Graham doesn't answer. He spins down the last bolt's nut and explains he's left them finger-tight; if I hit it good, I can spring myself—

"I found the charges!" Immediately I regret this, but there's no un-saying it. "They're going to blow this place sky-high the second you guys leave, aren't they?"

My voice rings up and down the ducts. Graham says nothing at first. In the distance, there are voices and clattering.

Dawson's men. On Twelve.

I wonder if my information about explosives is news to Graham, as it seemed to be for Eurasian Mumia. I sense sadness in his non-answer, which is a ludicrous assumption on my part— I can't even see his face.

Does he wish I hadn't found out? Is he feeling shame? About Vegas? About capitulating?

"When Dawson finds you," he finally says, "your best chance is to build the cursed thing. For your coworkers. For yourself. Just build it—and maybe we all come out the other end alive."

With that, he trots off down the hall.

# PART FOUR_

## CHAPTER FORTY

I CRAWL SEVERAL CEILING PANELS FROM THE VENT AND turn off Hedgehog Eleanor Roosevelt's display. I lay still on my side along the center of the duct—which I've learned is the quietest part, least likely to bend and pop when I shift. Placing my ear to the metal, I can hear a decent bit of what's happening.

The gang from Elite slams doors and rips partitions apart. They're either pounding walls with fists or throwing furniture at them. They curse each other.

One set of footsteps grows loud. Now very loud. The bolts in the nearest vent rattle and start turning in place.

*I'm a goner*, I think, and have a strong instinct to knee-clomp frantically in the opposite direction...then I remember what Graham said, that their men can't maneuver in the ducts.

I decide to hold my position. With a clatter, the vent is pushed up into the duct, then nudged aside. Then the top of a man's head appears. Again, it takes all my belief and self-control not to scamper off.

*There's no light here,* I tell myself. *He can't see. He can only hear.*

The man glances left, glances right, then sinks back down. I hear him perform a similar check of the next vent in this hall, and the vent after that.

Faintly I hear, "Where exactly did you see her last?"

Though distant, the voice is lashing: Dawson's. Probably in the adjacent hallway. I miss the next words, which must be Graham's.

Dawson says, "And why do you think that?"

This time I do hear Graham's answer: "Because I looked everywhere. Keep wasting time up here if you like. That's your prerogative. The manpower would be better spent on Eleven."

"We had men on Eleven. No one saw her."

"Were they good men? I don't know what to tell you. She's slippery."

For a while, I hear nothing. I wonder if Dawson is purple-faced and mashing that stress ball. Maybe he's threatening to resurrect that bloody knife from Vegas if Graham doesn't come up with a more convincing story. What did Graham say—"he has a way of bending people?"

Maybe Graham has already caved. Maybe he's whispering right now, gesturing for Dawson to keep quiet, to send someone ahead, I'm just around the corner.

I hold Hedgehog Eleanor Roosevelt by her quills and hope.

In another minute, the door to Twelve clicks open. Noises sound from the stairwell. There are no floors above me, so Elite must be heading toward Eleven.

I roll onto my back, exhaling, sprawling out what little I can in this cramped duct. It's pitch black. I could be inside a coffin.

I try focusing on my next move, escape, or some kind of telecommunications wizardry using Hedgehog Eleanor Roosevelt, but my eyelids have different ideas.

One moment, I'm muttering about sneaking messages out using Elite's outgoing email headers; the next, I'm snoring. I dig my nails into my palms and bite my lip, but lying prone like this —all I have room for—I can't do it. I can't stay awake.

I am envisioning my way through the ductwork...must move down...lying on a cot needing a tampon...not faking but actually needing one, badly...Dawson has a box of them, a gigantic cardboard crate of the super-absorbent orange ones...but there's an electric fence and I'm wearing this bulky collar...should send Raven, she could swoop in and pluck...

Wait.

Raven got blown up.

I jolt awake, my heel banging the top of the duct. I grab for Hedgehog Eleanor Roosevelt and check the time.

I was only out fifteen minutes.

I press my ear to the duct again and concentrate. I hear nothing. I risk crawling back to listen at the vent, whose open slats permit more sound.

Still nothing.

Dawson has probably given up and headed back to Three to harass the other engineers. What's the status of Blackquest 40 now? Will they forge ahead without me? Who'll fill in? Is Prisha being pressured to step up? Will Paul shift back into a programming role, revive his former code-ninja persona?

I need to know what's happening—whether they're giving it a whirl or packing up, planning to cut bait and blow us all to kingdom come on their way out the door.

Unfortunately Raven is no longer a surveillance option, and I get the feeling if one my dragonflies shows her pointy face to a yellow shirt, she'll get squashed like the bug she's meant to resemble.

The only workable option is my droid-Hot Wheels.

These do have audio, slick nano-microphones that are part of our Hot Wheels of the Future prototype for Mattel. I begged Paul for this project. Hot Wheels were my favorite toy growing up. I used to keep a plastic bag hung off Mom's cart, a dedicated receptacle of found cars, and stage races down the concrete slopes of overpasses.

I love 'em, and their tech is cash-money, but I haven't tested their hearing range. If Dawson is addressing the team, will they pick it up?

Depends.

On where exactly he is. On how their bin is oriented.

I roll over onto my tummy, Hedgehog Eleanor Roosevelt out in front of me. When I check HOTWHEELS_FLEET, the expected number, fifty-seven, reports for duty. I activate number sixteen at random and tap into her audio feed.

The sounds are so faint I wonder if her mic is malfunctioning. It could be she's buried in the middle of the bin.

I try a few other Hot Wheels. Their feeds are no better.

Grime is gathering between my toes—feeling it, I use the cuff of my sleeve to clear it.

What should I do? Sneak around through the ductwork and disable all the charges? Though I dabble in it for robotics, electrical engineering isn't my forte—and disarming explosives is nothing you want to wing it on.

I really need ears downstairs.

I think I have to knock over the bin of droid-Hot Wheels. If I can land one right-side-up on the ground, I can drive it within range of the action on Three.

When I considered this option before, I kinda tossed it off —*oh right, theoretically I could dump the bin*—but now I have to make it work.

The sides of the bin aren't that high, maybe a half-inch taller than the pile of Hot Wheels. It's even possible, with all of them revving and spinning their tiny rubber wheels like banshees, one could whiz its way up and out, tumbling to the carpet without toppling the whole bin.

I write a simple script instructing all to accelerate to infinity for ten seconds, beam it to the collective fleet, then run it.

Listening on number sixteen's audio, I hear the high whinny of many three-volt motors, metal knocking, and lots of static.

Ten seconds later, the feed returns to its former nothingness.

I tap out a command asking number sixteen for her position history. Hedgehog Eleanor Roosevelt blurts out a series of latitude-longitude-altitude numbers, every last one identical out ten decimal places.

She went nowhere.

Did any of them? Is the bin simply too heavy?

I write a script to find the lowest-altitude Hot Wheel, to see whether any managed to escape. I'm not wildly hopeful kicking it off, but the script finishes with intriguing news: a few Hot Wheels do show altitudes about four feet lower. I grab the first, nine, and give its audio a whirl.

I hear something. The hum of a hard drive? A faraway voice? It's better than sixteen, but still not that helpful.

She'll have to go for a ride.

This will not be easy. I can't cut her loose path-finding—she could zip right into Dawson's boot. I'll need to control her manually, and Hedgehog Eleanor Roosevelt is no videogame controller with joystick and buttons.

I'll have to turn, accelerate, and decelerate by text command, blind, guided only by lat-long coordinates. I'll need to get her close to Elite's command center on Three, where Dawson might be talking, but not so close as to arouse suspicion.

I inch her forward, ACCELERATE, 2—two being a speed value between one and ten. I listen closely to her audio.

A soft *bump*.

She's hit a cubicle border or a wall, I'm guessing. I send

SPIN_BACKWARDS, 5, then ACCELERATE, 2 again. She goes another few seconds before crashing again.

Driving like this is maddening. For five minutes, I tap out commands and the teched-up Hot Wheel dutifully executes them.

Finally, a dull tone in the audio feed separates from the background: a male voice.

Dawson's.

"...challenging, but very much achievable," he is saying. "Now you are rested. Great obstacles lay before us, but this is good. This is why we train. From great obstacles arise great teams."

A voice I can't identify asks, "What were all those noises? I —we thought we heard a gunshot. Or maybe a car backfiring?"

"Not a car," Dawson responds soberly. "It was a gun."

This causes an uproar. Hedgehog Eleanor Roosevelt's speaker fizzes with gasps and exhortations.

Paul's voice breaks through. "Is Deb dead, did your men kill her? We all have eyes—we see she isn't here!"

The feed goes silent. I imagine Dawson presiding over the collective anxiety, drinking it in.

"Miss Bollinger tried another escape," he says. "When a facilitator confronted her, she took his weapon and used it to kill him."

"Deb? *Deb* shot the gun?"

"Our personnel carry firearms as a precaution, but under virtually no circumstances do their rules of engagement permit them to discharge their weapon."

Confused murmurs meet this complete and total heap of donkey dung. Where is Susan? There's no way she could have slept through the racket of Raven's demise, the yellow shirts' pursuit of me, the gunshot.

Did she try putting her foot down? Have they locked *her* in the kitchenette?

And Carter? He was shaken last night—buyer's remorse about this horror show he punched our ticket for—but if it came to a bare-knuckle brawl between Susan and the Russians, whose side would he take?

Dawson continues, "Loose talk in the workplace can be as dangerous as loose talk on a battlefield. Rumors take us further from our shared goals. This is why I've told you all about Miss Bollinger—to remove speculation. The project becomes more difficult without her. With this in mind, we've reversed our prior decision to forgo injections..."

Susan's concessions—outside email, showers and clean undies—are out the window. All meals will be taken at workstations. Not only are forfeited stock options possible; now, any team member who fails to fulfill his module role risks demotion.

Susan *has* to be in the kitchenette.

"Counterbalancing these measures," Dawson says, "Elite facilitators will now be working alongside you. Their full-throated assistance will simulate Miss Bollinger's missing expertise."

Stunned, I lose my grip on Hedgehog Eleanor Roosevelt. The noise caroms about the ducts, and I miss several seconds of the Hot Wheel's audio.

When it comes back, the third floor is in revolt. Paul demands to see Susan. Prisha, with fervor I've never heard from her, wants to know who's responsible for defining "fails to fulfill."

Dawson gives neutral, dispassionate answers. "All this would be unnecessary were Miss Bollinger present. Despite her actions, we would accept her back if she returned. If any of you have information...information that might be used to, well, *persuade* Deb to rejoin the project...the reward would be handsome."

What crap is this? I'm trying to puzzle out what the creep has in mind when I hear new shuffling. I think it originates closer to the Hot Wheels' mic—big, honky noises obscure the feed, then fade.

Someone sneers. Someone else gasps.

A single pair of footsteps becomes audible.

Prisha calls, "Don't! You pig, what are you doing?"

Dawson waits out the commotion, then says, "You have useful information for us?"

The voice that answers is nasal and aggressively bored. Now I think I recognize those footsteps too—slow, draggy.

"I know what'll bring Deb in."

It's the irredeemable human phlegm-ball himself: Jared.

I ooch near Hedgehog Eleanor Roosevelt's speaker to hear, wondering what Jared could possibly claim to have on me. Will he threaten to reveal some inflammatory comment? I did once pledge to sneak cyanide into every vending-machine bag of T.G.I. Friday's Cheddar & Bacon Potato Skins—of which he's the sole purchaser—if he made one more suggestive groan about Susan's attire during a town hall.

The protests become louder, though, and now I can make out nothing but galled, generalized anger at Jared.

Dawson's voice cuts through. "Perhaps we'll discuss in private."

I can just see the look on Jared's face, glancing back at the other engineers with relish, acting like he's just scored mega career points when in fact he's entering the worst vipers' nest any of us have ever known.

## CHAPTER FORTY-ONE_

I DRIVE MY DROID-HOT WHEEL AROUND, HOPING SHE'LL stumble into range of Dawson and Jared's summit of the despicable. I catch snippets of other conversations, Minosh telling a database engineer "the query must go much, much faster!", Graham's silky voice asking Prisha to fill him in on my optimization logic. I steer past all this, banging walls, zooming blind, quite possibly sending her in circles.

I hear no Dawson. No phlegm-ball. They must've gone behind a closed door.

I can't waste any more time. I need to get out ahead of whatever Jared is telling Elite. Dire as my situation is, claustrophobic as these digs are, I do have an advantage: they don't know where I am or what I'm doing.

They also don't know that *I* know about the explosives, assuming Graham hasn't revealed our rushed tête-à-tête. I wish now I hadn't blurted out to him about the charges, but it was the right move at the time. He knows more—and it was worth the risk to see whether I could get it out of him.

The explosives are in the HVAC system, and I, myself, am in the HVAC system. It's a start. I crawl around Twelve, along one duct and back down its cross-floor partner, and find no charges.

Is it possible they just wired the one floor? Maybe they aren't bothering with vacant floors, or figure the top will cave once the bottom eleven crumble.

I crawl back to the vent Graham left loose, thinking to sneak down and check Eleven, but its bolts aren't loose. Then I remember the facilitator who poked his head up into the duct.

He must've screwed them beyond finger-tight.

I bang the vent three times with the flat of my fist before realizing I'm being an idiot.

*Why leave the ducts?*

The HVAC network extends all through the building. Why make a commotion getting down here and back up on Eleven when I can just use the intra-floor ducts?

I find the main trunk on the building's north side. I worm through a crinkly accordion section of duct to reach it, then lower myself in. The air from below billows my pant legs. The fit is so tight that I don't fear falling—my shins, hips, and fore-arms fix me in place against the stiff metal sides. I rattle my way lower until my toes find the next gap.

Feet first, I work myself into this gap and shimmy through another elbow segment. I turn myself around awkwardly—I feel metal compressing my hair spikes at the midpoint—and crawl forward over the eleventh floor.

I haven't gone five yards when a voice sounds below.

"Hey, did you hear that?"

I freeze.

A second voice says, "Hear what?"

"That noise," the first voice says. "In the ceiling. Here—listen for a sec."

I quiver from the effort of keeping still, one arm chicken-winged to the side, a strained smile fixed on my lips for no reason.

After a time, the second voice says, "Ghost. Must've been a ghost, or else rats."

The first speaker grumbles off the joke, and their footsteps fade.

Phew.

My mouth relaxes. I take it from their tone these weren't facilitators, but still: I must make less noise. Eleven isn't fully occupied, but it's not vacant like Twelve either. The problem isn't my knees and feet, which slide in steady contact with the duct and make only a low shuffle. It's my upper body, these pointy elbows and wrists that keep clonking against metal.

I raise my shirt and grip its tail in both hands, using it as an impact-deadening cloth underneath me. Now my stomach is exposed and my boobs're a bra clasp away from calling out "Bingo!" But I do travel more quietly.

I push Hedgehog Eleanor Roosevelt in front of me, her screen illuminating a few inches ahead. It takes five minutes to traverse the length of the floor. I scrunch through a U-joint to start back by the partner duct, and am just thinking Elite hasn't bothered with Eleven either when my nose tickles.

More almonds.

My pulse right back in my throat, I force myself to crawl ahead to another squat black cube. It blinks red like the first and has a similar tangle of wires leading out to a transmitter.

The placement seems hurried, not tucked against the duct's side or otherwise secured. Two coils of the wire are still bound in twist-tie, as though fresh from the original packaging.

They just popped the vent, slid this bad boy in, and moved along. They did it in the middle of the night. They wanted to get them all planted before anyone woke up.

These charges can't explode on their own. There must be a

trigger, some activator whose command cascades through the transmitters and kicks off the dominoes of doom.

But where?

My guess: someplace accessible to a certain corporate-training fraud who buys his stress balls by the gross. And separating said fraud from his trigger isn't going to be easy.

What if I disabled the transmitters? Could I neuter their antennas, climb through the building snipping all their connections—such that Dawson waltzes off at the end of Blackquest 40 with false confidence that the second he and his gang hit the Bay Bridge, he can annihilate us with a button tap?

It's an appealing plan. Except I'm no bomb tech. For all I know, these charges could be rigged to explode on losing link to their transmitter. The whole circuit could be rigged—one snip might blow up not only me, but Susan and Prisha and everybody in the joint.

Hm.

I move Hedgehog Eleanor Roosevelt's screen around, examining the cube and transmitter. The components seem solid. At both terminal points, the wires enter the devices' casing cleanly —no twisted-together copper, nothing a bump might dislodge.

I could gather them up. I could move down the ducts and collect them—at some point, I'd need a trash bag or some such container, but that's details.

What would I do with all these explosives? If I could get them underground to the parking garage, does that help? Couldn't a big blast there bring down the building just as easily?

How about high instead of low? If I stashed the lot in a corner of Twelve, the blast might necessitate a new roof—but people below could escape.

Maybe I should just quarantine them for now, stow them someplace like a ground-floor bathroom, then the instant Elite leaves, sprint them outside and hurl them far, far away.

How far—to the sewer? Into the bay? Would I have time?

It's a lot of questions.

I decide that one way or another, gathering charges is worthwhile. It opens up options.

I backtrack to the main HVAC trunk and lower myself to the ducts at Ten. This floor is packed with E-wing and other business personnel, so again, I must be quiet. Carrying around the one explosive doesn't help. It's only a few pounds, but the two units are unwieldy—especially holding my shirt tail in both fists.

That trash bag would be fantastic about now, but no way I'm going to risk dropping through a vent here. Maybe I'll hunt around for something when I get to Eight.

I push on. It's hot and sour and dry, and I feel like a turtle pushing its own shell through some smaller animal's tunnel.

Every time I slink low enough to graze the duct's bottom, my sweat absorbs more dust—they've mixed to a raunchy film on my bare midriff and upper hips. I wipe some away with my shirt and fall forward, landing on my sore ribs.

I hear fragmentary conversations below. I think about stopping over Susan's or Carter's office to listen, but don't have my bearings here and can't judge where their offices are.

They're probably detained anyway.

Now that I'm lugging my own almonds, my nostrils are no help finding the next charge—I smell it constantly. I nearly trample the next black box, smothering it with my shirt.

It doesn't blow.

Once my heart restarts, I follow the box's wire to its hinged-antenna transmitter. I am just considering how I'll carry another when I spot a second wire coming from the transmitter.

I shift Hedgehog Eleanor Roosevelt for light. This second wire is black and runs to a domed device at the side of the duct. I bump across on my forearms to examine.

The dome itself is wired down into the tenth floor through a dime-sized hole. When I pass my index finger along the nearby duct, it comes up with metal shavings.

Freshly drilled.

What's underneath me? It must be the trigger location—some utility closet or vacant workspace Elite commandeered.

What if it's not? What if I peek down and find Carter's office?

Or Susan's?

I don't know how or why this could be, but I fear it instinctively—that Elite might be co-opting her the way they've co-opted Graham. That somehow or other this will end with *Psycho* shower-scene music playing and my cherished mentor holding the knife.

Well, if it's going to happen, it might as well happen now.

I sidle up to the hole and try peeking down, but it's a no-go. The wire barely fits its hole, leaving nothing visible around its sides.

I crawl ahead for a vent, hoping to dip down possum-like for a peek at an office nameplate or other identifying feature. The nearest one is ten yards away, though. I'd have to descend completely from the duct and walk back an approximate distance through the hall.

No doubt I'd be seen.

I crawl back to the hole. I try again to orient myself, to gauge whose office I'm above from memory. My mind floats off the elevators and tries cataloging who sits where...but I get hung up on what color carpet I'm looking at. Sea foam? Ecru?

I can't. The synapses just will not hold.

Could I enlarge the hole? With what? There will be a corresponding hole in the ceiling panel too. Anything sharp risks piercing the wire and causing premature detonation.

I could make my own hole—safely offset by a few inches—if

I had a drill. Some battle bots have them, but not Hedgehog Eleanor Roosevelt. She's a peacenik.

One thing she does have, though, is GPS. And a whole-office GPS map lives on the network.

Tired as I am of tapping out scripts on her sticky, rounded keyboard, I have to. There's a programmatic solution—and right now programming may be all my damaged brain can manage.

I clack away. The script will get Hedgehog Eleanor Roosevelt's current geo-location, then cycle through every office on Ten, calculating her distance to its center coordinates. At the end, she'll output the employee whose office is nearest.

It should work.

I press RETURN on the last command, then, with an involuntary yawn, execute the script.

The result are back before my mouth has closed.

*O. MOHAMMED.*

I puzzle a moment at the letters before the face comes to me. Oh right, Omar. He's an account manager. I know him a little from Boeing. Carter had him do the terms and conditions of their Phase II contract. Dogged, detail-oriented. Outgoing. Sales type all the way.

Before I can form a hypothesis about why Omar appears to be at the center of Elite's *boom-boom* cover-up plan, the public address system clears its throat.

"*Hello, Miss Bollinger,*" I hear—everyone hears. "*This is Jim Dawson speaking. Wherever you are, please make your way to a computer monitor and navigate to the Intra-1 video channel. We have something important to show you.*"

## CHAPTER FORTY-TWO_

I KNOW IT'S GOING TO BE BAD.

There is simply no questioning the potency of an evil concoction featuring Dawson as the main ingredient and Jared as a spice. I badly want to ignore the message, to pretend Elite has no power over me and can't compel me to do one bleeping thing no matter what they broadcast...

But it isn't so. Dawson is trained in brutalizing people—brutalizing people in the service of his goals. I can't ignore this.

With cold dread, I prop Hedgehog Eleanor Roosevelt against the wall of the duct. Her display won't give me dreamboat video, but I'm not about to risk exposing myself in search of an empty conference room.

I find Intra-1 in the company directory and, hating to, tap its icon.

The feed takes several seconds to appear on screen, initializing, buffering. Finally an image, all green shades by Hedgehog Eleanor Roosevelt's monochrome. The background is faint, possibly taupe in real life, with eerily familiar horizontal stripes.

I've seen those strips. Wallpaper?

In the foreground, a woolly-bearded man sits at a breakfast

table. A sliver of his forearm is visible like he's holding the camera, most likely a phone. He wears a sweatshirt, but the tell-tale yellow collar shows at the neck.

Two people in hairnets pass behind. One pulls a tray of towels. The other carries food platters.

My stomach rears back against my spine.

When the man shifts, I see that his other arm—the one not holding the phone—is draped around a wicker chair. Sitting in the chair, looking groggy and confused, is Mom.

Dawson's voice returns, "We took the liberty of sending a facilitator ahead to notify your mother of Blackquest 40. It came to our attention that you often dine with her. We wanted to offset any alarm she might be feeling at having missed you last night. To assure her you were safe."

He draws out this last word like a bow across violin string.

I can tell, even though Mom is only a quarter-inch high on Hedgehog Eleanor Roosevelt's screen, that she's frazzled. Her eyes hunt about with the panic of broken routine. Her iris-print nightgown is rumpled, and her whorled, gray-blond locks—like my own spiked hair on speed—would make Albert Einstein look preppy.

The Elite facilitator is balancing a bite of scrambled egg on a fork, glancing at the camera as though for approval.

I want to reach through Hedgehog Eleanor Roosevelt's screen and yank his fork away and ram those tines larynx-deep into that over-muscled neck of his.

Mom bristles from the bite. "Where's the avocado? Who're you? I can use silverware, *where's my avocado?*"

The facilitator tries advancing the bite toward Mom's face, but she closes her lips tight. He moves a glass of orange juice onto her place mat. She eyes it suspiciously, then dumps it.

The facilitator dabs juice from his sleeve. After a tense look to the camera, he pulls Mom's chair closer.

Now the feed switches to Dawson, standing at the command center on Three.

"Apparently the orderlies were quite trusting of Benjamin," he says, "and did not challenge the documents proving he is your mother's nephew. When he offered to assist with her morning routine, they were grateful for the help."

This strikes me as depressingly plausible. Despite being the top facility of its kind in the Bay Area, Crestwood Psychiatric is criminally understaffed. Most nights I visit Mom, I end up filing nails or freshening the wheelchair blankets of some resident with no people of their own around.

Dawson says, "Your colleagues here on the third floor are facing their greatest challenge yet. They need you to make the right choice. Your mother needs you to make the right choice."

The feed returns to Crestwood, where the facilitator is holding both Mom's wrists against the table with a single hand. Glee flashes across the man's face before an orderly arrives to check the escalating situation—Mom is screaming incoherently.

The facilitator gestures to the spilled juice with a shrug. The orderly nods understandingly and hands him a dish rag.

I pound the side of the duct.

*Jared.*

How does he know about Crestwood? Maybe he tailed me from the office in the early days, sizing me up as a harassment target? I'm too angry to imagine.

The PA clicks. "Perhaps you are far from a monitor, and need extra time to reach one." Dawson doesn't know about Hedgehog Eleanor Roosevelt. *Good.* "We will replay the footage on Intra-1 for five minutes. After this, should you choose not to join your team, there will be consequences."

The feed reverts to Mom, the facilitator, and scrambled eggs.

What consequences does Dawson have in mind? Killing

mom—smothering her with a pillow or something—gets him nowhere. He will understand this. He'll find some intermediate cruelty to use for leverage. Maybe the facilitator takes Mom back to her room and slices off a finger, waggles it at his phone camera for Dawson to use against me.

This actually happened when I was twelve—Mom lost the top knuckle of her right ring finger. The woman who did it had been Mom's friend. I knew her as Sweets because her cart was always spilling loose Skittles. The two had been arguing about who had dibs on trash from a dim sum joint on Haight. It wasn't food they were after—there were tastier, more generous restaurants nearby—but discarded woks. Mom used them for street art, painting the rusted streaks bright reds and blues that always reminded me of betta fish. I never heard what Sweets wanted them for.

One day, three woks got tossed all at once. If it had been two or four, maybe they would've split the bounty and carried on, but that day it was three. Mom screamed and clawed and said Sweets had been scheming. Sweets kept her body between Mom and the woks—she'd shown up first and nabbed them—and, after Mom boiled over and kicked her shin, snapped open a pocketknife.

This only made Mom more convinced of premeditation. She lunged for the blade, and as I watched, shaking, holding myself up by a downspout, Sweets slashed an inch of flesh clean off.

Blood spouted from the finger, spraying both women. Their cries became frantic, and they seemed on the verge of doing worse to each other when I came back to myself and stepped between them. Sweets—whose son had been a good friend before he overdosed—dropped the knife at once.

I saved the fingertip in a plastic bag of ice. Cecil and I got Mom to the emergency room quickly, but the doctor there said reattaching "carried a prohibitively high expectation of failure." Meaning Mom didn't deserve it.

This incident didn't start Mom's descent, but it surely accelerated it. We avoided any spot Sweets might show up—which in Mom's mind encompassed half of San Francisco—and she never painted another wok.

What if a similar thing happens now? Crestwood is already pushing to increase her dosages, to "curb the increasingly antisocial impulses of her disease." I've resisted, but if a fresh trauma makes Mom even less manageable, what standing will I have?

On the spectrum of treatment versus living, Crestwood Psychiatric falls right about at the dividing line. That's why I chose it. Mom can swim. She can enjoy their garden courtyard unsupervised. If you can't color inside the lines there, you're looking at shackles and rubber walls. Around-the-clock sedation. Basically, loss of personhood.

## CHAPTER FORTY-THREE_

THE VENT IS STUCK. ITS BOLT HEADS AREN'T ACCESSIBLE from where I am—inside the duct. With a wrench, I could loosen their nuts until they drop out, but I don't have a wrench. I try my fingers, gripping the nuts by the scant light of Hedgehog Eleanor Roosevelt's screen, but my nails keep slipping.

At last, I manage to pry one loose and spin it off. Its bolt falls to the carpet with a satisfying *thunk*.

But the other three aren't budging. I bang them with the heel of my sandal, which only succeeds in making lots of noise.

I lean into the vent and am able to bend it away from the ceiling, a few inches down into the hall. First I push with just my knee. Then, convincing myself the vent's narrow opening will stop me from plummeting eight feet to a broken neck, I apply my full weight.

The remaining bolts creak and whine, threads grating against their nuts. I bounce a couple times. The vent keeps budging, lower with each try, until one bolt shears. Its nut and half its shank *plink* around the ducts.

Now the vent folds into the hall like a flap. I squeeze

through, elbows crammed into ribs, and drop to the carpet. My pupils constrict meeting all this light, and the office air is gaseous glory after so long in the ducts.

A small crowd has gathered.

"It's her," one says.

They're looking at me like I'm an Incan mummy who just woke up, which makes sense given the filth that coats my body.

I cough. "Yeah. It's me."

A woman in a sweater vest steps back. The man beside her mutters, *Hardcore*.

I leave them for the elevators. I see no facilitators on this floor, but then I'm not really looking.

I'm dizzy with resignation. I'm walking right into Jim Dawson and Elite's arms, and I don't care.

I am ready to deal: me for Mom. Dawson wins. Again. I know about the charges and about Omar Mohammed—and maybe this knowledge will pay dividends down the road—but for now, the power is all his.

Back on Three, I head past cube farms, drawing every eye. My coworkers have been told I shot a facilitator with his own gun, and their manner shows it. Keyboards go silent. Breaths cut short. Dimly, in a red corner of my peripheral vision that I don't have time now to address, I see Jared cowering under his trucker hat.

Jim Dawson waits in front of his doomsday timer. When I'm in hearing range, he says a single word: "Good."

"Not even remotely," I answer. The monitor behind him is still on loop, Mom and the facilitator bickering over the egg bite. "Call off the orc. Get him away from Mom."

"A discussion would need to precede that."

"Fine. Discuss away." I flop a hand aside—some bone or tendon cracks in my wrist. "Didn't someone say we were on a tight schedule?"

In the next row of cubicles, Graham is sitting by Prisha. He meets my eye and gives a slight shake of the head.

I can't tell if he wants me to ignore him, or not poke Dawson right now, or what.

Dawson says, "When a team is moving in opposition to itself, haste is counterproductive. We will make sure this time—make sure you're truly ready to participate."

What does he want, a pinkie-swear?

"Tell me where Susan is," I say. "Susan would never sign off on that stunt, sending some brute to a psychiatric care facility."

"Miss Wright is working with the module on Ten," Dawson says. "The business team has fallen behind in its checkpoints too."

"That phony spaceflight thing?"

He ignores my characterization. "As the senior executive, Miss Wright is best equipped to shape the messaging. We asked her to assist personally."

I'll bet they did—to get her out of the picture. What's surprising is that she fell for such an obvious trick.

*Did* she fall for it? Or is this pure fiction on Dawson's part?

My money's on fiction.

Dawson turns to the monitor and taps a remote. The looped scene of Mom and the facilitator cuts out, replaced by the live shot. They are in Mom's room—I recognize the signed picture with Ted Kennedy and dreamcatcher I gave her two Christmases ago. The facilitator is advancing inside while Mom shuffles back into a corner, face torn with distrust.

"Look, I'll participate," I say. "What do we have, twenty more hours? I'm cool for twenty hours. Lemme talk to my mother."

The rest of the engineers watch with palpable sympathy. Everybody has a mom.

Dawson considers me for some time, then places a call. The

phone of the facilitator on-screen rings. He answers. Dawson tells him to put Mom on the line.

I reach for Dawson's phone, but he pins it to his chest. "Not one more betrayal. This is a mercy we're showing you. A final chance to submit."

*Submit* makes me want to drive a knee through his pelvis, but I resist the urge. "Yep, got it, I'm on board. Now can I talk?"

Appearing less than convinced, he gives over the phone.

"Mom!" I say, hunching away from Dawson, away from everyone. "Sorry I missed you at dinner last night. Vegan chili, right? Aw, just my luck. See I—er, there's been a lot going on here at work."

"Deborah?" Her voice comes through clear but thin. "Deborah—he said they were 'training' you. Why? What're you being trained to do? Is what I wanna know."

I chuckle. "Yeah, I'd like to know too."

This was just a knee-jerk response, and I regret it immediately.

"*You* train *them*," Mom starts in. "Remember that. Training and assimilation are one and the same. I'm proud of you. *You* train *them*."

"Yeah, no—that's right, Mom. You're right."

"College should be a place for self-exploration—a *chapel* of self-exploration. You don't go to college to learn passively. You learn actively."

On the monitor, Mom is making the karate-chop gesture that accompanies this diatribe. I know it well. Expected duration is between fifteen and twenty minutes.

I'm just thinking how to redirect her onto a different topic when Dawson smirks.

My head boils. The idea that this piece of humanoid garbage is finding humor at the expense of my mother—of my mother's illness—is infuriating.

I cover the phone mic. "I am *not* doing this in front of you."

Without asking, I switch off the feed using Dawson's remote and take his phone to the nearest conference room.

A yellow shirt makes a move for me, but Dawson throws out a hand to stop him. He's trying to look casual, demonstrate that he's in control and won't go scrambling every time I throw a tantrum.

It's cockiness I must exploit.

Making a split-second decision, I take a deep step into the room, then two more quickies to the side—out of view of the doorway.

"*Mom, call the cops!*" I say. "Or have Hector call then, or Jeanette—anybody. These guys are bad news. They're holding my whole office hostage."

"Office?" Her voice is brittle. "I thought it was the college training you. Why would they do it in an *office?* Now they're partnering with big business? What's in it for the businesses, is what I'd be asking..."

"Can you just call? The cops? Just say who I am, say where I work, they'll figure out the rest."

Mom makes an indeterminate noise. I wish I could see her on the monitor to gauge her reaction. I feel the conflicting desires to scream into the phone, *JUST DIAL THE DUMB DIGITS, 911!* and run down to Crestwood Psychiatric and hug her dearly.

"Listen, Mother," I say. "These guys—the ones doing this to you? They're coming back soon, and I'll have to pretend we were talking about something else. It'll be confusing. I'm sorry. But just dial 911 after we hang up, okay?"

I hate adding to her distress, but I can't lose this opportunity. Most of those charges are still up in the ducts, armed. If I'd known about them earlier, I would have had Cecil contact the police—legal jeopardy or not.

But Cecil is long gone by now. Mom's my only chance.

I flinch at a noise. Slowly I look from my not-very-hidden corner of the conference room to the door.

Dawson stands at the threshold.

"Uh-huh, yeah, dinner tonight's also a no-go," I say into the phone, feigning indifference to his presence. "But I should get there for breakfast tomorrow. I'll work my magic with Hector, get you your double avocado."

Mom stammers, "Is this—I—the confusing part?"

"Yes, Mom." Tears begin to roll down my cheeks. "You're absolutely right. I'll see you soon."

"Tomorrow?"

"Hopefully. I'll do my best."

She says she knows I will. We end the call.

I straighten up and affect a yawn, handing Dawson back his phone.

"Well, she's not okay," I tell him, "but I guess it'll have to do. Back to the grind, then?"

I start past him, but Dawson plants himself in my way.

I try again.

He stays planted.

With admonishing lethargy, he moves the phone to his ear and taps a button. I'm close enough to hear the call initiate.

The facilitator answers on the first ring.

"Yes, me," Dawson says. "No, their conversation is over. You'll need to speak to the head orderly and explain that your aunt has been ranting wildly for the police. You made the mistake of mentioning her daughter's corporate employers, whom she believes to be war criminals."

I listen with a dying heart.

Dawson finishes his instructions and hangs up.

"You thought we would hand you a cellphone," he says, "an open line to the outside world—and not listen in?"

Stated like that, it does seem idiotic. I say nothing.

Dawson grins at my speechlessness, and I have the hollow hope that maybe this'll be enough—this rhetorical triumph will satisfy his ravenous control needs. After what Elite has inflicted upon me, they can't expect meek surrender from me, right?

But Dawson's grin lasts too long—and now an intensity comes into it. His scar twitches. He's not moving from the doorway.

"I should check in with Prisha," I try, "see how our module's coming."

When I make a third move to leave, he bumps me backward. The grin has vanished. "We are done being made fools."

At the finality in his tone, fear jolts me like water through a dead hose.

Dawson removes a gun from an ankle holster and black cylinder from his pants pocket. He begins screwing the cylinder onto the gun.

A silencer.

## CHAPTER FORTY-FOUR_

THE SOUND OF THE TWO DEVICES MATING, GUN AND silencer, is like the rattle of a steel snake. With each round of thread, my breath catches. I look left, right, behind me. There are no escapes.

"Are you *deranged*? You need me! You can't finish the project without me, I'm the one who—"

"That's been the assumption, yes." Dawson finishes attaching the silencer and squints down the barrel. "Perhaps it's a bad assumption. Perhaps the rest of the team can manage. You've proved so difficult that I'm forced to find another way."

"Execution—that's your other way?"

Dawson backs a boot into the hall, looks up and looks down. "The man who fell into the water statue was my cousin. The man you shot was my squadmate in Chechnya. We passed through the Gate of Wolves together."

He's glaring at me. I glare right back. "I didn't have much choice—they were both trying to kill me. But my sincerest apologies for tarnishing the memory of those glorious, minority-suppressing days of yore."

With the hand not holding the gun, Dawson twists the

conference room blinds closed. The stress ball, lodged in a pocket, bulges his khakis' fabric.

He tugs the knob of the door, starting it swinging shut, then trains the elongated barrel on me.

Fingers appear on the jamb before he can fire. The door rams them, and I hear a soft *"Owww"* before the door drifts back open.

Standing there is Paul Gribbe.

"If you kill her, you kill Blackquest 40. There's no way we get the software built without Deb."

Dawson doesn't lower his gun. "Miss Bollinger and I just finished this conversation. We'll sacrifice capability but gain focus. Codewise is the leading optimization company in the world—you have other assets. We'll squeeze more from them."

Paul grips one side of his hair donut, which has gone flat and wiry. "We *were* the world's leading optimization company. Now we're a husk."

Dawson's eyes budge off me.

Paul continues, "We've been losing engineers for two years. We've become a marketing and PR shop—that's where the head-count is. Even Deb. After they hired her, Carter and Susan did their big roadshow to tell everyone how hiring a genius like Deb recommitted us to the bleeding edge. It was pure optics. Susan created this public narrative, then Carter hustled it."

Dawson glances past Paul to the cubicles. With his attention diverted, I consider making a break. How far could I get? To the elevators? Maybe not even. I doubt Dawson would shoot me out in front of everyone—surely the "other assets" would freak and be useless to him.

Paul nods through the door. "See Jared just ambling around? He does that. He should be a mid-level coder. Instead we have him leading modules."

Dawson digs out his stress ball and begins punishing it. I

can't see from here, but Jared must be doing one of his trademark "slug strolls" (my term), where he wanders past his team's workstations, too gutless to challenge them point-blank about what they're doing, procrastinating from his own work by nosing into others'.

"Carter sold you a bill of goods," Paul says. "The complexity you need, the ingenuity—it far exceeds what's achievable without Deb. You might as well cut your losses."

Dawson's face darkens. "Perhaps we will. Perhaps we'll abort and reclaim your fee."

I remember what Susan told me a few hours ago. *We don't have millions of dollars sitting in the bank to pay Elite back.* The Russians must know this. Maybe it's why they targeted us—we were already desperate, our backs against a wall.

If they don't get their power plant or their cash refund, what will they do? They've waded awfully deep in the muck, with bodies and dumpsters and wrecked vans to explain. They've showed themselves to the 300-odd employees of Codewise Solutions, potential witnesses all.

This is not a thing easily stuffed back in a bottle and stoppered.

"Your only chance is Deb," Paul says. "Deb is...well, you've had twenty-four hours with her. You know. Deb is Deb. Maybe she can do it. Maybe she can't. I wouldn't bet against her."

In most circumstances, I hate being talked about in the third person. My graduate adviser used to do this, telling his department head about Hedgehog Eleanor Roosevelt and my natural language research with me standing literally feet away.

*Amazing, this one...her logical leaps stop you in your tracks...she may need a greater challenge, I'm kicking around ideas...*

Like I was some techno-engineering courtesan on campus for their amusement.

Now, though, I'll let it slide. Too many lives hang in the balance to be sweating gender politics.

Dawson's grip on the gun remains firm. "I've lost three men trying to secure her participation. What assurance can you give that this time will be different?"

Paul's eyes plead with me. *Just play along.*

"I'm her manager," he says. "Between the two of us, we'll come to an arrangement—Deb and I. We will. We have a rapport."

Dawson studies us. Paul's face is blotchy from confrontation. My bowels have been clenched for two solid minutes.

Before Dawson reaches a decision, Katie Masterson bursts in.

"Jim!" Her face blares at the firearm. "This doesn't help—you *know* that. Out! Go cool off."

He gives me one last scowl before allowing himself to be pushed from the room.

Paul mops his forehead. My core relaxes as we lose sight of Dawson, but my brain still rings from threats and anguish and near-death. I feel like that sadistic kid's kite strings got wrapped round and round my head and pulled hard from both sides.

I could cry for a month. If I escape this thing alive, I probably will.

Katie returns from ousting her brother, flashing an appeasing grin.

I talk first. "Don't bother—whatever you're about to say. I appreciate you stopping your psychotic KGB-operative brother, but you're complicit."

"No, Deb, please," Katie tries, "we're under extr—"

"Extreme pressure, is that it? You're under extreme pressure? Let's hear more about Columbus, Ohio. What a small organization you are. About doing your parents' taxes."

"That was true," Katie insists. When my face storm over,

she adds, "Not Columbus, but the rest. My brother is under tremendous pressure. Our organization is small."

"The KGB is small nowadays?"

"My brother doesn't work for the KGB."

"Did they change the acronym? Isn't it GPU now, something like that?"

Katie's mouth compresses to a pea. "You are so sure of yourself. We're all Russian dogs, right? We're filth."

My mouth opens and closes. It feels gummy at the charge of bigotry.

She says, "You know nothing about us. The Russian government is broke—it can't keep a vast roster of operatives on its payroll. It leverages private companies with ties to the West.

"My brother and I built Elite Development from nothing. We grew up in the Russian countryside—Kasimov, on the Volga River. My brother served in the army, then came to the U.S. and began training military contractors. I had the idea to use these same methods with corporations. We worked hard—our nationality was a great problem for many clients—and grew into a thriving company...until six months ago."

Katie's shoulders sag. "We were contacted by the GRU." She corrects my acronym stiffly. "The Kremlin had an opportunity—one uniquely suited to us. The payoff was large. My brother would be allowed to select his team. These aren't opportunities you can refuse."

She looks at me with none of that dynamism from the first hours of Blackquest 40. In its place is melancholy—but grit too.

"No," I say, swallowing. "I don't suppose they are."

## CHAPTER FORTY-FIVE_

Jᴉᴍ Dᴀᴡsᴏɴ ᴅᴏᴇs ᴄᴏᴏʟ ᴏғғ, ᴇxᴘʟᴀɪɴɪɴɢ ᴛᴏ ᴛʜᴇ Codewise team at large that his prior information was incorrect. It appears I didn't shoot the facilitator. I've been reinstated, pending an internal investigation of the accident on Twelve.

So here I am: back at the keyboard.

It's soul-sucking, and I can hardly fathom it, and innumerable bruises and lacerations make every fine movement of my fingers agony. My hemp satchel sits in my lap, a familiar elbow rest. I rustle my elbows soothingly into it—a small thing, but I'll take small things right now.

"You've been humping on this twenty-six hours," I say to Jared and Prisha, who've gathered in my cubicle along with Paul, "and your code has passed end-to-end Blackquest 40 testing how many times?"

The leaders of the two primary modules count in their heads. Prisha's hair sports an off-center peak, but otherwise she's come through okay. The same can't be said for Jared, who smells like brown cabbage and seems to have sprouted a new fringe of neck hair.

"Five," Prisha decides.

Jared whirls on her. "What? We've passed at least two hundred botlets through the sandbox."

"And the vast majority failed," Prisha says. "The simulator rejects 95 percent of your botlets' output."

Her glare has more venom than any I've seen from her in three months at Codewise. Either she's gained confidence or today's circumstances have melted her veneer of decorum.

Paul, who settles squabbles better than me, says, "Back up. Why don't you tell us what you *have* accomplished so far? Let's focus on that instead of the converse."

This restores civility. Prisha and Jared—whose betrayal I haven't forgotten, only tabled—stop attacking one another to describe their progress.

The optimization team has analyzed the matrix of seven variables and calculated a range of possible values for each. They can manipulate the matrix, store past values, track changes over time.

The injection team, Jared's, has crafted objects—"botlets"— that meet the handshake interface agreed to at the start of the project, allowing Prisha's team to receive and use them. The botlets can inject themselves into the host system, evade malware countermeasures, and intermittently slip through the randomly algorithmic security.

"That's a lot," I say, and mean it. "Now let's talk about that five number. That's five times we've tricked the simulator— beaten the sandbox, taken those seven variables and returned output that's lower, but within the simulator's accepted bounds. Correct?"

They nod.

"Great. And what's the specific requirement? We need to trick the system for how long?"

Chins fall to chests. Both engineers shuffle furtively.

Paul says, "Perpetuity. For as long as the—er, the simulation runs."

Our eyes meet, and I know we're both mentally replacing "simulation" with "nuclear power plant." The software needs to swap in allowably lower energy values (who knows what units we're dealing in—Joules, kilowatt-hours) for as long as it remains in place.

What happens if Elite installs our software and it passes a bad value to the plant's core? Does it revert to the old algorithm? Or could a terrible thing happen?

I'm suddenly sympathetic to their insistence on "one hundred percent-repeatable success."

We work through lunch, hot and heavy, trying to satisfy the simulator by different means. It's a fickle beast. Strategies work one time and fail the next. The process is maddeningly slow because Jared's botlets only slip through their sandbox once every few minutes.

"We need more from you," I tell him.

He whirls and seems about to argue, then stops—no doubt still fearing my wrath over Crestwood. "I—my code beats the sandbox. If you want to blame somebody, you should—"

"I don't," I cut in.

After a bit of thought, I ask whether his botlets have *clone.* *Clone* is a function many software objects support; it allows other parts of the system to make copies of itself.

"*Clone* wasn't in the original interface," Jared says.

"Didn't ask if it was."

He raises a shoulder, sulky. "No. It's trivial, though."

"You could?"

"Course."

I smack my mousepad and snap my fingers, reminding myself unwittingly of Carter Kotanchek. "Do it."

I give Jared a minute to write the botlets' *clone* function, then modify Prisha's optimization module. Instead of simply receiving each botlet and sticking in logic from one of our strategies, I clone each botlet a hundred times—scratch that, five thousand times—and give each clone its own strategy.

In the monitor's reflection, I catch Prisha's pupils spinning.

"The botlet brigade," she marvels.

When Jared's next botlet comes through the sandbox, another ninety seconds on, my screen erupts. Green and red text barges down the screen; jagged, urgent lines of it; debugging output from our now-wonderfully numerous botlets. None of us can read text falling this fast, but there's new electricity around us.

Stuff is happening—and quickly.

When the tempest stops, a final summary-stat line reads:

*Run time: 4.3 seconds. Botlets deployed: 30000. End-to-end successes: 73. Max consecutive successes: 3.*

"Yahtzee!" Paul roars, throwing up his arms.

Prisha and I exchange raised eyebrows at our manager's exultation while Jared turns his trucker hat around, all tough and *go time*.

In four-point-three seconds, our cloned botlets produced seventy-three successes: ten times the number achieved in the whole first half of Blackquest 40.

People are hooting about seventy-three, but the number that interests me—that worries me—is three.

Before I can disabuse everyone of their enthusiasm, I detect a familiar smell. Floral but woody, commanding. A moment after my nose processes it, my eyes find Susan.

"What're we celebrating?" she asks, swinging around my cubicle border.

Paul says, "Deb is absolutely on fire."

Susan looks at me with glittering admiration. She's changed into a suit one shade darker than persimmon. Her posture is assured, hair immaculate. She might've come from a day spa.

"So the software piece is on track? We're feeling good about this deadline?"

My mouse hand audibly flops over. *Did she just say 'feeling good?'*

Again, I wonder if her composure is an act. I know Dawson is about, cruising the halls; maybe she saw him out of the corner of her eye. Maybe she's cultivating the illusion that Blackquest is just another project, no biggie, we're swell, see? Here we are having regular-project interactions, par for the course, so you can leave us be.

Still. Susan did see the video of Mom at Crestwood, having eggs forked menacingly toward her face, right? Elite beamed it to every screen in the building.

I say, "It's still a longshot."

The three engineers' faces sour. I am not usually a downer, but somehow Susan's false cheer pries this sober—and undeniably true—estimation out of me.

Susan wrings her hands. "We knew this training would be challenging. We knew it would force growth on our organization, on our people. That was the idea."

And with an as-you-were tock of the head, she leaves.

*That was the idea?*

Paul and I wear nearly identical expressions of disbelief. I think about that comment he made about Susan's hiring of me being pure optics. Did he just say that to get me out of hot water? Or does he believe it?

It sure had the ring of truth.

If my coming aboard really was part of a larger public relations scheme, then I swallowed the hook—every inch as deeply as Dawson or cable news or the gullible Codewise shareholders. I believed I was joining the cream of the crop. I believed we were trending up—and when layoffs happened, I accepted the party-line explanation that it didn't matter, was only typical Wall Street-driven restructuring.

But everything Paul said squares. Why *is* Jared leading a module? How come Prisha, who's been in the workforce two measly years, is my best replacement option?

Did I really ditch Google for this?

## CHAPTER FORTY-SIX_

Paul asks, "Why a longshot, Deb? What do you see?"

I allow Susan's last vapors to clear, to fade away into our stale stress, then hold up the number on my fingers.

"Three."

Only Paul nods his understanding.

I explain to the others. We had seventy-three botlets make it through end-to-end testing, but the very best one only passed acceptable output to the simulator three times. It crapped out on try number four.

To fulfill the Blackquest requirements—and perhaps to avert nuclear meltdown—we need a botlet that succeeds in perpetuity. Not three times or three thousand times, or three million times.

Infinity times.

After bumming the team out with this reality, I try picking them up. "Remember, it's only software. Anything is possible."

This is a saying in our industry. It refers to the fact that software's raw materials all originate in the programmer's head—you don't need steel or plastic, or approval from some zoning board. You just need to imagine it, and have the skill to represent that imagination in language computers can interpret.

The aphorism produces no spark in my team so I dive into the debugging output myself, starting our quest to infinity.

I comb through readouts for that superstar botlet who fooled the simulator three times in a row. Turns out there were two superstars. I click into the first and am about to have Prisha dig into the second when a heavy *ploof* sounds from a previously-unoccupied chair.

Paul is folding open his laptop.

"Oh," I say. "Were you thinking *you'd* take a crack at it?"

I didn't mean to sound dubious. I know Paul used to rock code, but I've just never seen it myself. He's only been a manager during my tenure.

"Desperate times call for desperate measures," he says, but newly-light wrists give it away: he is stoked.

Working in tandem, Paul and I dissect the superstar botlets and trace back which optimization strategies each used. Mine weighted the third variable higher by half. Paul's did exponential smoothing.

Jared picks the bill of his hat. "Weird. What's the connection?"

Paul shakes his head. Those wrists are looking less light.

I answer for us, "There isn't one. They used totally different approaches."

It's troubling that two divergent botlets rose to the top. It suggests luck rather than some ingenious strategy we could identify and improve until it worked in every case.

Suddenly, we're all tired. God knows we should be, nearing thirty hours into this death march. Jared smears his palm into his cheek, showing his gums like a slobbery dog. Prisha, analyzing the next tier of botlets, dozes off and slumps into me.

They're slaving away on a project they have zero connection to. A project that relegated Paul to kitchenette jail, and keeps trying to kill me.

"This is rotten, coming and going," I say. "I wish we could turn back the clock to yesterday morning and all oversleep, but we can't. So no moping. The only way to give ourselves options is to beat the ogre."

They look at me with desire—I don't pep-talk often and they want to come along—but also desperation. Someone releases a huff that's like a sigh stripped of all attitude and judgment.

They think it's impossible.

I press both palms to the sides of my head and squeeze, squeeze, *squeeze*, until an idea pops out.

I start in a rush, "Prisha, what happens when the simulator rejects a botlet's output?"

She recoils from my vigor. "It—well, it throws an error. The botlet is terminated."

"Did you try catching the error?"

When software fails, it does what's called "throwing an error," which other parts of the code can "catch" and recover from if they have sufficient logic.

Prisha explains she already pored over the error messages. They simply say "Not in allowable range"—they don't even specify whether the output was too high or too low. *How would they recover from that?*

"For now, I don't care," I say. "I just wanna know if catching is possible, if we're allowed do-overs."

Paul, following our exchange, has already added a CATCH command. He runs the simulation again.

His machine spins for a while, that sort of lurching inactivity that makes you worry you broke something. A dejected look is just starting around the group when output comes back.

*Run time: 21.7 seconds. Botlets deployed: 6000. End-to-end successes: 73. Max consecutive successes: 3.*

Run time went through the roof! With stubborn hope, I open the logfile—which confirms our best botlets hit the simulator just over eight hundred times.

Every botlet did. Eight hundred tries apiece.

"Do-overs," I say, smiling.

"Super," Jared says with the enthusiasm of a rice cake. "Now instead of six thousand errors, we're making six-hundred thousand."

I want to say a snarky thing about his multiplication skills, but refrain.

"Do-overs give us space to tinker," I say. "Now our botlets just need to get smarter."

Paul and I split up the task of smartifying. Working into the late afternoon, dive-bombing Elite's sumptuous spread when our stomachs' rumbling gets too distracting, we try any algorithm either of us dreams up. We teach botlets to talk to each other. We give them adaptive strategies that evolve with failure. We try pure logic and pure heuristics and hybrids of the two.

By six p.m., with roughly ten hours left in Blackquest 40, the best any botlet achieves is seventy-nine consecutive successes: an improvement over five, but far from infinity.

Prisha wheels back in her chair to peek up the hall—Elite facilitators have been hovering, watching our progress.

"*They can't test perpetuity,*" she whispers. "What's the longest they would run the simulation for, once the forty hours is up?"

I glance to Paul. "What do you think? I doubt they're sticking around for brunch."

"Maybe ten minutes," Paul says. "Fifteen?"

Again Jared plays the spoilsport. "That's still gonna be

millions of hits on the simulator. Solving a million or solving infinity—same basic diff."

This takes the wind out of Prisha's sails. Unfortunately, he's right.

We try other ideas. Simple ones. Complicated ones. We invite Graham into our brainstorms to see if he can foil his own handiwork. He sits beside me squinting at the screen, scratching his biceps roguishly. His comments lead to minor improvements but nothing groundbreaking.

We keep banging through dinner.

Sporadically I hear the clomp of Dawson's boots, but he stays out of our grills. Now that I'm back in the fold and clearly working at max effort, he must see no profit in adding more pressure.

I'm swimming so deeply in the problem that I barely process time, the ticking of Elite's doomsday clocks. My head tumbles from one approach to the next, past fatigue, past self-awareness: a zone I've only traveled to a few times in life, that hackathon at MIT, the night before I signed paperwork committing Mom to Crestwood.

I cull every radical programming concept I've come across in practice or in the literature. I splice theories from radically different fields. I invent stuff.

Nothing works.

I mount my cubicle borders again.

"Listen up!" I shout from my perch. "I know everyone's busy finalizing their own piece of the codebase, but we have a blocker in the core and I need fresh brains."

It's not my nature to do this, to admit defeat and call in the hivemind. But I'm too close to the problem. I'm burning up my gears.

"Strip away all assumptions, forget every other programming riddle you've solved!" I say, shooting my fists away from clenched eyes, then popping hands and eyes wide.

I sketch the problem in the broadest possible context, just hoping somebody can give me a sprout, not the whole tree of an answer.

*"How do you beat a lock whose hole is never the same twice?* How do you solve the unsolvable?"

My gaze casts around to the grayest of the graybeards and greenest of the green. If there's a solution to be had, I imagine it coming from a whole new direction—some fount of insight I never even knew was on the payroll.

Or not.

Prisha calls out, "You cheat."

The corner of her lips just does raise.

*"You cheat..."* I say myself, trying on the sprout.

"Why solve it fresh every time?" Prisha says. "Cache the answers."

In the space of seconds, between our two minds, the concept matures to a nascent strategy.

I hop down from the cubicle borders. As a sideways look passes through the other engineers, the core team reassembles. Prisha, Jared, Paul, Graham.

The nearest doomsday clock reads 8:32.

"We save the answers," I explain on my and Prisha's behalf. "We run this thing a billion times and every time an output works for a given seven-variable matrix, we store the values. Then, next time our botlet gets passed that matrix, *boom*, it finds the answer in a lookup file. Spits it right out."

Jared says, "That's crude."

"And it'll get a whole lot cruder if we all..." *Get blown up* is what I'm thinking, but I finish, "Lose our Q4 stock options."

Paul asks, "Is that allowed, a lookup? Storing answers offline?"

We all turn to Graham, who's laced his fingers overhead with something like easy awe. "If it works, it works. They won't care how."

Exactly. Dawson just wants his power plant—beautiful code or ugly code, whatever it takes.

Paul, after momentary confusion at Graham's use of "they," gets cracking. While I change the botlets, he creates the lookup file. Meanwhile Prisha crafts a directory structure that will work in both the test and live environments, and Jared pre-populates Paul's lookup file with answers we've already found during previous simulations.

My cube is a dervish.

The first simulation gathers ninety-eight successful matrix-value pairs before the last botlet fails. Paul clicks into his file.

"Ninety-eight rows!" he reports, and high-fives each of us.

"We're dealing with large numbers, though," I say. "So let's assume that run was typical—we made about a hundred entries in twenty seconds. Call it five per second. How many seconds do we need before our file has an answer for every possible matrix of inputs?"

"Seven variables," Jared says.

"And you have the ranges, right?" I ask Prisha.

She rifles through her notebook for the values. Paul, ready with his laptop calculator, taps in the difference between high and low for each variable and multiplies the ranges together.

As Prisha reads off the numbers, I feel a black bubble starting in my stomach. These ranges are awfully wide...

Paul types the last number and computes the final product: the number of rows his file will need. His eyes wobble in place.

"*What?*" I say.

He tips the screen for us to see.

3,583,180,881,392,921,448,003.

The readout pulls every spore of hope from the room. The cursor blinks after it like some laughing hyena.

Jared assumes the keyboard. "At five rows per second, we'll be good to go in...oh, twenty-two billion years."

It's all I can do not to rip that disgusting hat off his head and feed it to him.

## CHAPTER FORTY-SEVEN_

I PUT THE SIMULATOR ON LOOP SO IT'LL KEEP RUNNING, keep gathering and storing successful matrix-value pairs. With grim faces, we all watch Paul's text file grow down the screen— about five lines per second, sometimes a little quicker, sometimes slower.

*What else is there to do?*

Maybe our calculations are off. Maybe some optimization from Serverzilla down in the parking garage will kick in, shaving orders of magnitude off our run times.

I watch ten minutes—like the boringest, yet most important television show imaginable—then check our results.

The file *looks* a lot bigger. Is it possible we're beating five per second?

Time for more math. Ten minutes divided into 2,981 new matrix-value pairs...4.968.

So no—we aren't beating five. We're actually down a tick.

Prisha groans. Paul raises his chin and starts drumming his Adam's apple in an annoyingly pensive way. I want to swat his finger off. Stress and fatigue are affecting me. Everyone in sight bugs me, even Graham, who just saved my life and is now pulling in a wistful breath.

*Quit acting like you care. What were you doing in a Vegas strip club to begin with?*

"I'm fixing this," I announce, and launch myself anew at the problem.

I close unnecessary processes; I inline local declarations in high-volume subroutines—every dirty secret in my coder's bag. The text file grows at its same pace: quick to the mortal eye, but molasses against what's needed for Blackquest 40.

Dawson slithers in from the hall. "We've been waiting for checkpoint seventeen. Has there been a setback?"

His eyes, centered in those thick glasses frames, are squarely upon me.

"I wouldn't call it a setback."

"No? What would you call it?"

After hearing Katie Masterson's up-from-the-bootstraps tale of how Elite came to be, I thought my interactions with Dawson might change. I might see past the style, understand he was only doing a job—same as the rest of us.

Now, though, as he looms over me speaking in the superior tone of a parent to a whiny child, I see no imminent détente.

"What've *you* been doing the last five hours?" I say. "Because we've been solving problems."

Dawson nods. "No doubt you've made progress. Progress and success are not the same."

"Thanks for that, Mr. Merriam-Webster."

Giving up talking to me, Dawson asks Graham for a status report. Graham explains our snag, dumbing it down, sparing Dawson the gory details of file storage and matrix-value-pairs-per-second.

The Russian passes his stress ball between hands. "We'll have to find a different way. Back to the drawing board."

I turn to Paul, who's still pleasuring his Adam's apple. A discussion takes place in our faces. We're too far down this path to ram it into reverse. Another approach is just going to yield another stopper. Our best bet is to accept the impossibility we have, rather than wasting another five hours uncovering a fresh one.

"We'll keep chugging," I say. "I'm hoping there's a breakthrough ahead. We'll get there."

"*Hoping?* You'll 'get there?'" Dawson charges farther into the cubicle. "Thousands of lives are at ris—" He stops, glancing at Prisha and Jared. "Imagine if this project were some mission-critical app, upon which the fate of thousands of people—"

"Oh, save it. They might as well know." I gesture toward Jared, whose mouth is caught in a dim, diagonal twist. "Maybe the sword of Damocles can inspire somebody to great new heights."

Dawson seems vexed at my usurping his authority, but does back out of my space in what I take for assent.

I tell the gang everything—aside from the explosives in the HVAC ducts, which I can't let on knowing about in front of Dawson. Vlast, the secret payments, the consequences of failure —which are essentially the end of Codewise Solutions.

Prisha's gaze hardens as I speak.

Jared has the opposite reaction. His eyes skitter to Dawson like he's just learned he's the target of some sting to catch online predators.

"An actual nuclear power p—p—plant?" He grips the sides of his chair. "When is it—erm, supposed to deploy?"

"At the conclusion of the project." Dawson checks a black-banded watch. "Six hours."

This is new information, I think, but not unexpected. They aren't wearing out their whips on us so they can sit on the software for months.

"*Six hours?*" Jared is thunderstruck. "That's insane."

"The timeline is beyond my control," Dawson says. "We paid an exorbitant premium to have the project completed in this duration."

"Right," I say, "and then you bullied, and lied, and threatened us with needles. Breach of contract much?"

His head ticks back and forth. "Excuses. Petty complaints. I expected more from you, Miss Bollinger. I expected excellence."

I hear a tiny *pfft*, and look down to see cotton fuzz poking out of Dawson's stress ball.

Now Graham stands and places a palm in Dawson's chest—an intimate gesture I'm surprised he allows. With mutters about *best among worst* and *allowing improvisational space*, Graham guides him out of the cubicle toward the Latrine.

When the conference room door closes, a scream sounds from within—muted but still audible through walls and glass.

"Yikes," I say. "He's cracking up."

Jared is staring out. His hat sits cockeyed, hair sticking through the adjustable closure. "If he—er, I mean, if we don't finish? What happens?"

If I told Jared at this point about the charges, and about Omar Mohammed—who I'd bet anything has a trove of phony ISIS propaganda on his computer, put there by Elite—it would finish him. He'd go blubbering off to a supply closet and melt into a puddle of dread. A big greasy puddle. And he would deserve it, after siccing those wolves on Mom.

Before I can say a rash thing, Paul—who's finally left his throat alone—speaks up.

"Nothing good," he says, fingers back on the keyboard. "So we'd better make this work."

## CHAPTER FORTY-EIGHT

THE CORE TEAM WORKS THROUGH THE NIGHT. MINOSH keeps nosing around my cubicle border so I finally drag him fully into the fold too, giving him a small bytecoding job that won't realistically move the needle on our twenty-two-billion-year problem, but should keep his jittery mind occupied.

We tell the rest of the engineers to sleep, and sleep they do —collapsing on cots like zombies back into graves.

All the window-dressing requirements of Blackquest 40 have been met. We're just banging on Paul's file, doing anything and everything to get all possible matrix-value pairs loaded so our botlets can beat the simulator.

Elite is packing up. Facilitators box supplies and tear down doomsday timers—kindly leaving one up right outside my cubicle. Katie walks past toting a stack of fat binders, which I take as copies of the phony private spaceflight business plan.

They must've gotten their busywork done on Ten.

We, on the other hand, are fighting it. Prisha gets hung up deleting extra decimal places from Paul's file, her finger quivering with over-effort on the mouse. Jared is nixing all tabs from his botlet code—which he must know the compiler does automatically.

I'm no better. As my upper eyelids crave their lower friends, I chase after any wisp of efficiency—bloated arrays, redundant logic forks. I'm jumping at imperfections like some sugared-up kid playing whack-a-mole.

At four a.m., the stink of desperation thick, Paul stands.

"Everybody stop," he says. "Let's work smarter. Let's be strategic."

I can't look away from my screen, which has become a tractor beam trying to suck my brain out through my eye sockets.

"You're in the throes of McGriddle withdrawal," I say. "There's no time for strategic."

Paul says there's always time for strategic. "Think: where's the bottleneck? Where is the payoff to optimizing large, where is it negligible?"

He adds some diagnostic bits to the code and runs it.

As we await the results, it dawns on me gradually—like chicks poking through eggshell—that Paul is right. We're flailing. All efforts are not created equal, and if we're going to pull off this miracle, we should be prioritizing. I wrest my eyes from my screen to watch Paul's.

The diagnostic stats return in another minute:


*RUNTIME SHARES*
  *Elite Simulator 0.003 percent*
  *Local Processes 99.997 percent*


Our faces swivel and meet.

"My machine's the bottleneck!" I grip the side of my laptop

screen—knowing the holdup is inside, I want to rattle it or wrench it or turn it upside-down and shake water out. "The simulator time is nothing!"

Paul says, "We need to run it on a faster machine."

"Yeah," I agree, but deflate as soon as I think it through. "If we have a faster one."

Both our gazes fall to my laptop, whose chassis still bears the chip-maker's dual fireball sticker. The principal software architect, show horse that (s)he is, naturally gets the baddest computer in the company. There might be a few speedier options in the server room, but no speedier than 30 or 40 percent.

We need orders of magnitude.

The doomsday timer reads 1:04:39. An hour and change.

"Could we..." Paul starts.

"...distribute the job across machines?" I say, but realize immediately the benefits aren't worth the effort of all that linkage.

"...or tap resources in the cloud?" he says.

"Data blockade," I remind him.

Prisha, Jared, and Minosh watch our volleys like spectators at the U.S. Open. Five people in a cubicle, even an oversize model like mine, can be claustrophobic. Our quarters feel all the more oppressive for what we just discovered: that the agonizingly slow processing that's dooming us to fail is happening right here, in this very air.

Jared yawns wide. "Too bad we didn't know about this six months ago. Could've beefed up the hardware."

His mouth closes to its signature schadenfreudic smirk. Revulsion seizes me...before I get an idea. A simple idea. It consists of two words. Two syllables. It's been a withering joke in the halls of Codewise Solutions, but not anymore.

*Yes.*

*This is too perfect.*

Jared narrows his eyes and asks what there could possibly be to smile about.

"Beefing up," I say. "We already did it."

## CHAPTER FORTY-NINE

THE CRAY.

When I speak the words, Prisha's mouth and eyes and palms all fall open as though she's ready to receive the Holy Spirit.

Paul, not so much. "That thing hasn't been online in years!"

"But it should be operational, right? Nobody sold off components, stripped out the goodies?"

"No, it—I suppose, yes, we just stashed it upstairs," Paul says. "If memory serves, it should still be up—"

"On Twelve, yep," I say. "It's there—I happened to be in the neighborhood earlier today."

Paul and Jared stare mistrustfully at me. Minosh's butt is frozen a quarter-inch over his seat cushion as though I've just uttered an ancient curse that could open a portal to some algorithmic bizarro world where AND is OR and XOR is NAND.

"Deb." Paul performs that full stop of his, the one that always precedes an idea squash. "We never even used the Cray. Not for a real project. Carter plugged it in to run demos for investors—that's it. I don't know that we ever installed the config files to put it on the network."

"So?" I'm standing now, flipping a pen end over end and

catching it, pleased by its lightness. "Five software engineers can't get one supercomputer up and running?"

There's a bad joke in there somewhere, but we have no time. I dash for the stairwell, groggily aware of the others following, not caring whether they do or don't.

The lobby shows only a tinge of early daylight, but pounding up the stairs, I can see boxes stacked near the entrance. Two Elite facilitators are wheeling hand trucks with more. A third facilitator stands at the double doors, glancing up Second Avenue.

They're prepping the getaway.

I swing around from Three to Four, Four to Five, stumbling and soaring and gripping twine. Minosh trails by just a step—who knew he was an athlete?—with Graham on his heels. Paul pulls up the rear, huffing a full flight below me.

At Ten, I encounter Fedor backing out of E-wing with a wary expression. His flattop ears, viewed from below, seem like mere lobes.

He asks where I'm going.

"The Cray," I pant, "supercomputer up on Twelve."

"You should be at your workstation. All software checkpoints have not—"

"You should *get out of my way*! I'm trying to make this Frankenstein-ware of yours dance, you should be pinning a medal on me."

The sinews of Fedor's neck stand in their skin, but he makes way.

I rip the door open at Twelve and run down two halls to the Cray. In its small room, I come across no body—Elite must have carried off Eurasian Mumia—but one side of the carpet is squishy and dark.

Prisha lifts her foot, examining the sole of her shoe. "What...what did I just step—"

"Nothing," I say. "I was up in the HVAC ducts earlier, they must've sprung a leak."

The others' faces do not exactly clear—Paul and Graham are steering well wide of the mess—but my frenetic work at the Cray pulls the rest through.

I boot 'er up. The display is monochrome, a bigger version of Hedgehog Eleanor Roosevelt's screen, and the keys are chunky beige, an old-feeling rig.

When I tap commands, though, I know I'm riding Secretariat. Output returns in a blink. Directory changes, hardware checks, file unzips—she eats it all like candy.

Paul, who knows the network architecture best, helps me with setup. We install drivers and enter security keys and dive around baseboards plugging in cables.

"Time check," I say once I'm staring at the successfully-linked botlet code.

Jared checks his watch. "Four thirty-two a.m."

Blackquest 40 ends at five.

I crack my knuckles. "Let's light the afterburners."

I kick off the Blackquest simulator. As the first botlets weasel their way through the sandbox, the Cray's various lights and indicators flash—a maelstrom of red, green, and yellow blips. Circuitry surrounds me, three hundred degrees of whizzing calculations that sound like my dragonflies might if I zipped a bunch up in a baggie.

Paul says, "How's the file looking?"

I click the matrix-value pair file. Digits start galloping down at a dizzying pace. Dizzying enough, though? There is no question the file is growing faster than five rows per second, but how much faster?

"Ready?" Paul says.

I nod, scratching neurotically at the spikes of my hair. We both know what needs doing.

We have to compare snapshots of the file from, say, a minute apart, and calculate the new growth rate.

"Taking snapshot number one..." I say, as Paul squints at the second hand of a wall clock, "...*now*."

I scribble the row count on a paper scrap. Our code roars along, processing botlets, catching simulator errors, saving good matrix-value pairs.

"Ten seconds left..." Paul watches the second hand. "Seven seconds...three, two...and...*stop!*"

I check the row count again. It has more digits than the first row count I scribbled.

A lot more.

I do the division. "We're there! Zooks, we're *right there!*"

I show him the new rate, which implies we can compile the full range of values in half an hour.

The building-wide public address crackles.

"*Your attention, please.*" The voice is Dawson's, hoarse, peeved. "*This training exercise concludes in twenty minutes. Please commit final work to your manager or the appropriate source-code repository.*"

I prance out of the Cray's C-shaped cavity, narrowly missing the blood. I take Graham's sleeve.

"Tell him! Go tell him we beat it, it'll be ready!"

But Graham's face is missing its usual hunky glow.

"It won't," he says. "You heard Dawson: twenty minutes."

"We. Have. The. Software!" I feel my eyeballs protruding from my head. "We can take over your nuclear power plant—the botlets work! Dawson's not going to sweat ten more minutes."

"The timeframe is not his. He's powerless to extend it."

"*What?*" I'm whirling about, checking walls and faces and fixtures for some shred of common sense. "We're *giving* you what you need! You can't keep the van running another ten minutes to get what you came for? What you crossed the

Pacific and violated multiple parts of the Geneva Convention for?"

Graham says nothing.

I press, "Does he just want the money back, is that it?"

"Ask him if you like."

"I will!"

I swivel to tell Paul to mind the store, but he's already taken my place at the Cray's keyboard.

I sprint downstairs. From the eighth floor, I peer down into the lobby and make out the top of Dawson's head. He is overseeing the exit operation, telling what goes where, passing off his box of phones to Security Kyle.

I'm winded by the time I reach him at the foot of *Semperinity*.

"Need a tiny extension," I say. "Ten minutes, possibly less."

He is marking up a sheet held in the claw of a clipboard. "Blackquest 40 contains no provision for extension."

"Right, but the software—I can get you the software!"

"The timeframe is not mine to—"

"Yeah, I heard, it's not your timeframe. But you can't let *ten minutes* stop us!" I pull him a step farther from Security Kyle and whisper, "Who cares if you hack your power plant at 5:05 or 5:15, right? As long as it's hacked."

Dawson continues marking—short, firm pencil checks. "The agreement becomes void in"—he consults a clock—"sixteen minutes. These are the terms of the contract, and I will abide by those terms."

I'm speechless. We have done the impossible, split the damn atom, and it's going for naught? How can the Russians walk away from this code—for which they were willing to pay many millions of dollars—because of *ten minutes*?

"I—I mean...it might speed up," I say. "The botlets keep improving, getting smarter, maybe they will finish in sixteen minutes. But I...again...why in the world wouldn't you just *wait?*"

Dawson gives no further explanation, only continues his methodical preparations to leave.

Where did his anger go? His rage? Has he so acclimated himself to the idea of failure that he can't summon up that former obsession?

Did it vanish when he punctured his stress ball, like some shaman's power disappearing when his voodoo doll gets tossed in a river?

I head back upstairs. I don't know what's up with Dawson. He lost it somewhere along the line.

I sit with Graham on the Cray's burnt-orange bench and dismiss the others.

"Go," I tell them. "They're about to hand back phones in the lobby."

Jared doesn't have to be told twice. He's gone.

Prisha says, "How can I help?"

"You can't," I say. "Just leave. Just go get your phone and wait there in the lobby, and the second Elite takes off, beat it outside. Don't look back."

She grudgingly agrees. I extend the same advice to Minosh and Paul.

Minosh goes.

Paul takes a hesitant look at the Cray, still chugging away. "Li Wei was concerned, and the kids...I-I just haven't been home in a while."

"Sure," I say. "Of course, go. Get outta here."

So he does, leaving just Graham and me. We set a chime to alert us when all matrix-value pairs have been found, then return to the burnt-orange bench.

I yawn. Graham pulls one foot, clad in a regular tennis shoe, up onto the opposite knee.

"Deb Bollinger, you're amazing," he says.

My head plunks back against the supercomputer.

*Ouch.*

"Thanks," I say, "but I am still gay."

He taps his chin sagely. "Good to know. Did I mention I was ambidextrous? Write with my left, but forks have always felt better in my right."

## CHAPTER FIFTY_

At the ten-minute mark, I stand and trudge to the Cray's inner cavity. I check Paul's file and find its growth rate has increased—slightly.

"We might make it," I call out to Graham.

He answers over the supercomputer's thrum, "If we do, you'll deserve one hell of a bonus for saving this place."

"From what, bankruptcy? Or being reduced to a pile of rubble?"

I return from the Cray's inner cavity to find Graham fingering his thermal undersleeve.

"As a coerced member of my team," he says, "I'm not privy to all aspects of the plan."

"Nobody told you about explosives in ducts?"

He shakes his head. "Though I can't say it surprises me." He rolls his tongue around his mouth. "You know, I'm certain Dawson would make space for you in the convoy. To have along, help debug any deployment issues."

I drop back onto the bench beside him. "I realize we've only known each other forty hours, but do you honestly think I'm the sort of person who'd ditch and jump in the runaway van with slime like Dawson?"

Graham smiles. "Sometimes the right move is beyond the character we thought was ours."

Our knees brush, and I don't pull away—his jeans feel like some luxurious balm for my battered bones. I look to him hoping for more, but his hazel eyes are ciphers.

*How is Dawson going to use those charges?*

I have been assuming they're the bleach to his cleanup job—blast us to the moon and pin it on Omar Mohammed. But is that a sound assumption?

"Does it even matter if we build Blackquest?" I ask. "If we succeed, do we gain anything?"

Graham, too, is leaving his leg where it is. "For all else he is, Dawson is a believer in due rewards. In accountability. That much is authentic. I think finishing the software would be all to the good."

The Cray's casing is warm against the back of my skull, its soft vibration like some exotic massage.

My eyes close. The code has been optimized to within a silicon wafer of its existence—I can't make it any speedier. It'll get the full range of matrix-value pairs when it gets them.

All it needs is time.

I recheck at five minutes, then at three, then at two.

Each time, the file size indicates the botlets inching closer to a rate that could push us over the top. If we do miss, it won't be by much. Maybe five minutes.

Where can I find five minutes?

*Where?*

I open my mouth and talk, just to start thoughts flowing. "When will Dawson run the final test?"

Graham stretches an arm overhead. "When the forty hours have expired."

"Okay, but specifically—is he going to kick off the test right downstairs in the lobby? Could I stall him? Get him talking somehow, buy us more time?"

"It's sound thinking," Graham says, "but no. I wrote the finalization code—at time zero, Blackquest 40 locks in the last commits, and that's the code that gets tested. Stall all you like, but the code is frozen."

I slump deeper into the bench, watching my toes in their sandals, the middle twisting over the big, then big over middle.

The building below us groans with activity. Stairwell doors to Ten and Nine keep opening in what must be Codewise and Elite personnel streaming down to the lobby. Boxes are surely being carted out for transport.

Time check: two minutes remaining.

We aren't going to make it.

Unless...

"Hey, at forty hours, does the data blockade come down?"

"Right. At the precise moment the codebase locks in."

"So theoretically, since the code gets tested *after* lock-in, it could call out to some cloud datasource."

"Theoretically," Graham says, "but any code like that would fail inside the forty hours."

"But the final test runs after the forty. Post blockade, yes?"

Graham twists his rugged mouth. "I suppose you could take a blind shot at it—commit some completely untestable code and hope it works." He shrugs. "What's this magic datasource you're imagining?"

I smack the Cray with the back of one hand. "I can keep this girl running, keep growing the file. The code can freeze at forty hours, but if I rig it to call the Cray over the internet whenever a botlet sees a new matrix-value pair, the file can grow right up until Dawson kicks off the test."

Graham makes a bemused cluck. "So it could. You might get another three or four minutes."

"Which might do it."

"Yes. Might. But you couldn't test your network code—it'd be like learning to ride a unicycle on the edge of a cliff, no margin for erro—"

I don't hear the rest, already inside the Cray at the keyboard.

I have ninety seconds to make the botlets call over the internet for the Cray's file. I pull up the code, fingers flying, eyes rabid, highlighting and typing over, scanning semicolons—a single one out of place kills the plan—and matching brackets and saving all with *control-s*.

Next, Paul's file needs to be on the internet. I write the bare bones-iest network script in the history of network scripts.

I've just rebooted the Cray—activating the script and making the file available—when a sort of air horn sounds over the public address.

Dawson's voice: "Ladies and gentlemen of Codewise Solutions, this concludes your training. The final test for Blackquest 40 technical compliance will begin shortly. All interested persons should report to the lobby."

I check Paul's text file, which is still growing.

*3,583,180,881,247,257,938,389 rows (99.99948%)*

So close.

Graham and I hustle downstairs. The lobby looks like the headliners' stage at some music festival—everyone crammed in, bouncing in place. People are wincing and rubbing out their eyes, but with a certain giddiness.

*It's almost over. We're almost out.*

Facilitators in yellow shirts congregate closer to the double-door exit, carrying last supplies to vans.

Supervising all is Jim Dawson. I spot his chunky glasses knifing through the crowd.

Susan is about too. I actually have to look twice, speeding down the last steps—it's been hours and hundreds of lines of code since I last saw her. She seems tense, both wrists curled under in the cuffs of her blazer.

She asks brightly, "Last second breakthrough?"

Her co-founders lurk nearby. Carter's Gatsby slickback is diffuse and bent like strands of licorice peeled back from a stalk. Paul waits with a shoe propped on *Semperinity*, leaning on his knee, probably thinking of Li Wei and their girls.

"Maybe," I say. "We pulled out all the stops."

Dawson consults a tablet. "It appears you were moving in the wrong direction. Your tries had been close—and improving —but I see here at the end, your last several simulations failed in all cases."

This is no surprise. Our botlets tried calling out to the Cray via internet and ran smack into the data blockade.

"I decided to swerve, left instead of right." I speak slowly, taking my sweet time putting together sentences. "I went with a radical new approach...I know how important this software is to you...I would be devastated if we let you down."

A group of fifteen or twenty Codewise employees is listening, pressed shoulder to shoulder.

Dawson says, "Blackquest 40 is a training exercise. The product you've built is incidental."

"Really? You're going to keep up the facade, even now. Even on your way out the door?"

I spread my arms obnoxiously and smile, saccharine, hoping to make an inviting target of myself.

Dawson won't be baited. "There exists a timetable, Miss Bollinger. And it is not a soft one."

"Right. I know you—nothing's ever soft, is it?" Mentally I

am tracking row counts as they tick higher, higher, inching closer to 100 percent of the matrix-value pair universe. "Gotta be hard-hard-hard, all the time."

Dawson finds Katie Masterson in the crowd. She is wading through haggard Codewise employees, carrying a laptop emblazoned with the Elite logo, that E with top stroke zooming skyward.

He accepts the computer and sets it on a high, pub-style table. He opens the Blackquest simulator and kicks off its initialization routine.

The row-count climb continues in my head. By now, the Cray must be mere millionths of a percent away from complete. It could conceivably finish as the first botlets of Dawson's do-or-die test are receiving their inputs.

Success or failure may come down to whether these early inputs happen to be among the matrix-value pairs we've already compiled, or one of the few oddballs we haven't captured yet.

In other words, pure chance.

Dawson clicks a rectangular gray button labeled SOFT-WARE COMPLIANCE. A dialog informs him, "Results of this test are final and cannot be reversed. Do you wish to proceed?"

I have a fleeting wish to dive in front of him, to get eyes on that internet code upstairs and make sure I used forward slashes instead of backward slashes in the network paths—my last project was on a Windows machine, which tends to screw with my head since Windows is the only modern operating system that uses backward—but of course I can't. The code is locked.

Dawson taps YES, and the test begins.

## CHAPTER FIFTY-ONE_

SUSAN AND I WATCH BETWEEN THE MUSCLED BACKS OF Dawson and Fedor. The laptop screen displays a dashboard of virtual meters: Number of Running Processes, Inputs Received, Outputs Replaced, Outputs Rejected, Total Duration of Output Circumvention.

This last meter—a bar—is larger than the others and shows a checkered flag at the end. I squint to read the value beside the flag.

*5:00 min.*

So that's the goal line. For testing purposes, five minutes will stand in for perpetuity.

The Russians must want this nuclear power plant of theirs back in a hurry.

As the various meters begin jumping with data, I catch Susan stealing peeks my way. The looks feel solicitous, as though she wants to express some sentiment or meaning, but I ignore them. I'm thinking ahead to the next phase—to escape, once Elite takes off with our successful (or not) code.

How long will they wait before detonating the charges?

*Will* they detonate the charges?

I have to assume so. Everybody will need to beat it outside, across the street. Should I yell that the whole place is wired to blow, or just gently encourage people to evacuate in an orderly fashion?

I have a feeling when the time comes, neither "gently" nor "orderly" will be doable.

I check the meter readings.

*Outputs Replaced: 973,124.*

*Outputs Rejected: 0.*

*Total Duration of Output Circumvention: 0:47 min.*

Has it really just been forty-seven seconds? This test is going to *feel* like perpetuity, anyway.

The Codewise group around us—engineers, account coordinators, middle managers—watches with rapt faces. Something like dog's breath reeks behind me, and elbows keep poking my ribs. The lobby monitors, which have been showing static for the last forty hours, are back on CNN.

Up ahead, Minosh inches toward the double-doors but is dissuaded by a glowering Elite facilitator.

As *Total Duration* passes two minutes, a smile begins on Susan's face. One wrist uncurls itself from her cuff. I feel a mild loosening of the gut, too. Those internet calls out to the Cray must be working—otherwise the test would have bombed immediately.

Dawson stands before the laptop with great primacy, stone faced.

*Outputs Replaced: 4,831,729.*

*Outputs Rejected: 0.*

*Total Duration of Output Circumvention: 3:55 min.*

With the *Total Duration* bar close to 80 percent full, a mere eighth-inch of screen from the checkered flag, a floaty sensation enters my legs. I'm excited and revving for action—for escape. No whammies in nearly five million matrix-value pair tries is a great sign. There's every chance the Cray finished, that its text file is sitting on the hard drive done, three sextillion-odd rows big.

*Outputs Replaced: 6,021,935.*

*Outputs Rejected: 0.*

*Total Duration of Output Circumvention: 4:41 min.*

Strange changes are occurring in Dawson. A vein near his temple begins throbbing visibly. His butt cheeks—I swear, they're right in front of me—clench in their khakis. His hand goes for his stress ball but, finding none, begins flexing and unflexing, stretching his pocket as though a furious rodent is trapped inside.

When the *Total Duration* bar fills, an up-chime sounds. The other meters stop. The laptop fan spins down. The screen background changes from neutral gray to cool green.

A message snaps across the monitor:

SOFTWARE COMPLIANCE CONFIRMED.

Susan throws her arms around me, wrapping me in her lush aroma. "I knew you'd do it, Deb! This was awful, but I knew you could—you're the best hire I ever made."

When we separate, she hikes up onto a glass coffee table to address everyone. It's a move I've seen her do before and admired—that bold stride up, commanding the whole lobby from an unorthodox spot—but now she staggers and has to right herself with both hands.

"Amazing, *amazing* job!" she calls once she's safely up. "Some mistakes were made—mostly by me, by us"—a spin of the hand seems to lump in Carter and Dawson—"but you persevered. You fought through it. I could not be more proud of what we've accomplished today. Well, today and yesterday. I want you all to take a moment and give yourselves an enormous round of applause!"

Tepid claps answer. A hacking cough rings out. The mood is

bizarre, bewildered. Susan's tone feels all wrong for the moment —which is less a victory part than refugee transfer.

I'm beyond confused. Has she forgotten about the nuclear power plant? Or is she referencing it—obliquely, to those of us who know? Is this more playacting for Dawson's benefit?

Is anything out of her mouth, any word or sequence of words slipping through those red-ribbon lips, real?

Dawson closes the test laptop. *Snick.* Then flashes some hand signal—pinkie and forefinger up, thumb twisting—to Fedor.

He says in an undertone, "Proceed with scenario A."

Both men start purposefully for the exit. All boxes have been loaded into the vans idling on Second Avenue: five black tanks with yellow shoulders showing through the windows.

Only a few facilitators remain. One is Katie, who approaches her brother with a stack of papers and carton of library-style half pencils.

I have the thought she'll seek me out, pull me aside and share some pearl of insight about East and West working together, muddling through prejudice and historical enmities...but she doesn't.

Dawson accepts the papers and pencils. "Many of you are eager to return to your families," he says, "and we are eager to get you back to them. The last item required by Blackquest 40 is feedback on the exercise itself—on Elite Development."

He passes the stack to Susan. I'm standing beside her and read the top sheet, a generic ten-question survey.

Were you satisfied with the quality of instruction? Did facilitators make clear the goals and objectives of the exercise? Et cetera.

The survey mentions "Elite Development" exactly zero times. It could be a feedback form for middle school band camp.

"I'm dinging you guys hard on number six, 'treated politely

and respectfully,'" I say, quietly reaching for Prisha, for Minosh, for everyone around me, ready to beat it. "I must be down a pint of blood, and I haven't gotten a single thank you for building your hijack-ware. For saving you from Siberian exile."

Dawson pays no mind to the perplexed faces around us. "We encourage everyone to be frank in these exit surveys. From you, Miss Bollinger, I would expect nothing less."

I'm holding hands with Prisha now, behind both our backs. Minosh has taken my cue and is nudging forward again. Jared, noticing, bumbles through the crowd and positions himself to leave, too.

"Did you pack out your trash?" I ask. "Clean up all your spills, wipe down the counters?"

Dawson's gaze, which turned light and almost playful after the successful test, becomes sober again.

"We have left behind no traces, no mysteries to be solved. I would expect you"—he bites the word—"to be most appreciative of this."

I fix him with my own glare, trying to hold his attention there—high in my face—while finding one of the exit surveys with my fingers, turning it over, pushing it to Susan.

I scribble blindly with a half-pencil, GET PEOPLE OUTSIDE FAST AS POSSIBLE.

As Susan reads this, I perceive only the slightest shudder. She takes the pencil, which I've set down beside the survey, and writes:

???

I take back the pencil and add to our running script, BOOM.

Susan clears her throat to cover a gasp.

Elite continues evacuating the lobby. Fedor has gone outside. Katie is passing through the double-doors now.

Besides Dawson, Graham is the last to go. He waits for our

eyes to meet, then purses his mouth—a pained, thankful expression. I'm sorting through a mishmash of emotions when he flits his eyes skyward.

I crinkle mine back.

His eyes flit skyward again. Is this some kind of prayer? Or appeal to an afterlife meet-up?

Is he telling me to head upstairs? Could there be some failsafe switch on Twelve or Ten?

Before I can even guess, Susan has climbed back atop the coffee table.

"Everyone, please listen carefully!" she announces. "These surveys are important, but I'm going to suggest we tackle them tomorrow, with the benefit of rest. I know I feel like I could sleep for a week—and I showed up halfway through Blackquest 40."

Halfhearted chuckles are heard. Paul, whose shirttail hangs about his amorphous hips, bobs in place near the double-doors. Jared shifts between feet and digs a finger in his ear.

Dawson matches our CEO's volume. "The surveys must be completed now, while the exercise is fresh in your minds. The feedback loop is a vital part of our process, and ensures we're providing the very highest caliber of training."

Susan, still standing on the table, sets both hands on her hips. "We delivered your software." Her tone is low and gritty. "We fulfilled the contract."

This, finally, is no act. Her heel is dug into the glass—I'll be surprised if she hasn't made a chip—and her chin is cocked resolutely.

For his part, Dawson stands in front of the double-doors with legs bowed, looking ready to bounce all comers into *Semperinity*.

"You did," he says, "and now we must insist on fifteen further minutes of your time."

Fedor approaches from behind, from outside. He's carrying an oval slab—dark, possibly metal, definitely heavy judging by the slope of his shoulders.

What *is* that? A kind of flattened barbell?

I feel one ear start to sail up my head, losing it, that sadistic kite runner again.

Dawson backpedals through the double-doors. I grab my coworkers and push forward and Susan is shouting, gesturing, diving down off the coffee table.

We're all too late.

In one slick motion, Dawson takes the slab from Fedor and snaps it over the door handles from outside. The lock engages with a deep *clunk*.

Our eyes meet one last time. Behind the glasses, his shine with that same furor that's gripped this building for the last forty hours, but there is something else.

Respect.

I think about him and Katie playing blocks in the country-side, founding Elite, having to gladhand corporate dunces like Carter Kotanchek in order to make it go—then having it all co-opted by Mother Russia.

As he slips into a van and speeds off down Second Avenue, I can't say I respect Dawson back. He could've said no. He could've gone about his task with less cruelty. But I know something of his burden.

## CHAPTER FIFTY-TWO_

Hysteria seizes the lobby. Only a few of us know about the charges, but anyone can look at Dawson's industrial-grade padlock and recognize bad intentions.

Jared and Minosh grip the inner door handles, heaving, leaning—to no avail.

Some salesman is shouting. "*You said forty hours, not one minute more!*"

"Break a window!" I yell myself. I try hoisting the pub-style table in front of me, but it's bolted down.

Susan directs other efforts, marshaling small teams, calling out specific windows to target.

Carter struggles under one corner of a loveseat.

Prisha dumps fake apples off a porcelain platter and slings the thing discus-like at the glass, which bows and *thunks* and trembles in its frame, but doesn't break.

"Paul!" I say. "You know some electrical engineering, right?"

He is grinding two knuckles into a crack of a south window, but the crack isn't getting bigger. "I—well, yes, I minored EE at Carnegie."

"Let's go, *come on!*" I plow through the roiling crowd to pull him away. "I saw the trigger—I know where they put the trigger!"

Cursing myself for not disabling the charges when I had the chance—when I had *time*—I race upstairs to Ten. En route I grab wire cutters from Security Kyle, ripping open his toolbox, upending nails and nuts and stud finders. Paul hustles after me.

We zoom through E-wing to the workspace of Omar Mohammed.

*Do I have minutes?*

*Seconds?*

I have no idea. Dawson doesn't know I saw the charges—assuming, again, Graham didn't sell me out—so maybe he'll wait, make some progress on his getaway before blasting the place.

Or maybe he won't. Maybe having slapped on the mega padlock, he'll figure we're going to try escaping immediately and jump onto his metaphorical bomb plunger the instant they've rounded the corner.

Omar keeps a neat workspace, only a left-behind windbreaker sagging off the back of his chair. I motor into his cubicle and dive underneath his desk to the baseboard. Two wires run here from a hole in the ceiling—I saw the other side earlier from inside the ducts.

Somebody has stapled the wires to the wall and painted them over white—a slapdash job, but nothing you'd notice at a glance.

Here at the baseboard, connected to the wires, is a steel box. Lunch-pail size. A lone indicator light along its top edge, currently solid green.

The detonator.

And up in the ducts is the bang-bang.

Separate detonator from bang-bang, problem solved.

I spread the jaws of my wire cutters and slip one between

wall and wire, separating them, breaking a thin coat of fresh-dried paint. I'm about to squeeze the handles and snip before second thoughts come.

*Maybe it's less simple.*

*Maybe what sounds infallible inside your brain is actually...fallible?*

Footsteps pound nearer. I decide to wait for Paul. In the meantime I stare at the detonator, willing it not to change state or otherwise bring three floors crashing down on my head.

Paul lunges into the cubicle, clutching his side.

"Here's the detonator," I say, pointing to the box, "and there are the explosives"—to the ceiling—"and eight or nine floors have 'em, all in the ducts, all connected wirelessly. I was gonna snip both wires to take the detonator off the circuit."

He tips his face one way, then the other. "That probably works. Unless they wired a brownout circuit closer to the charges."

"Brownout?"

As precious seconds tick away and indeterminate cries sound from the lobby, Paul explains you can plug a small power source into a larger circuit and wire it such that the system is fail-open (rather than fail-safe), meaning a break in the main circuit triggers the positive case.

I say, "Meaning explosion?"

He nods. "The only reason you'd bother is out of extreme caution—if you were worried about sabotage."

I pull the wire cutters back farther. "At least one member of their team is operating under duress—and Jim Dawson isn't the incautious type."

Paul sighs in agreement. "Did the charge on this floor look different? Was the mechanism the same size as other floors'?"

I squinch my face trying to visualize, but the duct scenes are all running together in my brain. "Eh, I'd be guessing."

We move a table under the nearest HVAC vent, and one last time I hurl my body up into that dusty, stifling tunnel.

With Paul shouting instructions through the ceiling, I push Hedgehog Eleanor Roosevelt and her barely-still-kicking flashlight ahead.

I find the charge. It does have a small additional mechanism, domed like a smoke detector and adjacent to the ceiling hole. That's right—I did see it before.

*"That'll be a 'yes' on brownout circuit!"* I call down. *"Want me to crack it open?"*

Paul shouts back sure, but how about twisting rather of cracking? I twist. The top half lifts off.

This circuitry, which I keep having to prop Hedgehog Eleanor Roosevelt at different orientations to see, contains half a dozen wires sticking out of a simple breadboard, with a nine-volt battery for a power source.

It looks like something a kid put together at Radio Shack while her dad was ogling speakers.

I ask, *"Can I just pop out the battery?"*

"They could've wired to fail-open here, too," Paul says. "How many transistors do you see?"

I count. "Nine."

He doesn't answer.

I yell, "What? *What does nine tell you?*"

His voice returns, "It could be fail-open. A simple brownout circuit shouldn't require more than two or three transistors."

Fantastic.

In a parallel mental process, I'm figuring how far away Dawson has gotten—how much time we have. Will he wait until his brigade of vans has crossed the Bay Bridge? Or until they're out of San Francisco proper and closer to the airport?

Are they flying home across the Pacific?

Would the FAA ground planes for an explosion of this size?

"So...what, now we have to disable both power sources simultaneously?" I ask.

"Correct," he calls up. "You left the wire cutters down here —let me go grab them."

There are scrabbling sounds, then more footsteps—but different, crisper than Paul's.

My stomach plummets as I think for a second Elite has discovered our rebellion and come back.

But the voice is Susan's. "*Deb?* Deb, where are you? We've been trying but the glass won't break—"

"*I got this,*" I yell. "We got it—we're doing it. Just stay back!"

She gives no verbal answer, and I imagine her closing those long lashes, biting her lip—chastened by this fiasco that's taken place on her watch.

But who the hell knows? At this point, I have no claim on what lives inside anyone else's head.

"Paul!" I shout. "On three, yeah?"

He answers, "On three!"

I poise my fingernails at either side of the nine-volt battery. I bring my face so close I can see my own breath condensing on the terminals.

Sweat dribbles down my neck. I lie flat against the duct's bottom, heart beating into cold steel.

I start, "One!"

Paul follows, "Two!"

I rock between my elbows, double- and triple-checking my grip on the battery and its connector.

Together we say, "Three!" and I jerk my battery free at the exact moment that Paul—I hope—is clipping his wire.

## CHAPTER FIFTY-THREE_

FOR TWO PRESSURIZED SECONDS, I HOLD EVERY BODY PART over which I still have control away from the duct's metal. The nine-volt battery is alive between my fingers. The whir of the HVAC fan, pushing air at me from many floors down, whispers in my ear.

Trying to keep perfectly still, I lean too far forward and start tilting toward the brownout mechanism.

Nothing has happened yet. It occurs to me that electrical circuits are fast.

One second becomes two.

Two become three.

My tilt continues and is turning into a teeter—I'm about to pitch forward onto the brownout circuits.

Will anything happen if I smash them? Could some spark be produced and do the job of this battery I just snatched?

Not caring to find out, I duck my shoulder at the last moment and crash into the empty corner of the duct. The noise is stupendous, my head knocking around the inside of a tin-can drum.

Three seconds become five.

Five become ten.

We're safe.

I squirm over onto my back and fill my lungs with hot, filmy air. The duct's metal sides pin the spikes of my hair against my head. My skin is a petri dish of grotesqueries—sweat, dirt, blood, scabs, stuck clothes.

And I don't care.

Paul calls up, "Deb, what's your status? Are you okay?"

I exhale. "All good up here."

I crawl back to the removed vent, plodding on all fours, sore in my butt and back, nudging Hedgehog Eleanor Roosevelt ahead. Of forty original quills, she might have seven left.

Paul is waiting under the vent. He's helping me down onto the table we pulled over earlier when I lose hold of the ceiling panels. He stops my fall by bracing my heel, and as he releases it, we're both watching the contact.

I think about my belief, forty hours ago, that Paul had impure thoughts about my feet. It seems such a strange, petty inference now. So cavalier.

"You need to get to a hospital," he says, looking from one abrasion to the next.

I pick a dust bunny from a gash on my elbow, pulling a thread of blood with it. "Hospital later. I have a few to-dos ahead of it in the queue."

Paul grins. In the fullness of his face, I don't see condescension or fatty breakfast sandwiches—only warmth.

"Why am I not surprised?"

We plod to the lobby together. My heart is still pumping double-time, but my brain has given up the fight, processing the scene in a happy haze. People stream through the double doors, gushing out to sidewalks or Muni, anyplace but here. The evacuation is hasty but controlled; Susan went ahead the moment the detonator was disabled and let everyone know the threat had been removed.

Though the lobby glass shows cracks, none of the panels got punched out. Apparently Security Kyle ran downstairs and escaped by the parking garage—which Elite had secured with a simple padlock, circumvented by bolt cutters—then circled back around front to disable Dawson's double-door lock.

"Take your time, let your body readjust to the natural world," Susan is saying, raising her nose with a savoring air. "Again—you have my apologies, your families have my apologies —please, relax, take as long as necessary coming back to the office."

Her message is having its intended effect. People pause to buckle their briefcases or be sure of keys. A few even linger watching the lobby TVs.

Paul retrieves his stuff, which he dropped by *Semperinity* before scampering off to help me defuse the charges.

"Don't spend all day on Carebnb fixes," he tells me. "Whatever the data says, remember: it's one day. Launch is important, but it's still just one day. Don't go trying to solve every last issue."

"Gotcha," I say. "No, I won't. Just a quick peek. I promise."

He chuckles, surely tallying up how many of those I've broken these last two days.

We hug.

When I pull away, I find Carter Kotanchek waiting, fidgeting in place behind us.

"Perfect. Two birds, one stone." He smacks his hands slickly. "Look, I have something to say to both of you. This disaster's on me. Truly. I whiffed big time. Jeopardized everything we built here. Regardless of anything else, how it all shakes out...I'm done. Goin' upstairs now to clean out my desk."

I reach out to smooth his summer-weight suit. The shoulder won't lay flat.

"Good," I say. "Don't swipe any pens on the way out."

Carter lets this go.

I walk up with him as far as Three, veering off for the engineering area. The place is Times Square on the morning of January first: paper shrapnel littering the halls, half-drunk cups of brown liquid. Somebody toppled Minosh's sit-stand workstation, and purple gel is oozing from the monitor.

I need to get out to Crestwood Psychiatric. It occurs to me, though, that if I leave the office immediately and this place turns into a crime scene, it could be days before I get back inside—before I can check Carebnb.

I'll take ten minutes. Mom has either compartmentalized the episode with Elite's scrambled-egg forcer, lumped it in with the rest of life's indignities and moved on; or she's flipped out utterly. Ten minutes won't make a difference.

Back on my workstation, I punch up the Carebnb map. Blinking dots for Wanda, Cecil, and 135 other unhoused beta users inch about the screen.

I tab into *Nightly Report*, which gives me a chunk of numbers. I never bothered creating some snazzy dashboard since I am the only one—for now—who'll be using it to monitor Carebnb performance. The numbers come straight from the database, unadorned sums or percents. They look crappy.

The story they tell is even crappier.

Carebnb didn't work. Though 34.7 percent of active users checked into a host location (I had been estimating between thirty and thirty-five the first night), only 1.8 percent stayed through the night.

I click through comments left in my auto-feedback prompt, which appears every time a user quits or logs out.

*"lady kept looking in at me like i'm a rat. i don't need that."*

*"Cool idea but my 'guest' insisted on insulting art my wife's friend makes, extremely uncool."*

*"Just left."*

There were a bunch like this last comment, people who seemed to think they had to type something just to get the app to release their phone or wristband.

The data is imperfect, but I draw one fundamental conclusion: people didn't help each other.

When placed in situations where they could either bail or overcome some issue, they bailed. They held tight to their own interests. I knew the host-user relationship would be vital to Carebnb's success, but I believed people would goodwill their way through glitches and misunderstanding. They'd make it work. Love would trump inconvenience.

*Stupid.*

After all my fretting over servers and ports and uptime statistics, it wasn't technology that sank me. The tech was golden.

People were the problem. The very premise, the idea that if you enabled people with tools and the opportunity to help their fellow human—and be helped—they would. They would recognize the opportunity and seize it. They would run with it.

Instead, they ran away.

I'm deep in dread when Susan appears at the threshold of my cubicle. She props her forearm against the border, one hip opposite, making a delicious line of her body.

"How did launch go?"

I look from the screen, surprised.

She explains, "Paul told me last week. I had him allocate another few gigabytes of bandwidth to the T server."

I bob my head at the disclosure, which is meant to encourage me, or endear me to her—neither of which works.

"Big fail," I say. "Users left. Hosts judged them, I guess. I dunno. Everybody found something to complain about."

"People do that." Susan lolls her head to one shoulder, then straight back, some yoga-studio stretch. "That doesn't make it a failure. It's only a failure if you quit."

I look at her.

"Wow," I say. "After all that, a pep talk."

She flutters a hand apologetically. "You don't need my advice—we both know that. But look, Deb, it's homelessness. Right? It's hard."

I know she's right. I know hard problems don't melt in a single day, just because you ache for them to. Still—in this moment, she has no business telling me that.

"Have you called SFPD yet?" I ask. "Dawson took three bodies home, and I know where every one of them fell, if the cops need to collect fibers or whatever."

Susan looks at her slim shoes.

I say, "You aren't calling them?"

An intellectual shock registers in my brain, but the rest of my body doesn't feel it. That elastic has been stretched too far.

"For better or worse," Susan says, "Blackquest 40 is settled. It's over. The casualties were all on their side. Nobody got injected or lost their job. The company is solvent—more solvent than ever, thanks to you."

I raise my arms listlessly overhead. Muscles whine in my back.

"Hooray."

She steps into the cubicle and takes both my hands in hers, a touch that reminds me of the one she used in the dead of last night (the night before?) to keep me in the fold.

"The person who's suffered the most here is you, Deb. If you tell me you need to press charges, we'll go to the police. We will. I can explain how the training was all a charade—how Elite fooled us, how we signed a contract under false pretenses. Just say the word and I go."

She releases my hands and pivots as if ready to go do exactly that.

The offer is clever—what else would I expect from Susan Wright? She's been careful in her wording, not saying she'll come clean, only that she will "explain."

The moral choice has been laid squarely upon me. If I need justice, or revenge, or mollifying, I can have it—at the expense of my coworkers.

"Forget it," I say. "I'm good. I still don't see how this is going to work, though. Three hundred employees, and nobody's going to report this to the police?"

Susan says she expects somebody will. With a resigned wheeze, she concedes the authorities will have questions. She'll have to bite the bullet and answer them.

I'm sure she will—and equally sure none of those bullets will graze her.

I could challenge her with more logistics, but what would be the use? Susan with corporate politics is like me with algorithms: she plays seven steps ahead.

"Well, back to reality." I click over to the depressing Carebnb comment log. "Enjoy the rest of your day."

I retrain my eyes on text.

Susan crimps her brow. "Going home soon, right?"

I nod. "Yep. One last thing, then I'm gone."

She pauses, and in that pause I read calculation. *She is digging into Carebnb, right?* She gives me a long look but leaves without further questions.

Once she's gone, I switch from Carebnb—which I will dive into in a second—to the low-level financials database. I can't access the journal entries from my machine, but my superuser access can get me into the granular underlying data.

Because I've seen those murky cash flows firsthand, I know just what they look like under the hood.

I open the *finance_journal_detail* database. The payer ID is still seared in my head from those frantic moments in Carter's office. I search on this value and request all fields back, sorted by user.

This will show me every time the Russian money was added, changed, or viewed.

The results are back in a blink—nobody's doing any work now, network traffic essentially nil. Red rows flood a black screen.

Of thirty-four times the secret money was accessed over the last months, thirteen belong to the user name *carterK*.

By now, the user name of the other twenty-one is no great mystery. I scroll anyway to be sure.

*susanW*.

## CHAPTER FIFTY-FOUR_

I DROP MY FACE INTO THE KEYBOARD AND CRY. FULL-OUT bawling, dripping into the keys, teeth grinding, plastic corners scraping my eyeballs. *H, Y, U*, and *7* are all depressed, characters streaming across the screen and the machine bleeping in my nose.

I'm wrong about everything.

I idealized Susan knowingly, wholeheartedly, believing her true flaws were beside the point. They weren't. She's no unicorn defying the patriarchal morass. She's a wolf: shrewder and stronger than the males but fundamentally the same. My greatest ally here was Paul Gribbe—who two days ago I wouldn't have left alone with my toiletries.

Carebnb didn't tap some vast well of latent social power, or unleash people's innate charity. It exposed them for the selfish cowards they are.

I'm sure of nothing. Even sexuality. What were those twinges I felt around Graham, sitting beside him on the Cray's vinyl bench? That part of me has always been gospel, unshakable. It was never a choice—never anyone's choice. It was simply who I was. My identity.

Why should that tenant be any firmer than the rest?

Through my tears, I spot the Polarity of the Universe toggle, currently set to *Evil*. I would love to leave it there, to foist the blame fully on the Russians who terrorized me, to nurse my own convictions until the world made sense again.

But that world isn't coming back—the black and white version. I reach my middle finger across the workspace and flip the toggle to *Amoral*.

I just hacked a nuclear power plant on behalf of the Kremlin.

The most important product launch of my career tanked.

I misjudged basically everyone.

I got Raven blown up.

Actually, Raven's brains are backed up to the cloud. Well, almost—thanks to the data blockade, she never uploaded her RAM record of Blackquest 40, but those are memories we're probably all best without.

I could build her a new body. Better—maybe she needs localized, micro-missile defense. Will it really be her, though?

I only take a moment pondering this, in no mood for some existential sci-fi contemplation. What I feel like doing, honestly, is biking one last time around Lands End and up onto the Golden Gate Bridge, pedaling to that first pylon, gazing down at the swirling whitecaps, then casting off all my pain.

I think about that.

*Ah, shut up,* I decide.

To occupy myself, I pull over my bin of droid-Hot Wheels. The bin is light a few cars, those brave girls who hopped out to be my ears on Dawson. They're strewn about the carpet. Now I bend low and collect them, replacing them one by one in the bin.

I'm starving—and Elite took all its scrumptious food. I keep a stash of flaxseed bars in my desk. I tear two open at once and chomp both.

I drink half a bottled water.

I'm just pulling out of my psychic tailspin when I hear a noise. It's somewhere above my head—for an instant, I think it must be Raven's ghost.

The sound is shallower than what her propellers made, though. When I glance up, I find one of my mechanical dragon-flies weaving drunken figure eights.

"You still suck at flying."

Her path is even wonkier than usual, pitching and rolling forward at once, then recovering a line, only to wobble off in her next series of wing-beats.

I'm sure she took a beatdown from Elite in the melee, but her components look sound. She should be recovering better. Are her state variables not re-calibrating?

When she veers closer, I squint into her buggy eyes.

"Whaddaya say? Shall we fix you up?"

I punch up the Bailey's Buzzy World modules. It's neurotic and pointless and I really need to get to Crestwood, but maybe some coding will be therapeutic. After all, I was just contemplating a header off the Golden Gate.

I find the flight logic. The main algorithm, which I wrote so long ago I've nearly forgotten, is *produce_lift_output*. It receives a matrix of values, then compares the values to previous matrices, then churns through a series of complex calculations, then...

All breath vaporizes in my mouth—like my lips closed around a lit match.

*Oh God.*

I mentally zoom through the two algorithms side-by-side, comparing, contrasting.

The contrasts are small.

*Oh no. No, it can't be.*

*It can't.*

But I click the matrix's name for details and see that it is. The set of variables required to simulate flight—the inputs needed to calculate future lift vectors—contains the exact number of variables I feared it would:

Seven.

## CHAPTER FIFTY-FIVE

I SPRINT UPSTAIRS TO TEN, TO E-WING. MY UMPTEENTH time making the dash is the loneliest, my sandals echoing out across the lobby like a lost percussionist's cymbal blast through an empty concert hall.

Notions swirl and snap and unknot themselves in my head.

Through the glass balustrade, I can just make out the lobby televisions. CNN is showing a live shot from Cape Canaveral, scaffolding towers being wheeled away from a spacecraft.

*That is scaffolding, right? Not clouds?*

I can't spare time to confirm.

On Ten, I once again zoom past the business side cubicles. Spaces are unkempt here but not as messy as in Engineering. Susan is reclined in her office, feet crossed on her desktop.

I waste no more than a glance.

I keep running to Carter's office. The CFO—soon former CFO—is packing up his belongings. He always kept personal effects to a minimum in accordance with a modern aesthetic and has already cleared half his wall hangings. He's just laying the framed portrait with Phil Mickelson flat in a bin, grinning crookedly—maybe remembering some tryst or fantasized tryst—when I accost him.

"*Whose idea was the newspaper?*" I yell, catching both his lapels in one fist.

Carter squints repeatedly as I push him into the nearest wall. Like mine, his cheeks are wet with tears.

"You picked the business plan subject off the front page of the Chronicle!" My knuckles bore into his chest. One nail pierces linen. "It wasn't your idea, was it?"

His confusion clears and he curls his lips inward, groping back in memory.

"I—well, now that I think, he was the one who suggested it. Dawson." Carter's eyes telescope forward as the memory falls into place. "He said private spaceflight had a lot of interesting business questions... and even if...even if the biz side mission was a decoy—"

I don't wait for the rest. I release his lapels, dropping him in a heap, and run. I plow through the stairwell door like a rugby player through a scrum, jolting my wrists, slamming the door into the exterior wall.

I barrel ahead to the glass balustrade, nearly hurtling over into *Semperinity* like the guard I ninja-kicked yesterday. My forearms slam the rail and save me. I lean forward, squinting at the broadcast, tuning my ear.

*Has the countdown started? When would they deploy the hijack code? After launch, definitely—but how long after?*

I can't believe I missed it. The clues were right there, dancing on my face. The seven-variable matrix, same as the dragonflies' lift equation. Graham moving his eyes up—either to the lobby monitors or sky, take your pick. Dawson's bizarre insistence that we complete the software by hour forty, a deadline that would've been completely arbitrary if his goal was to recapture a nuclear power plant Ukraine had been controlling for decades.

No: it had to happen *right now*. Any earlier and they risked somebody putting two and two together, hearing echoes of Blackquest in media coverage of OurSpace's innovative security and blowing the whistle.

The software we just built has zilch to do with power plants —with saving thousands of Ukrainian and Russian lives. If I found a computer now and typed "Vlast" into a search bar, I'd get back information on some caffeinated gum or vodka.

The stairwell door opens behind me. I whirl. Carter and Susan stand on the same step, breathless.

Carter says, "You think they're using Blackquest 40 to take over the launch? Or spacecraft? But it was a decoy, Dawson said it—"

"Yeah. He said plenty."

The faces of the Codewise founders blanch. Their oversight —facilitated by the promise of cold, hard cash—is as bad as mine. The business piece of this equation was equally obvious, Russia sitting on all this aerospace technology, experts and cosmonauts and doodads from the International Space Station gathering dust.

What can you do with these elaborate Space Race assets? How do you monetize them?

If you're Russia, you do the same thing you do everywhere else: you privatize, leaving one foot safely planted in governmental control. The same playbook that's worked with Gasprom, Rosneft, Sberbank.

I think back to Katie Masterson grilling Shaggy and team about their hypothetical roll-out message. She was riding them so hard because there was nothing hypothetical about the exercise. The oligarchs really did want our advice on how to enter the market.

Still, our primary use to them was software: landing a fatal blow on OurSpace, the industry leader. Russia wasn't about to let some pie-in-the-sky Silicon Valley upstart stand in their way. Oren Andreassen, with his grand talk of open-source and interoperability, must've made a gleeful target for the hardliners at the Kremlin.

Susan says, "Tell us how we can help."

Ten floors below, faint on the distant screens, smoke billows up the sides of the spacecraft. The vessel disappears for a moment, then an orange flicker begins, growing to a flame.

The smoke dissipates. The body of the spacecraft—slender, shaped like half of a tilted boomerang—becomes visible again. It trembles fiercely in place before the nose starts its skyward ascent.

I run not down to the lobby for a better view of the launch, but up: up the stairs, splitting Susan and Carter.

*How can they help?*

"Stay out of my way," I say, ramming through their shoulders.

## CHAPTER FIFTY-SIX_

O<small>N THE TOP FLOOR OF THE BUILDING, IN ITS OWN SMALL</small> room—a room that until ten hours ago seemed destined to be its final resting place—the Cray supercomputer runs.

I speed through one hallway and half of a second, tapping what's gotta be the last of my legs' energy. I have the notion to slide feet first into the cord, to disable the Cray in a World Cup-worthy takeout.

*Bad idea. Power loss is erratic—no telling how the spacecraft might respond.*

The proper fix won't take long anyway. I keep running, panting, into the Cray's cavity now and caroming off its humming inner panels, spinning to the keyboard.

Even though I expect it, the sight of debug output scrolling down the screen—blocky green text puked out in gluts —chills me.

*The algorithm is live.*

*Blackquest 40, devil spawn of my brain, has been deployed.*

The OurSpace flight controller has been hijacked. Its thrusters are receiving lift values marginally lower than what they should be.

I imagine the passengers—two men, two women, an astronaut and civilian of each gender if I'm remembering correctly—and what they're feeling. Relief that liftoff is behind them...anticipation at entering outer space...but still plenty of nerves at the remaining work to be done.

Have they detected anything wrong? Probably not. The under-thrust is subtle.

*How will the craft fail?* Will they bump into the top of Earth's atmosphere and burn up? Take a slow-arcing nosedive into the Pacific Ocean? How many bogus vectors will it take to doom the flight?

I think about Oren Andreassen watching in his silk bodysuit, triumphant, believing his goal of democratizing private space travel is within reach. Not so different from me thirty minutes ago, thinking Carebnb was toppling its own giant, unfathomable problem.

My fingers find keys. I don't sit. I navigate to the directory containing Paul's file.

The Cray is the tiniest bit laggy, each directory switch taking an extra tick—which is stunning given its processing power. The spacecraft flight controller must be seriously slamming the file.

I type *delete value_pair_lookup.txt* and press enter.

The Cray answers with a brief message confirming the file's removal.

In the debug window, the green-text waterfall freezes. A cursor blinks once before yielding to a peevish message:

URI FORMATION ERROR: FILE 'value_pair_lookup' NOT AVAILABLE ON SERVER.

Then nothing. The screen stays gloriously fixed—no scrolling, no new text.

No thrusters receiving faulty lift values.

*The botlet only gets one fail, then the host reverts to the prior algorithm.*

*Incursion over.*

In another minute, platters inside the Cray spin down. All bleeps and bloops cease. The room is silent.

The machine—vinyl and silicon, big and ugly and dated—is back to being a dust collector.

I stand. About fifty parts of me crackle. Everything else is sore or bleeding.

I lope to the stairs without hurry. Shooting pain in my knee forces that foot to one side, and my next few steps follow, making for a long, loopy route. Someone shouts from the lobby.

I keep not hurrying.

I arrive at the stairwell door. Laying my forearms against the push bar, eyes half closed, I bump. The door opens an inch, than slams back shut.

I push again. The door budges wide enough for me to squeeze through to the pine steps.

Now I can discern words.

"It's still airborne!" Susan is calling up. "No explosions, nothing strange!"

Carter: "Deb, *Deb*! Are you done? Did you do your—er, whatever you were doing?"

I don't answer. They wouldn't hear me unless I shouted too. I'm not going to shout.

"Two minutes post launch and it's still up!" Susan's voice is delirious. "Deb—that's you on the stairs, right? Is the patch in place?"

I mumble, "It's not a patch."

But she can't hear. I've only descended one flight. My strides are glacial. I lower each sandal carefully, pausing to breathe at each footfall, yawning often.

"...confirm the patch is uploaded, we're out of the woods?"

"*Deb! What's the scoop up there, we good...?*"

Susan and Carter begin seeing me at Five, catching glimpses as I make the turn from one flight to the next.

"Good? Are we good?" Carter hops up onto the lip of *Semperinity*, wingtips clacking. "Deb talk to us, we golden?"

I say out the side of my mouth, "We're not golden."

"What? Deb, *what'd you say*? Do they look okay, the space-ship readings? A-ok?"

"Can't see readings from space." I reach Three. "Not a bidi-rectional information flow."

Despite my reticence, the bosses are figuring it out. I wouldn't be doing my grumpy sloth routine if there were still dangers afoot. Smiles stretch both their faces.

Susan collapses into an upholstered couch, kicking her heels end-over-end to the floor.

Carter plunges both hands into *Semperinity*'s basin and splashes water over his Gatsby slickback and in his eyes—a joyful, baptismal act.

This company, the work of their lives, is saved.

Somewhere, Dawson is watching the OurSpace craft regain its course and enter orbit—and wishing for a new stress ball.

Will his masters in Moscow blame him? Will they cut him loose, disavow any connection when the US government comes sniffing around? Will he and Katie make it back to the coun-tryside?

I realize I have no idea where the Volga River is.

It's two more flights down to the lobby. I take them in a trance—*what ungodly number of stairs have I covered?*—and keep moving when I reach the ground floor.

Carter rushes up with arms outspread and those white, white teeth. Seeming to read in my body language that I'm not coming in for a bro-hug, he drops theatrically to one knee.

"Deb Bollinger," he says with one hand over his heart. "That. Was. Epic."

I walk out the double doors.

THREE MONTHS LATER_

CHAPTER FIFTY-SEVEN_

I STRETCH OUT ON A GENTLE SLOPE OF SHARON MEADOW, my favorite lightly discovered nook of Golden Gate Park, and rub my eyes. The temperature is a natural seventy-one degrees, no climate control here, the sun shining its best behind cottony clouds.

I've been coding three hours straight and need bánh mì. Badly.

A girl, five or six years old, keeps looking between me and the sky.

"Is that thingie, um, yours?" she asks, pointing shyly. "Are you controlling it?"

Her mother, wearing baby brother in a sling, takes a step to discourage the girl. I wave to her that it's cool.

"Sort of," I say, tilting my laptop screen so the girl can see. "Right now she's controlling herself, making her own decisions about how high or fast or where to fly. But I did make her brains."

The girl recoils, probably imagining me manipulating squishy gray goop. "How do you do *that*?"

"Well," I say, "it takes a lot of work. A lot of determination.

You have to go to school and study." I tap my forehead, then immediately wonder when the concept of corniness enters a child's awareness. "This brain I actually made a long time ago. It's an amazing brain. I didn't want to lose it."

Together we watch Wren traipse through the air, flirting with leafy willow branches, dodging Monterey pine needles. She has a more aerodynamic look than Raven—minus the repurposed arcade claw, plus a parabolic silver chassis. The waterproofing (I'm anticipating more outside use) has softened Raven's pricklier edges.

When a real bird approaches, a splashy male cardinal, Wren rises to let him pass underneath.

The move is encouraging. I've been worrying about her paths, which can feel jerky compared to her mom's—twin sister's?—but that looked smooth. The algorithms are byte-for-byte identical; possibly I invented the deficiency in my head.

Preoccupied with the girl and drone, I don't notice Cecil until he's right behind me.

"Lil Deb."

His deep voice spins me around.

"Look at you, healing up," he says. "I believe the new office digs suit you."

The girl leans to one side, peering around me to Cecil. Her eyes hitch on his cart, parked between two bushes.

"Now I do keep lollipops in there," he says. "But only for girls who've been nice to their little brothers."

Her face is frozen for a moment until Cecil's breaks wide in a grin. She grins too. He glances to the mother, a question in his eyes. When she nods, he pulls a goofy-relieved face and heads for the cart.

Once the sucker is delivered, he and I sit in the grass chatting. Cecil catches me up on the giant Obama he's wheatpasting with friends onto an I-80 overpass. I tell him what a difference it's made seeing Mom twice a day, how Crestwood Psychiatric has cut her dosages by two-thirds.

"*They* cut the dose," Cecil says, "or you *made* them cut the dose?"

"Made. They just raised their fees so they're feeling especially accommodating."

He drums his fingers over his belly. "You okay on cash, them raising fees?"

"Pshaw," I brush off his concern, then think twice—what am I, Miss Moneybags?—before remembering who I am talking to. Cecil has known me since I was making rain catchers out of milk jugs. "I'm still suckling at the Codewise teat. Little contract stuff. Last week, I had to teach my old dragonfly pals a few hand signals."

"Pay nice?"

"Nice enough."

"And you're okay going back? Walking in that building..."

I shrug. "I do the work remotely—here, in cafes. The coding. But I'll pop in for a meeting if need be. It's just bricks and glass. It doesn't have fangs."

He pulls back his face, as though not quite sure.

Dawson, at least, is unlikely to return to the scene of his triumph-turned-defeat. He fled the country the day Blackquest 40 ended, and according to Susan the FBI has placed his name and likeness on various watch lists.

As for his masters? I have no idea. Katie's story did check out: Elite Development has a website—last updated ten months ago—and "Jim Dawson" has a LinkedIn profile to match. Whether or not they were coerced, to what extent they were coerced, I don't know.

I also don't know about Graham. I like to imagine he split off from Dawson at the airport, hopped a train up to Banff or Park City and caught on with some startup, where he's going to build a snazzier framework than anything they thought possible. That he hikes the Rockies on weekends—finally someplace those thermal undersleeves make sense.

I did have it out with Susan. I yelled questions until I felt all lies had been exorcised. Yes, her midnight indignation had been an act to keep me in the fold. Yes, she'd been aware Russia was the client—but no, absolutely no, she'd NEVER known or had the faintest suspicion about OurSpace.

"You used me," I said.

She nodded.

"I don't believe in people. I believed in you."

Susan kept her lip stiff. "I could apologize every day for the rest of my life, it wouldn't be enough. I know."

She didn't try then, but a week later Susan showed up at my apartment, startling Liz—the new woman I'd been seeing—and asked if I would consider staying on.

She had come clean to the police. Turned over copies of all Blackquest contracts with Carter's and Dawson's signatures on them, plus paperwork on that murky Elite revenue.

(What became of the revenue itself remained murky.)

"Come back," she begged. "We'll do it different. With clear eyes."

Carter Kotanchek was history, and so was his brand of oily hucksterism. Codewise would rededicate itself to bleeding-edge optimization. No more Sales hires. No more corporate training. She was committed to changing the culture.

Saying all this, given what we knew of each other, a lesser executive might've struggled looking me in the face. Not Susan. Susan pitched with lucidity and conviction. *This company can be great again, but it needs you to be its greatest.*

I don't know that she broke eye contact, or so much as blinked. Not once. She's that good.

But not quite good enough. I'll do her contract jobs when

they fit my schedule, when the Carebnb coffers demand it. Susan gets me, but she doesn't get all of me.

Twenty-five percent, tops.

Cecil asks, "What time are we supposed to meet?"

I look toward the sun. "Two. Ish."

"You know what we're gonna talk about?"

I finger a stack of papers in my hemp satchel. "I printed up agendas, I dunno. They're rough. We can play by ear."

He nods warily. Cecil and the other unhoused members of the board aren't big process people. They bristle at structure, preferring a baggier, free-flowing exchange of ideas. Which is fine. I started out casual myself, but over the last month I've decided basic meeting topics and objectives have their place. Much as I value diversity of opinion, six people talking over each other about the symbolism of a blue house icon versus a black one gets you nowhere.

Wanda and Earl arrive next. The clouds thinning, they slough off outer layers as they settle in and josh about the Niners. Cecil hugs them both and says they're both wrong—the Raiders are the only team in the Bay Area going to the playoffs.

Theresa Braun, my host representative, shows after them. She is finishing a call, chin pinning her phone, twisting to confirm her parking spot's legality. She works for Seagate in Cupertino. I thank her heartily for trekking up here.

Everybody claims a patch of grass in a loose circle around me.

Cecil angles his tremendous form toward South of Market. "You sure he's coming?"

I nod. "He said he was. We can count on him."

Sure enough, a minute later at what I can only assume is the stroke of two o'clock, Paul comes cycling up. He dismounts, sets his kickstand, and removes a bike helmet that's flattened his hair.

He joins the circle puffing hard. Google has put him in their Spear Street office in the city, which beats Mountain View but is still a solid twenty-minute pedal.

I scoot to make space, patting the ground. "Plenty of room."

He wedges his legs into his lap and looks haltingly around the group.

I announce, "This is my friend, Paul Gribbe, a conventional white male who frequents McDonald's. He's okay. He's going to help us."

Paul waves, a swipe over his chest pocket. "Pleasure meeting you all."

These words don't match his flummoxed expression, but I am not worried.

He'll warm up.

With all parties present and accounted for, I break into my satchel and spread a dozen bánh mì sandwiches—half lemongrass tofu, half five-spice chicken—in the middle of the circle, a metaphorical gavel bang.

"Welcome to the seventh official meeting of the Carebnb Board of Directors. We've accomplished a lot so far. The feedback system has incentivized"—I can hardly say the word with a straight face—"both hosts and users to behave better. The personal space guidelines have helped, too. Every time I dig into the numbers, I'm seeing higher occupancy and satisfaction metrics."

My report is met by smiles and gratified murmurs. It's a talented mix that surrounds me—a mix I'm just learning to harness, accustomed as I've been to flying solo. Wanda hates every idea the first time she hears it, but understands the realities of the unhoused community and will eventually listen to reason.

Theresa, who finds my solutions over-technical, needs to see any proposal on the printed page. Once she does, though, she knows at a glance what six tweaks it'll take to work.

"Still, there's more to do." I tap a command for Wren to make us some shade—the glare is brutal on this screen. "And we're going to do it. Together. We are absolutely finishing this job."

CPSIA information can be obtained
at www.ICGtesting.com
Printed in the USA
FSHW022129310519
58636FS